For my Family

PROLOGUE

She could see the light on the hill, pale white in the dark. There was a frost forming and the mist rolled through the streets like a ghost creeping out from the woods. The pubs had shut over an hour ago, the last of the few drunk and weary punters stumbling down the main road to their wives and kids and wood-burning stoves.

She wished she'd brought a warmer coat. Silly cow. It was common knowledge the temperature could drop quick around here. As soon as the sun went down—not that there was ever much sun—that was it. The chill would be here in no time at all. She wrapped her knee-length woollen cardigan around her and focused on keeping her feet moving, tricky as it was in these heels. She knew as soon as she'd bought them that they weren't really for her. She was a trainers and jeans kind of girl, but was persuaded to buy them for this bloody party. It had been Kurt's idea. She knew of course that he'd only said to buy them because she was distracting him from Stranger Things. Seemed like half the world was addicted to it, Kurt included, but she could never really get into it. So she'd bought them on a whim, really, despite knowing she'd probably only wear them once. Which had been tonight. She wouldn't have minded but she'd stuck out like a sore thumb, anyway.

It had been a while since she'd been to a birthday party. The fortieth had been one of those gatherings that a friend of a friend of a friend was throwing and she'd been invited, she guessed, just so she could make up the numbers. Turned out she was the only one overdressed for the occasion. She'd wished Kurt could've been there with her, but she knew these big parties were never really his thing. Sometimes, she thought he'd reached the pipe and slippers stage far too soon. Much sooner than she would've liked. So it had been convenient for him that he was working nights, anyway. She knew he wouldn't have wanted to go. Driving trucks for a living didn't exactly do wonders for their relationship, especially when he worked lates all the time, but she loved him and he loved her.

She believed he did, anyway. They'd been together long enough to want to keep going. She'd been holding out for a proposal but was still waiting. All she wanted, really, was a family. Kurt would make a brilliant dad. They'd tried already but she'd lost it. Time was probably running out for her, she guessed, but they'd made a commitment to keep trying. In a way, the miscarriage had brought them closer together. She just wished he'd give up his stupid job and find something more... normal. Something more convenient. That way, he'd be able to come with her for these kinds of social dos, and she wouldn't end up stood in the corner looking like a spare part.

She'd gotten used to the fact that he was rarely there in their bed with her these days. Work, of course. She never really thought he was the type to play away. She knew he hadn't had many girlfriends before her, either, so it wasn't as if he was a ladies' man. Truth was, he could be a bit of a slob. Give him beer and telly and he was happy as a pig in shit. But she didn't mind.

He was her man. He made her laugh, gave her something to be happy about.

She pulled her phone from her handbag and checked it for texts and calls, but there hadn't been any. She guessed he was probably too busy driving his truck somewhere up the M6. He usually sent a quick text when he was at a service station. Mainly in the middle of the bloody night when she was asleep, but still. It showed he cared, didn't it? Showed that she mattered to him. That was all she needed, really. To be loved. She sent him a quick text herself—On way home babe xx—and left it at that. He'd probably get back to her soon enough. He usually did.

When a car swept past, speeding down the road at fifty, she almost went on her arse. There was a bit of ice around, just a touch coating the pavements in patches, but it was enough to add to the problem of trying to get home. She'd thought that maybe the walk would do her good, help to sober her up a bit. Not that she'd had too much. Chance would be a fine thing.

The speeding car was swiftly followed by a speeding white van. Whatever they were up to, they were crazy to be going so fast on these roads. One wrong manoeuvre or a lapse in concentration and they'd likely go skidding off into a wall or something. It had certainly happened before now. You'd think people would learn the lesson, but no. Strange for a white van man to be out at this time, but it took all sorts. A lot of people seemed to have second jobs as bloody delivery men, these days. Making drop-offs at all hours. But at this time? Gone midnight? Maybe it was a rogue plasterer who'd had a few beers with his fancy piece after work and got carried away, forgot the time, fell asleep after a quickie, and now had to get home sharpish before the wife suspected the worst.

Or maybe she just had an overactive imagination.

She stumbled on. The odd taxi glided past, and she thought about trying to flag one down, but she was only twenty minutes from home by now and it seemed pointless to cadge a lift. She fancied a quick brandy by the fire when she got home, too. It was way too late to pick up a takeaway, though, so she'd have to make do with raiding the fridge and cupboards.

Come to think of it, she was bloody starving. She'd barely eaten a thing at the party and red wine always made her hungry. If Kurt had been here, he'd have picked up a dirty kebab and kept it warm for her. Another reason to love him.

Just as she passed the school, the white van pulled in and rumbled to a stop twenty yards ahead of her. On this side of the road. People just didn't give a toss, these days, did they? Then the driver got out. He had this funny look on his face, like he'd just been told some inappropriate joke or that he knew something she didn't.

When he started to walk towards her, she did a double take and almost stumbled again in the bloody heels. She was just about to ask if he was lost or something but then someone grabbed her from behind and wrapped a thick, pudgy hand over her mouth and nose. She instantly thought of Kurt and wished he was there.

But he wasn't.

The driver guy got close to her and whacked her on the head with something hard. It looked like a flask or something chunky like that. She started to drift away almost immediately. She could smell his blue checked shirt as the world swam, and he grabbed her in a bear hug—the most unloving hug she'd ever had—and then she really started to fade.

She could feel something wet drip into her eyes, then cold air going up her legs as she slumped to her knees. Somehow they'd gotten her up and the next thing she knew, she was lying on a metal floor with the smell of damp rags all around her. Felt the hum of the engine and the wheels roll beneath her.

She had no idea what had happened to her phone. Or her bag.

She hoped Kurt had gotten her text message.

On way home babe xx

Except now she knew she wasn't. She didn't know where she was going. She let herself drift into darkness and hoped it would be over quickly.

ONE

'And don't forget, Izzy's got a birthday party to go to on Saturday. One o'clock. Until three-ish, or whenever you're sick of the screaming kids. The invite's in the rack on the dresser. One of the dads at school handed it to me yesterday.'

'Wonderful.'

'And also don't forget, I'm going out with Mel for dinner at seven. You know we haven't been out in ages. What are you gonna do Saturday night?'

'A few beers on my own. *Match of the Day*. Might get some peace...'

'You're not working?'

'I told you, I never work Saturdays now. Unless they want me in for something extra special. But nothing ever happens around here.'

'Just the break-ins, the beatings and the... bollocks.'

'What's up now?'

'Forgot my keys.'

'Izzy, can you please get a bloody move on?'

'You know she wants to take Elmo, Rob. I mean, get with the program.'

'Oh, fuck off.'

Detective Sergeant Rob Logan wrestled with the car doors while Vic ushered Izzy out of the house and locked up. Looking up at the sky and the teenagers shuffling their way into the school down the road, each of them slip-sliding on the ice, he was thankful for small mercies: he wasn't expected in work until ten. It was about to piss down hard, or snow, and this was the chaos before the calm. The madness before the sanity. It was a good job he'd had the foresight to text Kel and get her to order their breakfast before yet another averagely shite day on burglaries.

Six years on the job and nothing much had changed. Nothing much happened. If it wasn't for the odd domestic gone wrong or the city gang violence gone crazy, he'd probably have packed it in long ago. Yet there was something keeping him in it. This was it, really. His career. What he'd finally settled on. He supposed it was a good thing to have that security he craved for his family—Vic's nursing career seemed a long way behind them after the pandemic had almost ruined their marriage—but they'd held it together and Vic was far more excited about life now that she was pursuing her real passion: food. A street food business was around the corner if she could secure the finance for a little truck, and Izzy was more than settled in school. There was a lot to be grateful for.

But lately, his heart hadn't been in it at all. The Job had become just that: a job. Any excitement his young mind had found at the beginning of it all had faded into the odd fragment of interest every now and again. Occasionally, DI Murray would throw him a bone, but those were few and far between. Since he'd made DS, the paperwork pile had gotten bigger, and the days were often filled with monotony and boredom. There was only so much staring out the office window he could do. Only so many pens he could push. For the past few months, he'd been aware that his thoughts often drifted when on the job, and that probably wasn't a good thing. Ever since he could remember, he'd always wanted to be a copper. And now he was here, achieving his dream, he had little to no enthusiasm whatsoever. Perhaps it wasn't for him, after all.

After they'd dropped Izzy at school—she had to be persuaded to leave Elmo in the car—Vic brought up the subject, like she knew what he'd been thinking. She had a knack for this.

'Hypothetically speaking,' she said, 'what would you do if you packed it in?'

'I'm not just going to pack it in, am I?'

'But if you did?'

He shrugged, careful to keep his eye on the road and his wheels steady on the black ice. 'I don't know. Not thought about it. There's nothing else I've ever really wanted to do. Police was always it for me. I can't imagine myself doing anything different.'

'Maybe it's just a blip. A mid-life crisis.'

'Mid-life? Jesus, Vic, I'm not that old.'

'You know what I mean.' She was busy applying mascara. 'But it's not too late to change, is it? Thirty-seven is still... well, maybe not. Or maybe it is. I mean, look at me. I thought I'd be in nursing forever but since the pandemic, when everything went tits up, I was in the same boat. I could never go back to it now. The stress...'

'It's not the same for me, though. I'm just... bored. With you, it was the pressure, wasn't it? I just feel like I can't be arsed anymore. You know what I mean?'

'You've never really been arsed about much, though, babe. You're that type of bloke.'

She was wrong, but he didn't feel the need to argue the point. Instead, they drove in silence until she put the radio on, and that was how they left the conversation, all the way into Bury.

DS Rob Logan dropped his wife at the bank, then spun the VW around and drove to work. Greater Manchester Police, Bury HQ, was just two minutes away.

LOGAN TURNED into the car park and found his usual bay down at the back end. By now, the drizzle had turned to full-on icy rain, and if he could have turned right around and go home to a roaring fire right then, he wouldn't hesitate. But then his phone pinged as a text came through. DS Kelly McCulloch didn't like time-wasters.

Tomatoes or beans you lazy twat?

He never liked beans and he wasn't going to start now. He fired a quick text back and locked up, before making his way into the main building.

There was the usual quiet at this time of the morning. Most would be out on patrol, the rest upstairs doing paperwork. The canteen had usually emptied by now, except for a few occupied tables, and the desk was relatively peaceful. The Custody Sergeant, Martin Hobbs, gave a quick wave as Logan swiped his log-in card then went up the stairs two at a time. He was hungry.

He found DS McCulloch on their usual table, busily slurping her flat white and mopping up the juices from her breakfast with a pale round of toast.

'What time do you call this?'

'The time I clock on,' he said, taking the seat opposite.

His own breakfast was now merely lukewarm. 'Not like there's anything to get me here sooner, is there?'

'That might be about to change, though,' she said, her light Scottish accent pleasantly melodious. 'DI Murray wants to see us both, pretty pronto. Must have something other than the usual shite, 'cause it's not like him to summon a couple of lowly DS's.'

'As long as it gets us out of here, I'm not arsed.' He stabbed a sausage and went for it. 'Need to get out of the fucking office for a change.'

'Yeah, but it's bloody cold out there, eh?'

'Only a bit of snow. What's up with you? You're no stranger to that, being Scottish.'

'I hate the bloody cold, Rob.'

'You sound like Vic. It's a woman thing, isn't it?'

'It's a weather thing. Come on, don't act like you don't have your wee long johns on today.'

'Temperature's dropping quicker than your knickers.'

'Ha bloody ha.'

'How is that love life of yours?'

'Non-existent. Simon turned out to be a bit too much of a softy for my liking. I like a man who's done a day's work in his plumbing pants, not a soft wee shite pushing pens and crunching numbers.'

'Not your type, then?'

'Not anyone's type, if I'm honest.'

Logan nodded and went in for demolition while McCulloch sat back and dug her phone from her bag. No doubt there were one or two dating apps for her to check in on. Logan left her to it and ate quickly.

Just as he was about to drain his coffee, DI Dave Murray grabbed the chair beside him and whacked a file down.

'Not being funny but that bacon looks shit,' Murray said.

'It's all right from where I'm sitting,' Logan said. 'Come on, then. What've we got? Chubby little gobshite at it again, is he?'

'What, young Clarky? Not today. No, this is much more interesting.'

'Old lady been done in with a loaf tin?' McCulloch said. 'Or a sledgehammer?'

'Not as straightforward as that, I'm afraid. But it will get you two out of here for a day or two, if you're up for it.'

'Get me out of here,' Logan said. 'Before my brain melts.'

Murray nodded. 'You got some wellies? We can sort you out in no time if need be.'

'Hang about,' McCulloch said. 'Are you gonna have us slushing through the bloody woods in this weather?'

Murray shook his head. 'The moors. Up on the hill, actually. Holcombe Moor.'

'What, no man's land?'

'Where the army train?' Logan said.

Murray nodded again. 'I've started a file for you. It'll probably turn out to be nothing, but we need someone to head up there, so I thought it might as well be you two, given that you're always moaning to get out of the office. You'll thank me later, I'm sure.'

'What is it?'

'A dead sheep.'

'You what? You serious?'

'You're sending us out to investigate a farming incident?' McCulloch said. 'Wee sheep get trapped in the bloody fence?'

Murray gave a wry smile. 'Something like that, yeah. Now if you'll excuse me, I'll leave it in your capable hands.'

TWO

The traffic was light. They took Logan's car and drove up Brandlesholme Road in the mid-morning gloom. A blanket-grey sky was moving in from the north, bringing sweeping rain and an icy blast. January in the northwest of England could be enough to make you lose the will to live.

A dead sheep, though. Logan could be forgiven for thinking that DI Murray was taking the piss.

'I mean,' McCulloch said, 'it's not exactly what you'd call a murder scene, eh? Sheep get whacked every day, right? Farmer's probably done the poor thing in because it's got some weird disease or something.'

'Actually, I think these particular sheep are farmed for their wool.'

'Probably been a shearing accident, then, eh? Poor wee sheep got sheared in the parts he wasn't expecting and the next thing, there's blood everywhere.'

Whatever it was, Logan wasn't expecting to find a shearing accident. To be sent out to the body of a sheep was more than a bit strange, though. As far as he knew, there weren't many predators around on the moors that could do any serious damage to the animal. More likely the poor thing had been a victim of a teenage prank gone very wrong. Or perhaps it had been poisoned accidentally by some kind of farming chemical. Or maybe it had been run over by a quad bike or something just as dangerous. He'd seen how those young farmhands ran around on those things. Half of them were probably pissed most of the time. They worked stupidly long hours, so it wouldn't be a surprise for one of them to lose it completely, fall asleep at the wheel, go off track and smash one into the mud.

'I say we might as well take our time with this one,' McCulloch said. 'Drag it out all day if need be. We could maybe pick up some lunch at the Hare and Hounds, eh?'

'Just as easy to pop into mine. Vic'll be home. I could get her to warm us up some soup.'

'I was thinking more of a cheeky pint or something but whatever you think.'

'Too early for me,' he said. 'And anyway, you know I never drink on the job. Unless I'm desperate.'

Soon, they were further away from the town centre and heading into the more rural area of Bury. Now there were fields on all sides dotted with sheep and coated in yesterday's snow, and ahead, dominating the skyline, stood the imposing Holcombe Hill, with the Peel Tower monument standing proudly at the summit. Logan knew it would be bloody freezing up there and was thankful he had his police-issue winter coat in the boot.

’So, where exactly are we going?'

Logan checked the notes in the file. 'Morton Farm. Contact is Frank Morton. It's not very clear on here but I've got a vague idea where it is.’

When they reached the top of Longsight Road, they had

two options. Right, towards Ramsbottom, and left towards Hawkshaw. Logan took them left and they pulled over about a hundred metres down the road. Logan took out his phone and dialled.

'Jesus, the houses around here,' McCulloch said. 'What do these people do for a living?'

As far as Logan knew, not much. He raised a hand as the phone picked up on the other end. 'Yeah, good morning. I'm looking for a Frank Morton. It's DS Rob Logan of Greater Manchester Police. Bury division.'

FRANK MORTON HAD TOLD them to drive up the narrow side lane, which became more of a dirt track the further down they ventured, and Logan's VW was clearly not up for the job. When they pulled into the grounds, flanked by a tractor on one side and a quad bike on the other, he killed the engine as Frank Morton came out to greet them walking like John Wayne and wearing a hi-vis raincoat and industrial boots. Logan and McCulloch had clearly not come dressed for the occasion.

'Thanks for coming. I was expecting you yesterday, though.'

Morton was tall and broad and looked like he lived on raw meat and potatoes. He had massive hands like garden tools.

'Ah, sorry about that,' Logan said. 'We've only just been given the job.'

Morton led them into the house. 'You brought boots?'

'Wellies,' McCulloch said.

'Better than nothing, I suppose,' he said, taking them into the kitchen: a huge old place that had an Aga on one side and a wood burner on the other. The wood crackled away, blasting pleasant heat into the room. 'Help yourself to coffee while I just nip upstairs to let my son know you're here.'

'This is bloody nice, eh?' McCulloch poured herself a cup from the jug but Logan declined. 'God, I'd love a kitchen like this. Far cry from my shite little flat.'

'And mine.'

'They work hard for it, though, I expect.'

Logan nodded, taking in the vast space. Through the door at the back wall, he could see into the lounge, which was equally impressive. There was an open fire burning away in a hearth beneath a mantelpiece taller than Logan.

Five minutes later, Frank Morton reappeared with another, even more imposing, man trailing behind him.

'This is Michael,' Frank said. 'We'll take the pick-up.'

MICHAEL MORTON TOOK the moors like a pro. They made the ascent onto the moor itself via a dirt track that led onto Holcombe Hill. Going past the Peel tower, they'd gotten some funny looks off the nosey bastards that should've been taking in the sights instead.

'Great view,' McCulloch said. 'I should come up here more often.'

'Even better on a clear day,' Logan said.

Michael drove the pick-up across the moor, expertly bumping over rocks and frozen earth, and soon the tower was a blip somewhere behind them. He eventually brought them to a stop in the middle of nowhere and they all got out into the freezing cold. Above, the sky had turned black and was threatening a downpour.

'It's this way,' Frank said, leading them through a muddy trail.

The wellies DI Murray had found them were half decent but rubbish at keeping in heat. Logan's feet were like blocks of ice. McCulloch was clearly suffering, too. Her wellies were more suited to a rainy day in the town centre than up here in the frozen wastelands. She was visibly traumatised by the cold.

They dropped down into a two-foot-deep ditch. The sheep's body lay frozen in the mud.

'He's an old boy,' Frank Morton said. 'But he didn't deserve to bow out like this.'

'Where's the head?'

'Well, that's just it,' Morton said. 'It's been cut off. His heart's been taken out. His feet are gone, too. Look.'

The hooves had gone in four individual clean cuts, as if the butcher had gotten to the animal while it was still alive. And where its head should've been, there was now nothing more than a stump, the raw flesh bright red and frozen in the snow. There was a gaping red hole in the animal's chest where the heart had been removed, with the ribs broken and sticking out.

'Did you bring a camera?' McCulloch said.

And suddenly, Logan felt incompetent as well as bloody frozen. He shook his head. 'Just my phone.'

'I suppose it'll have to do. I'm gonna get back in the truck.'

Logan took out his phone and noticed a missed call from Vic. He made a mental note to call her back just as soon as they were off the moor and back into civilisation, then circled the dead animal and snapped away.

Michael Morton was hanging around behind him while Frank had seen sense and got back into the passenger seat.

'So, what do you think?' Logan said.

Michael shrugged. 'Not a clue, mate. But taking his head off like that would require a hefty blade.'

'There's no sign of the head?'

'We've been all over the moor. I suppose it could turn up, but it could be anywhere.' He swept his arms across the vast expanse. 'Not that it matters now.'

'And what about the heart? And the feet?'

Michael shook his head. 'Them either.'

Once Logan had finished taking photographs, they got back in the pick-up and Michael drove them back.

'Any ideas?' Frank Morton said.

Logan had to admit that it wasn't what he'd thought it would be and told Frank Morton as much. 'Have you any clue what this is about?'

Frank shook his head and was quiet for a minute as Michael manoeuvred around bumps and dips. 'He was a ram. Quite a grand-looking beast. But he was old as well. Unless someone wanted his head as a trophy or something, I'm lost. And that doesn't explain his heart and feet, either.'

'A ram?' McCulloch said. 'They the ones with horns, yes?'

Frank nodded. 'Male sheep. He'd sired most of my stock. The oldest animal in the flock.'

'Could it be a jealous farmer or something?'

'Nah,' he said. 'I doubt it. Not around here.'

'Can't rule that out, though,' McCulloch said.

'But no one's really mad enough to chop a ram's head off in the middle of nowhere,' Logan said. 'Could they have grabbed the animal, killed it somewhere else, then dumped it on the moors?'

'I suppose it's possible,' Frank said, 'but I doubt it. Who would go out of their way to do that? And for what reason?'

'He's got a point,' McCulloch said. 'Some weirdos about, though.'

'Nevertheless,' Logan said. 'I feel like I should call it in. Better to be safe than sorry, you know. That old chestnut...'

THEY SLOWLY MADE their way back to the car, sludging through grime and snow. A daylight moon was rising in the pale blue sky. Logan dialled up Murray to update.

'So, I suppose if a ram's head turns up, it'll be ours.'

'Get yourself down to that antiques place in Helmshore, maybe they've got one of those wall plaques with his head on it.'

'Come on, Dave,' Logan said. 'As daft as this sounds, you've got to admit it's a bit weird. And quite serious, actually. The poor animal was killed in cold blood.'

'Happens every day in abattoirs up and down the country.'

'You know what I mean. So are we gonna get the lab on this or not?'

Murray sighed. 'I'm not sure our resources can stretch to putting a sheep on the slab. Though I believe a leg of lamb is up thirty percent these days so it might be worth it in the long run. I'm sure the canteen might be interested in doing a mutton curry or something.'

'Forget it, then. If you're not gonna take this seriously, I'll leave it to you to let Frank Morton know we're not gonna do anything about it.'

'I'll make a few calls, Rob, but I'm not promising anything.'

Logan hung up before putting it into gear and leaving Frank Morton's farm.

'He's an absolute bell end at times.'

McCulloch smiled. 'One of those things, eh? I can see why the lab might not be interested. They'll probably see it as a waste of their time. I believe a man's been pulled out of the Elton reservoir this morning, so they'll be on that. Kind of takes precedence over a sheep.'

'A ram.'

'Aye. But you know what I mean.'

They were quiet for a moment or two as they made it to the main road. Logan swung the wheel towards home. He called Vic, who answered on the third ring.

'Hiya, love,' she said.

'You pay it in okay? What did they say?'

'They said – eventually, after they fucked me around a bit – that it was a good thing. But yeah. Looks like it's on. I'll speak to you later.'

'Well listen, we're heading back for something to eat. A bowl of that chicken broth would go down a treat.'

'You bringing a guest?'

'Kelly McCulloch.'

'You two skiving already then?' Vic said. 'Oh look. It's starting to snow again.'

Logan hung up and hit the wipers. It was already coming down heavy. 'Who would chop a ram's head off like that?'

'Don't forget the heart and feet.'

'Exactly. And how? I mean, what did they do, go up to the moors and attack it in broad daylight? Swing an axe at it?'

'It's horrible.'

'And it was just left there. Frank Morton said they just found it like that, with the body parts missing. I can't wrap my head around it.'

McCulloch whacked the blowers on. 'It does seem a tad bizarre. So let's run through the possibilities. Just who would do such a thing? They've obviously got to be some kind of nut job, eh?'

'It would probably take at least two people, I'm guessing. Unlikely they've done this in broad daylight, even if there was no one around. The army train up on that moor, so I doubt they'd have killed it there. Too much of a risk.'

'So, how would they get it off the moor? Wrap a dog lead around it and lead it off?'

'Maybe.'

'I was joking.'

'It's possible.' Logan turned into Cemetery Road and killed the engine outside number seven. Home. 'But a bit unlikely, eh? Can you imagine?'

'All they'd have to do is walk it off the moor and into a van or something. They could drive off the hill down that dirt track and off they go.'

'I'm more interested in why, though.'

They headed inside. Vic was in the living room.

'You know, you've barely even started work and here you are back home already. You should really think about addressing this attitude, Rob.'

'You sound like Murray.'

They all slumped in the living room in front of the fire. Vic added a few fresh logs. 'Bloody freezing, innit?'

'How's the business plan coming along?' Logan said.

'Slowly. I keep getting distracted by Facebook and TikTok. Soup'll be ready in five minutes. So what brings you home so early?'

McCulloch filled Vic in while Logan warmed himself up. He knew that coming home for lunch was a bad idea. He'd never want to leave again. But being so close to home, it was a no brainer.

'And what?' Vic said. 'Its head's missing?'

Logan nodded. 'Got to be somewhere, though.'

'Not necessarily,' McCulloch said. 'They could've burned it. Destroyed it in some way.'

'Maybe it's a rogue butcher or something,' Vic said. 'You know. Putting special meat in his sausages, that kind of thing.'

'Don't be ridiculous,' Logan said. 'It's gotta be something else. Kids being dickheads or something. A couple of crackpots into sacrifice.'

'Now you're onto something,' McCulloch said.

'I was thinking out loud, Kel.'

'I think it's a valid assumption, though. A sacrificial lamb, that kind of thing.'

'Sacrificial ram,' Logan said. 'Sacrifice for what, though? A good summer? A plentiful harvest for next September?'

'She's got a point, love,' Vic said. 'A bizarre killing like that. Maybe it is a sacrifice of some sort. You've said yourself about all the weirdos around here. I bet you there's one or two nutters who wouldn't think twice about chopping an animal's head off and dumping the rest of him on the moor.'

'But why would they do that?'

Vic shrugged. 'You're the coppers. You two figure it out. Come on, let's get that soup.'

THREE

Logan's phone rang while Vic was busy in the kitchen and Kel was telling her all about her latest dating disaster with Simon. It was unusual for Murray to follow up so quickly.

'The lab are sending a crew out to retrieve the animal this afternoon. They'll also have a good look around the area for anything else. Say, "thanks, Dave".'

'It's the least you can do,' Logan said. 'You told Frank?'

'Spoke to his son. I also told him that would probably be the end of the matter, unless the lab come up with something. Our resources are limited, all that.'

'What did you say that for?'

'You really want to go racing about looking for a sheep's head?'

'Ram.'

'Whatever.'

'Well, yeah. I do. Because it's been killed in cold blood for a reason. And I want to find out why.'

Murray sighed at the other end. 'Come on, Rob. Don't give me that shite. You just want to make sure you get away from the office for a few hours every day. I think we should put this one down to reckless teenagers having fun.'

'As reckless as teenagers can be, I honestly don't see them swinging an axe at a sheep.'

'Come on. You know the shite they get up to on that hill. Getting pissed, doing drugs. Shagging.'

'Killing animals...'

'There you go, then.'

'I was taking the piss.'

Murray scoffed. 'You should be on stage.'

'The point I'm making,' Logan said, 'is that it's a big leap from getting pissed to murdering animals.'

'So, you're ruling it out?'

'I'm not ruling out the possibility that kids could be involved, no. But I highly doubt it.'

A sigh. 'Just get back here, Rob. I'm getting lonely on my own.'

Logan hung up. 'Knobhead.'

'What's he on about this time?' McCulloch said.

'He's getting the lab to pick up the animal. Thinks we should knock it on the head now. As if.'

'Let's see what they come up with.'

'Probably four legs, plenty of chops, a shoulder...'

'Now who's being silly?'

She had a point. McCulloch ladled another bowlful of chicken broth while Logan went to the front window, thinking. The snow was pelting down and the roads hadn't been gritted, which wasn't unusual. He thought about the possibilities. What would someone want with a ram's head? The horns? Were they worth something? And what about the feet? What about the heart? The fact the feet were taken was bizarre. There had to be a reason. If they wanted the animal, why not take the whole lot instead of dumping the torso back where they'd got it from? None of it made sense. But nothing much did, these days.

He turned back to Kel, who was busy devouring Vic's homemade broth. 'Come on. Let's go to the butcher's. I fancy a chat.'

'What, now?'

'Well it's either that or the station. Which would you prefer?'

'Give me ten minutes.'

VIC HAD ASKED Logan to pick up a couple of fillet steaks while he was there—the girl had expensive tastes—and now he was shoving the packet in his jacket pocket while Paul Brown, the local village butcher, led them into the back of his shop, to the place where the magic happened. The smell of raw meat hung around like damp. Two of his staff were busy cleaving into whole animals, making cuts for the front counter. A butcher's block the size of a tree and coated in red reminded Logan of the slab at the station mortuary.

'So, tell me again,' said Brown. 'You found a ram's head?'

'No, we were called out to the remains of a ram up on the moor. Turns out the ram's head, heart and feet were all missing. We're just trying to piece together a few things, that's all.'

'Well it wasn't me, before you start jumping to conclusions.'

'No one's jumping to conclusions,' Logan said. 'We just want to bend your ear, that's all. A bit of advice on the subject.'

'Well, I might be a butcher. But it's not us that kills the animals. We just cut them into little pieces.'

Was that a glint in his eye? Logan thought so. 'Is there an

office we could go to or something? Don't want to give your customers something to talk about, you know.'

Brown led them upstairs to a tiny box room with a computer and printer and one window. There was a kettle, and tea and coffee paraphernalia on a little side table. One chair.

'I wouldn't really call it an office,' Brown said, taking the chair. 'But it's the best I can do. So what do you need to know?'

What did they need to know? 'Well, to be honest, we don't really know. But I suppose there's a few things. One, would it be possible to kill an animal with a heavy blade, like an axe? And two, is there some kind of black market for this kind of thing?'

Brown pondered a moment. Offered them a brew, which they both declined, wisely. 'It's unlikely the animal was killed with a blade like that. I assume you mean someone taking an axe to it and *whoosh*! Off it drops. Yeah?'

'I guess so,' McCulloch said.

'I find that highly unlikely. For one, a ram is a sensitive beast. It would know if it was being attacked and run.'

'The ram was an old fella, apparently,' Logan said.

'Even so, it would be hard to keep it still. It would need at least two people, maybe three, to hold it down while someone swung the blade. And it would have to be a very sharp blade and a very clean cut to take it out in one go. And that's not even mentioning the downright messy business it would be. You know what I mean? More likely that a bolt gun was used. That's probably why you haven't found the head. Wherever it turns up, it'll no doubt have a huge hole in it.'

Logan realised he was probably spot on. 'You're talking about what they do in an abattoir?'

'Yeah,' he said. 'You know, they walk the animal in through the traps and then stun them with the bolt gun. It's a lethal weapon. It'll kill the animal instantly, and conveniently, which I realise is a horrible thing to say. But that's how it is.'

'Doesn't account for the head, though,' McCulloch said. 'I mean, let's say that's what happened. A bolt gun. What would they want with the head?'

Paul Brown shrugged. 'Who knows? And that brings us on to the second part of your question. As far as a black market goes in this industry, yeah. Yeah, I've heard a few things over the years. Is a ram's head worth anything? Maybe.'

'What would anyone want with a ram's head?' McCulloch said. 'Seriously.'

'What about the feet?' said Logan. 'Can you shed any light on what that might be about?'

Brown shrugged. 'I'm stumped.' He raised an eyebrow.

Logan didn't have much time for people who laughed at their own jokes.

OUTSIDE, the snow was tumbling down even heavier. But now it was sticking, too. They headed down through Tottington and got stuck behind a tractor and a bus that had met at a narrow gap just beyond the road works.

'So,' McCulloch said, 'a black market in sheep heads. The real world is stranger than fiction, eh?'

'Well he wasn't exactly confirming it.'

'He said he'd heard a few things over the years.'

'Hardly anything concrete, then. I suppose it's like anything, though. A big industry like this, there's bound to be some dodgy shit going on.'

McCulloch nodded, deep in thought. 'I wonder how many butchers there are in Bury.'

'Not just Bury, but the whole of Greater Manchester. I don't think it's a butcher we're after.'

'Could be.'

'Connect the dots, Kel.'

'But there aren't any to connect yet. So let's say it's someone with a bolt gun. That means that someone who works in an abattoir has used it on this ram.'

'Not necessarily. If the killer had gotten hold of a bolt gun, it doesn't mean he or she works at an abattoir.'

'But they could've got it from someone who does. Oh for fuck's sake, come on!'

Logan grimaced. 'Bus driver looks pissed off.'

'Probably twenty minutes late now, eh?'

The traffic started moving again and Logan sailed her down the hill. 'We could do with getting hold of the weapon, if indeed a bolt gun was used.'

'Could've been a bloody sledgehammer.'

'I'm going for bolt gun. Seems the most logical right now. So what next? How do we keep this thing moving? I really can't be arsed with Murray keeping us locked up at the station.'

McCulloch nodded. 'There's an abattoir down Newton Heath way. Should keep us busy for at least a while.'

FOUR

Logan pulled into the station parking bay. The ground hadn't been gritted and was turning to sludge. There were a few semi-enthusiastic PCs dotted about, no doubt heading to the canteen for lunch. McCulloch retreated to her car for what she called 'quiet time', though Logan suspected she was keen to check over her various dating apps. They agreed to meet again for a coffee before heading out again.

The snow continued to fall steadily as Logan left her to it and skipped up the steps into Bury HQ. He'd heard on the grapevine that there had been a few incidents over the weekend that had turned the midday lunchtime into a bit of a buzz. A poor guy had been pulled out of the Elton Reservoir, dead. Probably an accident. Two gangs of youths had beaten each other up with metal bars and other assorted tools over on the Walmersley Road on Saturday night. It had quickly turned into a bloodbath. Several had been arrested. The rest were wanted for questioning. And a thirty-four-year-old woman had been found dead in her flat with a kitchen knife in her neck. She was a known victim of domestic abuse, and it looked like this time her partner had finally done her in. The community was calling for heads to roll at GMP. Logan couldn't blame them, to be fair.

He slumped at his desk and closed his eyes. It was either lack of sleep or stress or something else entirely, but he had a headache he just couldn't shake off. The cold and damp of winter wasn't exactly helping, either. He longed for warm spring days and summer evenings out in the beer garden. Instead it was all rain and dead people. And dead rams. And when he wasn't outside in the cold, he was here at his desk feeling hopeless and bored of what he'd become. Of what his job had become. Perhaps it was time to admit to himself that he just wasn't up for it anymore. Perhaps get a job at B&Q or something.

DI Murray joined him at the desk opposite and slurped on his tea. 'How did it go?'

Logan shrugged and filled him in. 'I mean, what is there to say? A farmer's found his prize ram up on the moor without a head and there's no reasonable explanation.'

'Any idea where the head might turn up?'

'If it turns up at all. You know how it is. It's probably burnt to the bone now or tossed into the tip in a bin bag.'

'Has to be a reason.'

'You know, I don't think there is. Probably just a bunch of weirdo kids messing about.'

'A bit extreme, though, don't you think?'

Logan nodded. 'So, what's the motive?' he said, as much to himself as to Murray. 'I can't think of one.'

'Any leads?'

'Not really. We spoke to a local butcher who reckons no one would be mad enough to take an axe to a ram without stunning it first. And that points to a bolt gun. You know, the kind they use in abattoirs.'

'So, we could be looking at an employee of one of these places?'

'Possibly. Though I doubt it. Bit of a mad one, to be honest. And anyway, I heard our favourite couple have had another row. And this time it's fatal.'

DI Murray sighed. Took a sip from his tea. 'Don't look at me, Rob. Nothing to do with me.'

'You know we should've had him in weeks ago, don't you?'

'I know, I know.'

'The poor woman's dead now. She didn't deserve that.'

Murray nodded. 'I know. But it's best, right now, that you just crack on with your job and let DCI McKenna get on with his. We all know mistakes were made. Best to stay out of it and keep your mouth shut. You can keep me updated on this ram thing when the need arises. Until then, have a word with Miss McCulloch about these cranks she's dating, will you? She's starting to worry me.'

There wasn't much point in replying. Logan watched DI Murray walk off and disappear into DCI Warburton's little hideaway.

Kayleigh Matheson had complained no fewer than fourteen times about her boyfriend, Ian McNamara. Logan had seen for himself how she'd kept her bruises hidden. Or tried to. She'd been on the phone, emailed, even called into the station in person, and each time her cries for help had fallen on deaf ears. Even an emergency visit to Fairfield Hospital with a broken wrist wasn't enough for DCI McKenna to take her situation seriously. Even though McKenna had been on secondment from Oldham, and had probably come into Bury HQ half-arsed, a copper of his experience should've been on the ball. Kayleigh was a known crack user, and she wasn't without her alcohol issues, either. Logan had often wondered if that was partly why they let her complaints go over their heads. Maybe they thought she was a liability, was best left alone. You couldn't trust her. But now the town was up in arms about it, after her body was found by a neighbour in the early hours of Saturday morning. And conveniently, Ian McNamara was nowhere to be found.

Logan pulled out his phone and fired off a quick text to McCulloch, though he needn't have done, because she was weaving through the office with two coffees just as he hit *SEND*.

'Right,' she said. 'You want me to drive? We can take my car.'

Didn't matter either way but he took her up on the offer. Grabbed his coffee and drank. It was scalding hot but would warm his hands up for the journey ahead. 'Where are we going?'

'Newton Heath abattoir. We can drag it out the whole afternoon, eh? Not much point in hanging around here with all the bloody death and hooliganism. Duty will be over by the time we get back to Bury, anyway. And it's bloody freezing.'

'So, come on then. Who's the lucky guy?'

She grinned as they made their way out of the office. 'I don't know what you're talking about.'

In the car, he quizzed her before she'd even started the engine. 'You can't keep it from me that easily. So who is it this time? Another banker? Estate agent? Don't tell me it's a footballer.'

'No!'

'So, when are you going out?'

'Don't make assumptions. I'm not going out anywhere yet.'

'Ah, I knew it. Be careful though, Kel. Make sure he's not just after one thing, you know what I mean?'

'It's not like that. He's nice.'

'Plumber?'

She shook her head. Tried to hide her grin. 'No, he's one of us.'

'What, you mean—'

'A copper, yeah. Merseyside CID. And that doesn't mean you can go telling every fucker in there, by the way.'

'Fucking hell, you'd better watch out then.'

'Why so, eh?'

'Scousers...'

'He's from Chester, actually.'

'A wooly back then. We should get him down to look at this ram, would be right up his street.'

'Don't be a dick,' she said, starting the Kia. 'Now let's find this bolt gun, eh?'

'I'm still not convinced a bolt gun's got anything to do with it,' Logan said. 'We can't just go off what the butcher said, can we? Guy seemed a bit unhinged, if you ask me.'

'I'm glad you said that,' she said. 'I thought he was a bit weird myself. But it's what we've got to go on. It's a better lead than anything else we've got.'

'It's still early days, though.'

McCulloch drove through Bury and took it down to the M66. The abattoir at Newton Heath was only a thirty-minute drive at best. They pushed on at a pace until they came off at Chadderton and turned towards Failsworth and Newton Heath beyond. The snow had turned to rain and the traffic was piling up as the day turned towards the dreary winter afternoon. Darkness loomed and there was a distinct chill in the air.

Of all the jobs Logan had been sent on in his police career, this had to be up there as one of the strangest. Yet he could see why the farmer would want justice for his prize ram. Mustn't have been a nice sight when they stumbled upon it. Who could murder a beast like that in cold blood? Who would have the balls to do that?

And then a thought occurred as McCulloch got up too close to a white van in front. What if the animal had been drugged? If whoever had killed it had somehow knocked it out, the job of removing the head and heart, and feet, would've been that much easier.

'There's no way they're gonna sanction this for any further investigation,' McCulloch said. 'Resources won't stretch that far.'

'Yeah, that'll be their excuse. You can kind of see why, I suppose.'

'At the same time, it's not every day a decapitated sheep turns up.'

'Ram.'

She paused a moment as the traffic began to move again. 'Do you think the farmer's got anything to do with it?'

'What, Frank Morton? Nah...'

'I guess so, eh?'

'Doesn't make any sense. Why would he want to do that to his own animal?'

McCulloch shrugged. 'Maybe he's a weirdo. Lot of weirdos around.'

Logan pointed at the road to keep her on track. 'Yeah, but killing your own ram's a bit much. Maybe it was sick, and he decided he wanted rid. No. No, that's stupid.'

'Could've been sick, though.'

'Probably had some kind of disease, yeah.'

'Hardly a humane way to take it out.'

Logan put the radio on and caught the tail end of the news. The doom and gloom was enough to send him into a pit of despair. Another thing adding to his sense of loss and his withdrawal from the job. What was the actual point to any of this?

Maybe his mid-life crisis had arrived.

'How's things with Vic?'

'Fine.'

'Only you don't seem yourself, eh?'

'It's not my marriage, Kel. It's the job. It just doesn't cut it anymore. You know what I mean?'

She was nodding but Logan wasn't quite convinced.

'Not exciting enough for you?' McCulloch said.

'Yeah. Well, yes and no. I mean, this is okay. It makes a change, getting out like this. And this is what I always thought it was gonna be like, if I'm honest.'

'Sounds like you want more action.'

But Logan couldn't quite agree. 'I don't know what I want. All I know is, I just... can't be arsed anymore. You ever get that feeling?'

'God, you sound like you're depressed.'

'Nah.'

'You sure you're not depressed, Rob? If you see your GP, they'll be able to sign you off on the sick or something, eh?'

He sighed. 'Yeah, that's if you can even get to see your GP. But I'm not depressed, Kel. Not a chance. I'm just... in a malaise.'

She looked over at him. 'Let's get down to the meat and bones, Rob. You hate your job, and you want out. Am I right?'

'Well, when you put it like that—'

'Do you really hate it?'

'I don't hate it. And maybe it isn't the job at all, more a case of me being stuck in... I don't know.'

'A mid-life crisis? Maybe you should go out and blow a couple of grand on a Gibson Les Paul and never pick it up. Or how about a Harley Davidson?'

'Don't be ridiculous.'

'Take up rock climbing?'

'I don't need anything else, Kel.'

'But maybe that's exactly what you need, eh? A decent hobby to take your mind off all the shit. Actually, that's something we all need, right? I mean, I like doing jigsaws.'

He winced. 'Jigsaws?'

'Yeah, you know. I'm working on a massive one at the minute. Five thousand pieces. It's a picture of the Colosseum in Rome. Fucking doing my head in, to be honest.'

'So, you don't like it that much, then?'

She shrugged. 'It takes my mind off things. Just for a while. And it helps.'

'You really do need a man, don't you?'

'Is it that obvious?'

Logan laughed. He could picture her sitting at her coffee table getting wound up over a corner piece. She deserved a good man to look after her.

'So, tell me more about this copper,' he said. 'Merseyside CID, was it?'

'There's nothing to tell. We've not even been out yet.'

'Where's he taking you?'

'Mind your own business.'

Logan took that as his cue to leave it, for now. 'Fair enough.'

McCulloch drove in silence for a moment, her lips sealed, and her eyes peeled on the road ahead. Logan sat back and thought of all the things that he would quite like to do as a hobby, to take his mind off things. He couldn't think of anything. He liked the odd sci-fi novel now and again. Although he was a Manchester City fan, he rarely had the time to go to a match, thanks to the job. He'd never had the inclination to take up an instrument, and anyway, it felt like it was way too late now. So what did that leave? The gym? Perish the thought. Cycling? Not a chance he would pull on those stretchy pants. Golf? Fuck, no.

'We're nearly there,' she said. 'You thought about what we're gonna say when we get there?'

Logan shrugged. 'Just do some digging around, I suppose.'

Five minutes later and McCulloch pulled into the abattoir's car park. The building was painted in grey and black, its horrendous architectural design screaming 1960s industrial slaughterhouse panic. The brick façade and the privacy glass windows seemed straight out of a hellish dystopian nightmare; a place where not just the animals went to die, but the workers too, each of their morning steps to the front doors taking a little bit more of their soul away. She found a space near the back fence, which gave them a good view of the complex upon leaving the car. Over near the main entrance, a lorry load of sheep were crying into the afternoon, as if they knew what fate awaited them. Logan felt a twinge of anxiety as they stepped towards the reception doors.

'Poor things, eh?' McCulloch said.

'I bet you don't say that when you're eating a nice lamb chop.'

'Actually, I'm not a fan of lamb. Too fatty for me.'

They pushed open the glass-and-metal doors and stepped into a cold reception area. There was an old and battered black leather couch at the back wall, and Logan wondered if it had been made with the skins of the very first animals slaughtered here. A glass coffee table—circa 1979—sat in the middle of the room.

'Can I help you?'

She was a bored twentysomething brunette examining her nails behind a harsh-looking marble counter.

McCulloch showed her a warrant card and kicked things off. 'We're from the police. Is there a manager around we can speak to?'

For a moment, the girl—her name badge said Donna—mouthed a perfect 'O' as if she'd been anticipating this day for a while now.

'You can take a seat,' she said. 'Someone will be down soon.'

The radio was on low, but Logan could make out a tune by the Arctic Monkeys as they collapsed into the couch and waited. There was no offer of coffee.

'Do you think they call her Kebab?' Logan said.

'What?'

'You know. Donna Kebab. Seems appropriate for this place.'

'Fucking grim, isn't it?'

It was. From somewhere behind these walls, a mass execution was in full swing. Logan could picture the machinery of murder : a conveyer belt of raw meat going around and around like a perpetual nightmare of flesh and blood, the souls of half a million farm animals haunting the grounds forever.

'I was thinking,' he said. 'About whoever's taken the ram out. Maybe they've drugged it, you know? Before taking a blade to it, I mean. Give it something to knock it out, then do the business.'

'I suppose it would be a lot easier.'

'Less messy. And less risk. I mean, there wouldn't be much chance for it to go kicking and screaming while a few sickos tried to hold it down.'

'It would have to be some strong drug. What is it they give to horses? You know, the street drug.'

'Ketamine.'

'Yeah. I suppose it would have to be something like that, eh?'

'Here we go.'

Logan nodded and stood as a man he guessed was the manager came towards them. He held a flabby arm out and Logan shook his hand, which was coated in sweat.

'Malcolm Leonard,' he said. 'I'm one of the managers here. Hope this is nothing for us to worry about.'

Logan plastered on a smile and introduced himself and McCulloch. Leonard was a little overweight and unkempt, like his hair hadn't been washed in weeks, and his stubble was uneven, as if his clippers had gone on the blink halfway through shaving. By the smell of him, Logan had him down as a twenty-a-day man. The tips of his fingers were yellow with nicotine.

'Not often this happens, I have to say,' Leonard said. 'Any of our lads in trouble?'

'No, nothing like that,' McCulloch said. 'Not yet, anyway.'

'Shall we go to my office?'

They followed as he led the way through a set of double doors beyond the reception desk and up a flight of stairs that reminded Logan of the ones in his old school. Leonard's ill-fitting baggy trousers were stained with something resembling coffee. At least that was what he hoped it was.

He took them through another set of doors and down a narrow corridor before ushering them into an office so small you could barely swing a cat, or a chicken. Leonard sat behind his desk after pulling up two chairs for them both. The office smelt of Benson & Hedges and the windows looked like they hadn't been cleaned in months.

'So, what can I do for you?'

McCulloch went first. 'Putting it straight out there, Mr. Leonard, and this is gonna sound a bit weird, I know, but we're investigating the gruesome death of a ram.'

'It was found decapitated in a field up in Bury,' Logan said. 'It was pretty brutal.'

'We believe it might've been stunned first,' McCulloch said. 'You know, with one of those guns you guys use.'

Leonard was nodding. 'And you think it might've been stunned with one of our guns?'

'Not necessarily,' Logan said. 'But we'd like to get your thoughts on it. It's early days in our investigation.'

'And you reckon one of our lads might've had something to do with it?'

'No, nothing like that,' McCulloch said. 'Not at all. We just want to get a picture of what we might be dealing with, that's all. The farmer's distraught. We just want to get to the bottom of it as soon as possible, you know?'

Leonard thought for a moment. 'It's been a long time since I used one. I'm going back ten years at least. I've been a manager since then and we don't get involved in all that. We just deal with the paperwork and the arseholes down there.'

You were an arsehole once, Logan thought. *Still are...*

'Let's get you some protective gear on,' Leonard said. 'And we'll have a good look downstairs. I should warn you, though. It's not for the faint hearted.'

McCulloch looked queasy all of a sudden. Tried a smile. 'Is that necessary, Rob?'

'Won't do any harm,' he said. 'I suppose we need to know what we could be up against.'

LOGAN AND MCCULLOCH stepped out into a cold and noisy expanse: a warehouse made of white tiles and walkways that had been walled off with stainless steel. They stood on a balcony overlooking the abattoir, with the animals ushered through one large open door at the back wall. Logan watched McCulloch's eyes fall on a stream of cows that were rolling in looking bewildered and scared. Could see the fear in her big brown eyes. The shouts were deafening.

A group of workers helped to push the animals through, with others standing ready with the stun guns at the other end of the weird-looking stainless steel trench, and the rest at the top end of the building, moving the dead animals up onto a conveyor belt so they could be shifted into the next room in a streamlined and well-rehearsed fashion.

Techno music blared from somewhere, tinny over the loud animal noises. This was a special kind of vibe and one which neither of them found particularly pleasant.

'Jesus,' Logan said. 'This is fucking awful.'

Leonard nodded. 'I did say it wasn't for the faint hearted. Come on. Follow me.'

It was hard to hear him over the noise, but they followed behind, looking and feeling like a pair of clowns in their white overalls and their hair-net hats and safety boots. A guided tour of an abattoir wasn't exactly high on Logan's bucket list, and he was pretty certain this was going to be his last. He wasn't exactly blind to the kind of stuff that went on in places like this but seeing it up close was something else:

nauseating, anxiety-provoking, and downright fucking frightening.

'You get used to it!' Leonard shouted as they passed a machine the size of a double decker bus that was pumping out all kinds of screeching noises from behind its steel walls. Steam rose from a chimney at the top and Logan could only wonder what the hell was going on inside.

'Oh my God,' McCulloch said. 'Get me out of here.' She gripped Logan tight as Leonard led the way. 'Why the fuck did you agree to this, eh?'

'I thought it would come in handy,' he said. 'Might be useful, you know...'

'The smell's knocking me sick...'

'Not good, is it?'

They followed Leonard up a flight of stainless-steel stairs and onto what could only be described as a viewing platform. He ushered for them to join him. McCulloch gripped the red-painted metal bars, looking pale. Logan tried to switch off from the chaos around him, but it was impossible. The whole place was a factory of death. Fear was imprinted on its walls. Maniacs were employed as key staff.

'Down there,' Leonard said, pointing, 'is where the animal is killed. It happens very quickly and humanely, and the carcass is then put onto a conveyor belt where it travels through to butchery. The animal doesn't feel anything. There's no pain. It's all over in seconds.'

Logan begged to differ. He would bet a million pounds that having a bolt gun stun the top of your head wasn't painless at all. They watched as a ginger psychopath raised a gun and a loud hydraulic sound like air being sucked from a room whooshed and popped and a cow flopped onto the floor. Four more handlers dragged it onto a conveyor belt that sloped upwards and off into the next room about sixty feet away, where Logan assumed it would be skinned and butchered and hung out to dry.

All very humane.

'See,' Leonard said. 'It didn't feel a thing. And here comes the next one.'

Logan turned to McCulloch, but she was facing the blank steel wall behind them with her eyes firmly shut. 'Kel, you okay?'

'I just don't want to see it, eh?'

Logan left her to it and nodded for Leonard to continue the tour. 'She's not feeling herself. Can we move this on quickly?'

Leonard nodded and led them away again across the viewing platform, which skirted the perimeter of the building. By now, Logan was convinced they needed no more of the guided tour, but the manager insisted. They followed down another set of stairs—steel everywhere—while on the other side of the tiled walls around them, animals that were now slabs of meat were carted into another room to be butchered some more.

The whole process was cold and calculated. The machinery of mass production. They went through another set of doors—this time made of rubber and Perspex—and into a busy thoroughfare where hordes of men in blood-stained white overalls were busy hooking the animals up to let the blood drain from their bodies. McCulloch's expression had become glassy and vacant. It was clear she wanted no more of this.

'Why don't you head back to the car, Kel? Wait for me there.'

'I'm okay,' she said. 'Just trying to think of something else. I'll leave all this to you.'

The pools of blood on the floor were being washed away with giant mops and drained through various grids at each corner of the room. Down the back end, which Logan was thankful of as it was just about far enough away for him to handle, was a massive plastic industrial waste bin that was home to the many severed heads of the cattle that had already been killed. He watched as a couple of workers tossed the heads into the bins as if they were footballs. They were obviously so used to it that it was all just part of the job. The chatter around them was loud and the soundtrack had moved on from harsh German techno to 'Living on a Prayer' by Bon Jovi, a staple of Smooth FM.

As work environments go, the incident room at HQ was a much calmer affair.

'This way,' Leonard said and led them through the massive room where hundreds of the cattle had been hung out to dry.

They took a walkway painted in yellow and Logan watched what seemed like a thousand butchers take to the animals and virtually strip them of everything, filling the massive industrial waste bins with everything from skins to bones. Logan almost threw up on the spot when he spotted a spinal column hanging from one.

'I think I'm gonna need a drink after this,' McCulloch said, who had finally found her voice, but it sounded like she was about to throw up, too.

'Just don't look,' Logan said. 'We'll be out of here in no time.'

Leonard marched off towards the back of the room, and Logan and McCulloch followed. Logan kept his eye on proceedings, impressed with the handiwork of the butchers who were turning the animals that had been killed less than an hour ago into what passed as food. McCulloch kept her head straight and her eyes still.

Pretty soon they had walked into an industrial-sized fridge and the temperature dropped considerably. This room was as big as an average school hall and the walls were frosty. More butchers were scattered around at enormous red tables, chopping up the meat and putting it back on the hooks. Bodies swung from one end to the other as the blood swilled away down the grids in the floor. Logan caught the eye of one of the butchers: he was grinning as he went to work with a boning knife.

'I think I've seen enough now,' McCulloch said. 'This is pointless.'

They went through a set of rubber and Perspex doors, which thankfully led away from the slaughter, and through a corridor that was much warmer and whose walls were adorned with framed photographs of animals on the field, various men in suits, a staff team photo, and an aerial view of the complex itself. Leonard offered them a coffee from the drinks machine, but both declined. McCulloch whispered 'thank God' to herself as they followed him through the winding complex of corridors with offices banking off on either side, and up another flight of stairs that again reminded Logan of school.

'I know it's not a pleasant experience the first time,' Leonard said. 'But you do get used to it.'

'In all honesty, Mr. Leonard,' McCulloch said, 'I don't think I'd ever get used to it.'

On the landing, there was a glass cabinet housing various implements and Logan's eye fell on a weapon that looked like it was straight out of *Star Trek*. Leonard dug in his oversized trousers for some keys and unlocked the cabinet. He reached in for the bolt gun and pulled it out.

'This is only a model,' he said. 'But its good enough to illustrate how it works. Let's get back to my office.'

LEONARD TURNED the gun over in his hands and handed it to Logan. This version was made of pale blue plastic, like a cheap kid's toy. Logan examined it up close.

'The pistol is placed on top of the animal's head,' Leonard said, 'and when the trigger is pulled, the bolt is catapulted straight into the brain. The animal is rendered unconscious immediately.'

'Jesus.'

'It's safe and humane. The real guns are made of steel and are either black or chrome. Some of them have coloured handles, depending on the animal they're designed to cull.'

Leonard handed McCulloch a circular steel bar he retrieved from his drawer. 'This is the bolt we use for pigs.'

Was that a touch of glee in his eyes? Logan couldn't be sure. He only knew that to work in one of these places, you had to have a little bit of psychopath in you.

McCulloch handed Logan the bar. It was cold and heavy, like the atmosphere in this whole place. It was time to leave.

He handed the gun back to Leonard and stood. McCulloch followed his lead.

'I think we have enough for now, Mr. Leonard,' he said. They shook hands. 'Thanks so much for your time. We may be in touch should the need arise.'

'Glad to be of some help,' he said. 'At least you have a bit more understanding about what goes on in here. So you think an animal was slaughtered outside of this environment?'

'We're looking at all potentialities,' Logan said. 'But, yes, it's possible.'

'Any suspects?' he said, raising his eyebrows. 'Sorry, it's just like this is like one of those cop shows, you know. *Police Camera Action!* Something like that.'

McCulloch smiled and nodded. 'Stand by your phone, Mr. Leonard. Just in case.'

'JESUS. Thank fuck we're out of there, eh?'

'It wasn't exactly pleasant,' Logan said. 'Can't see us going back in a hurry.'

'He was a fucking nut job.'

'He was, wasn't he?'

They walked back to the car, a little snow drifting in the air. Logan thought he would probably end up dreaming of cattle tonight and wake up screaming in the early hours.

'So, what do we reckon?'

Logan shrugged. 'Not much, really. But at least we know what one of those things looks like.'

'Did anyone stand out in there?'

'Other than Malcolm and that ginger psychopath who was pulling the trigger, no. Just another workplace, I suppose. Can't say I want to go back.'

'Me neither, but we might have to. You never know.'

'Nah, I'm not feeling it. Unless this ram's head turns up and we find something linking it with this place.'

They got in and McCulloch fired her up, switching the heating to full and the blowers on high. She was putting her into gear when Logan's phone rang.

He retrieved it from deep in his pocket. 'It's Murray. Just hang on.'

'Probably wants us to pick up a couple of steaks, eh?'

'Hello?'

'Rob,' Murray said. 'Something's come up. I'm gonna need you two back here. As soon as.'

'Well, what is it?'

'It's another one.'

'What, another ram?'

'I'll fill you in when you get here.'

CAITLIN

The smell of horse manure had been drifting in the air for days now. At least, it felt like days. She had no idea how long she'd been sleeping but when she did wake up to darkness and heard the rain lashing at the walls around her, she guessed she was somewhere fairly dry. Apart from the wetness underneath, the surrounding space seemed dry enough. She'd spread her arms out as best she could, but it was awkward because something was tied to her right ankle. A chain of some sort. She didn't know what it was attached to, but it bloody hurt when she tried to move. The floor was cold, but they'd covered her in a massive heavy blanket which kept her fairly warm, but still. There was a nasty lump on her head, and it often throbbed, sending her into a dizzy spell.

She had no idea what they wanted with her. No idea what she'd done to deserve this.

She'd been dreaming of Kurt, waking up in tears because she'd realised it was only a dream. She'd hugged him tight, and he told her it was gonna be okay, and there was no need to worry. Easy to say, of course.

She remembered the walk home. The light from Peel Tower

on the hill, the ice on the pavement. If it wasn't for that stupid bloody party...

Sooner or later, someone would come looking for her. At least, she hoped so. Kurt would be back home by now, surely. He'd have raised the alarm and called the police. A search party would be out there right now and any minute the door would crash open, and she'd be rescued, just like on those crime dramas she loved watching on a weekend when she could relax with a bottle of wine and a curry and no work until Monday.

That's what would happen.

That's how it always happened in the end.

FIVE

What little light remained had faded to wintry darkness by the time they got back to HQ. A dense fog was descending over the town and the traffic was moving slowly. The gritting lorries were out again, which was about time, and the temperature had dropped below zero. It was going to be a cold night.

'So,' McCulloch said, 'going on your theory that a drug was used on the ram first...'

Logan shook his head. 'It's not so much a theory. More a stab in the dark, I suppose.'

'Well, it's a more likely scenario than a stun gun, eh?'

'They could've tranquillised it first, then stunned it.'

'Before cutting it up.'

Logan nodded. 'Has to be a strong tranquilliser. Probably Ketamine, something like that.'

McCulloch pulled into HQ, the road slushy but gritted. Fresh snow was on the way, according to the radio. 'Would they even need to stun it, if it was tranquillised? I mean, doesn't a tranquilliser knock it out, anyway?'

Logan shrugged. 'I suppose.'

'Maybe we need to talk to a few vets, eh?'

'It was just a thought,' he said. 'I think we'll need to know what the post-mortem brings up first. You know, see if there's a trace of any drugs in its system.'

'They'll probably need a vet for that, eh?'

'I'll get onto it. Speak to Murray.'

McCulloch pulled into a parking bay near the door and killed the engine. 'It can't be another ram, surely.'

Logan pushed the door open. 'Let's go and find out.'

The incident room was busy with around fifty coppers milling about and waiting for a briefing on the Kayleigh Matheson case. Both Logan and McCulloch wanted to join them, but Murray was waving a jar of coffee and beckoning them over to his office. What fresh hell was this?

'Sit down. How did it go at the abattoir?'

'Not a pleasant experience, sir,' McCulloch said. 'I don't think we'll be repeating it anytime soon.'

'We had a call not that long after you left,' he said, making the coffee at his little brew station. 'A woman up in Tottington had opened her door to a dead bird. Or, to be more precise, a bird nailed in a crucified fashion across her porch. I've got two PCs up there. They were in the area, so called round after it went out on the airwaves.'

'A bird?' McCulloch said. 'What, like a sparrow or something?'

'Jesus, Kel...'

'Alright, a starling, then.'

'You'll be saying it's a robin redbreast bobbing along any minute.'

'Who are you? Bill fucking Oddie?'

'Guys, guys,' Murray said. 'I'm told it's a raven. Or I suppose it could be a crow.'

'Jackdaw, maybe?'

'Could be a rook. I don't know. They all look the bloody same to me.'

'Blackbird?' McCulloch said.

Murray shrugged, spooning in a heap of instant coffee. 'Could be, I suppose.'

'Nah,' Logan said. 'Different species, I think. If it looks like a raven, it probably is.'

'Jet black, so I'm told,' Murray said. 'So, that's pretty close.'

'You think it's connected to our ram?'

Murray handed out the coffees and took his seat behind the desk. 'Who knows? Bit weird, though, don't you think?'

'A ram and a bird,' McCulloch said. 'What's next? A horse?'

'How long ago was this called in?' Logan said.

'About an hour.'

'Has it been moved?'

'I don't think so.'

'Get onto those PCs and tell them not to move it until I'm up there. I want to see this in person.'

'You sound keen, eh?' McCulloch said.

'I suppose I am, yeah. A crucified raven doesn't happen every day. Gotta be a reason for it.'

'Fair enough. I'll just drink this then I'll be with you.'

'No, actually, you stay here. Maybe get onto a vet or something about that theory.'

Murray slurped his coffee. 'What theory's this?'

'The theory,' McCulloch said, 'that the ram was drugged before it was killed.'

'They might be connected,' Logan said. 'Then again, they might not be. But it would do no harm to check things out properly. I'll update you both later.'

. . .

MURRAY HAD GIVEN Logan the address, and this time, Logan took his own car. He'd been given strict instructions to leave the scene untouched. Photographs had already been taken, Logan had been told, but he also wanted some of his own.

A *raven*.

What kind of shit was this? First a ram, now a bird. Had the bird been decapitated, too? It couldn't have been a nice moment for the woman, opening her front door and seeing the bird hanging beside her flower basket. And why her house? Why her house in particular?

He headed up Bury Road, which became Tottington Road about halfway up the hill. The snow was falling once more, and the afternoon had turned dark. It was the dead of winter and dead things kept turning up. The schools had kicked out about an hour ago but there was still plenty of traffic and people around. The temperature had dropped considerably. He'd switched the radio on, only half-listening, and it was all warmongering and the cost of living. Logan wondered if the ghost of Kayleigh Matheson was sitting in the car with him, in the back seat, gazing out the window at the world she once inhabited.

When he pulled into the road in question, he could see a pool car down the bottom end and two PCs waiting for him. There were no blue lights, which was just as well. Drawing attention to this could prove troublesome. It was a strange road for a house, with a garage on either side: a place that did repairs and MOTs, and one that specialised in tyres. There was also a welder's yard and, bizarrely, a Turkish barber. The house was a converted three-storey property that had once been a school, closed in the 1950s. Logan had seen various incarnations before someone had finally bought it and converted it into a home. He'd always wondered who lived here. Now he was about to find out.

He parked up in front of the closed garage and walked the stone path up the slope to the property. There was a porch light illuminating the front and a few people dotted around: a middle-aged man and woman, and the two PCs. As Logan drew nearer, he saw the bird—definitely a raven or a crow—splayed and nailed up, crucified style, between two chunky wooden pillars either side of the large front door. Logan was keen to get a closer look, already retrieving his phone for a few photographs.

Logan nodded to the two PCs. He recognised Stefan Hartmann but didn't know the girl. Hartmann introduced her as PC Claire Walton.

'You took your time,' the woman said.

'Mrs?'

'Braithwaite. Annette. This is my husband, Clive. Look, I'm not being funny, but we'd really like this thing removed.'

Logan nodded. 'Of course. I'll make arrangements to sort that in just a moment.' He doubted that the station would send anybody up to bring a dead bird back for examination, but he had to deal with this properly and call it in, anyway. Murray would just have to suck it up.

'Well, can't you just take it down yourself?'

'I'm afraid not, Mrs Braithwaite. As disturbing as this might be, I have to stick with protocol and deal with it as such. I know this sight might've come as a bit of a surprise to you. But I'll get it removed as soon as possible. I'm sure you understand.'

Before she could answer, Clive took her by the elbow and suggested she make tea. Logan accepted the offer and asked Hartmann to radio in for a scene-of-crime unit, stipulating that it had to be here as soon as possible. Hartmann wandered off, his air wave crackling. Logan stepped up to the porch for a closer look at the dead bird.

'It's a raven, I think,' Clive said. He was softly spoken and calm, bespectacled and balding. 'You can tell by its tail. And its beak is much bigger than a crow's. You can see how big it is, as well. A crow would be smaller, I think.'

'Could be a big crow.'

'Could be, but I doubt it. It's an impressive bird, I'll give it that. Though why it's been nailed to my porch is a mystery.'

'And a concern, no doubt?'

'It's probably kids. Annette's a bit freaked out, to be honest with you. Sorry about that.'

'I can understand. But it's not the kind of thing kids do. They're too busy getting high or stuck at home with their games consoles. I don't think this is a prank. Do you have CCTV?'

Clive shook his head. 'No, but the garage across the road does. Maybe ask them?'

Logan nodded, as Annette Braithwaite returned with three mugs of hot tea. He was glad he accepted the offer as the chill was beginning to bite. The snow was icy, the air bitter.

'Sir?'

Logan turned to Hartmann. 'You on it?'

'There's a unit coming,' he said. 'Control said they'd send one straight away.'

'Good.'

'Oh, and sir,' Walton said. To Logan, she looked beat. 'We did take our own photos. Sent them to the desk ten minutes ago. We've had a good look around. There's no sign of any intrusion. The Braithwaite's are certain the bird wasn't here this morning.'

'Would be good to take a look at the CCTV locally,' Hartmann said. He glanced at Walton, who nodded. 'Trouble is, it's all closed up right now.'

Logan nodded. 'Maybe you guys can come back tomorrow. See what you can find. And do me a favour. Log everything.'

'Sir.'

Logan took a sip of tea before resting it on a nearby step to take a closer look.

The bird had been strung up, with nails hammered into each of its wings, penetrating through the thick feathers. Its head, as big as a tennis ball, hung limply, with its beak pressing upon its chest. The beak itself was shiny black, curved and broken at the tip, as if the creature had fought hard to stop whoever had taken it. Had it still been alive when they'd strung it up? Judging by the hole in the middle of its chest, that was a no. Someone had gone in and removed the heart. All that remained was a cavity more than three inches across, the blood around it dried into the feathers and thin tendrils of flesh and sinew hanging loosely. It was as though the organ had been carefully removed.

Logan retrieved some nitrile gloves from the boot of his car and returned. He was now at least able to touch the bird, though he shivered when he did, lifting the head from the chest slowly by the beak. Its eyes were glassy, like some kind of rare black pearl. Up close, the dense black of the feathers was tinged with a sprinkle of emerald green, and its feet were leathery black, the talons sharp as a knife. The wingspan was at least four feet across. It was a majestic beast. How anyone in their right mind could've done such a thing was beyond him.

Which of course begged the question: just who *had* done this? And why?

It couldn't have been the actions of someone sane. Just like the ram. And maybe it was more than one person.

Someone to kill it. Someone else to do this, whatever this was supposed to be. Was it really a crucifixion? Given the bird was probably dead before they took the heart, probably not. The display was bold. Daring. But what was the reason behind it? Was there even a reason at all?

'Mr Braithwaite, if you don't mind my asking...'

'Clive.'

'Clive. Have you or Annette fallen out with anyone recently? I mean, have you any idea who might've done this?'

Clive thought for a moment, sipping his tea, which prompted Logan to grab his own. 'Not that I can think of, no,' he said. 'We're not the type to make enemies of people. But I can tell you this. That poor bird wasn't here this morning. So, whatever happened, it must have happened in broad daylight, which bloody worries me.'

'We'll get that CCTV from the garage checked out,' Logan said. 'It should show us something.'

'If it's pointing in the right bloody direction. I just can't understand it. If you ask me, it's some kids messing about, to try and scare people, you know. Well, it's worked on Annette but not on me.'

'Have you both been at home all day, Clive?'

He drained his tea and nodded. 'We were just about to go out until we opened the door to it. Now I don't think we'll bother.' He tipped his head in the direction of the main road. 'Looks like your friends are here.'

The scene-of-crime unit was turning the corner. It was no surprise they'd only sent a small van but at least Logan could now get out of the cold and head home. He finished his tea beside the empty stare of the raven as the SOCO team parked up and Hartmann and Walton joined him.

He took some photos of his own before handing over to

SOCO, spending the next ten minutes briefing them. Given this was the second animal found in recent days, the raven would now return to the lab for a more thorough examination.

Logan was tired. And bloody cold. Not exhausted, just ready for a rest. He called Vic, who asked that he pick up a few things on the way home, and left the scene. He called Murray on the way back to update, then McCulloch. She was particularly intrigued about the missing heart. Maybe it really was connected to the ram and its missing head and feet.

And there was something else. This mystery had awakened something in Logan that had lain dormant for a while. For the first time in ages, he hadn't once caught himself clock-watching.

VIC WAS busy in the office when Logan got back home. He found Izzy on the rug in the back room, far too busy playing with her *Frozen* dolls to acknowledge her dad. But he scooped her up anyway.

'How was school, Iz?'

'Good.'

'Did you learn anything new today?'

'Can't remember.'

'Playtime fun?'

That sparked her interest, and she told Logan all about the fun she'd had earlier as he made a pot of tea and called for Vic to join them. For the past few years, it had been easy to switch off from the day job when he got home. He'd crash around eight o'clock and open a beer, thinking about how it was now too late to leave the force and start a new career.

Tonight was different, though.

Tonight, he was thinking about that raven: its glassy eyes, and the open cavity in its chest.

The missing heart.

The ram's missing head.

As they settled into the evening for tea at the kitchen table, Vic twice told Logan to snap out of it and pay attention to their daughter. But there was something niggling him.

He made a point of going in a bit earlier in the morning.

SAM

The light from the kitchen inside was calling him. It was freezing out here but there was also a certain thrill knowing that it was almost done. He walked across the field, the frozen snow packed down and crunching beneath his boots. The pale moonlight faded as the clouds rolled in, but it didn't matter. Besides, the clouds were moving fast out here. There was probably more snow to come, and the wind was picking up, too. There was work to be done but plenty of time to do it. He wasn't worried about that.

He turned to look back at the barn, beside the house. It wasn't always locked, and he'd said to the others before now that they had to be careful, just in case she tried to get away.

He liked it out here. It offered a great view of the city. Those distant twinkling lights had him mesmerised for a few moments. He wondered what was happening down there tonight. All those people. All those lives. All those opportunities. But it was never a place for people like him. Not that he cared about that.

He took the plastic bag from his pocket and carefully untied the knot. When the break in the clouds came, and the moonlight shone down, he plucked the bird's heart from the bag and held it in the palm of his hand.

There was blood.

This was good.

He took the fleshy muscle and brought it to his lips. Touched his tongue with his fingertips, tasting little droplets of the raven's blood like a fine and incredible wine.

He knew he should probably share it, but he wanted this moment all to himself. It was selfish of him but fuck them. This time it was his turn. After all, he'd been the one to do all the dirty work. He deserved it.

He took a deep breath and laughed out loud. Flakes of icy snow drifted on the cold air. Up above, the Milky Way sparkled.

He opened his mouth wide and dropped it in.

He ate quickly and hungrily, the blood bursting all over his mouth like the juice from some wild fruit, and swallowed.

Christ, what a fucking rush.

SIX

The phone was ringing, dragging her out of a deep and wonderful dream.

DS Kelly McCulloch rolled over in bed and grabbed her iPhone before it fell off the bedside table. It was Rob.

'Yeah?'

'You coming in, then?'

She checked the time. 'Rob, it's not even half-six. I don't get up 'til seven.'

'Nonsense. We've got work to do. Did you chase up a vet?'

'Can't talk about this now, Rob.'

'Just get here as soon as you can. I've done a day's work already.'

'No you haven't,' she said, sitting up and sending the cat jumping off the end of the bed. 'Give me an hour. I want coffee.'

McCulloch wrestled her way through the canteen. Eight o'clock in the morning was peak time and notorious for being bloody noisy. She spotted Logan on their usual table with DI Murray. Within half an hour, the place would be empty, and she might be able to hear herself think. There was a hot coffee waiting for her.

'What time do you call this?' Logan said.

'The time I clock on, eh? So, come on. What's new? Any news on the heart?'

'Nothing as of yet,' he said. He took out his phone and showed them both the photos he'd taken the previous evening.

'Christ,' McCulloch said. 'Poor wee thing, eh?'

'Not so wee,' Logan said. 'The bird was bloody massive. I could've sworn it was looking right through me.'

'So, what now?'

'It's in the lab,' Murray said. 'Along with the ram. We'll know more as soon as SOCO are done with it. Could be a few days.'

'A few days?' McCulloch spluttered into her coffee.

'They're busy, Kel,' Murray said. 'There's a lot going on. Resources are thin as it is.'

'You're telling me.'

'And meanwhile,' Logan said, 'we're none the wiser. It's a bit bizarre, to say the least. The heart could be anywhere. Probably in a bin somewhere. Flushed down the toilet, whatever.'

'Why the fuck would the heart be removed?' McCulloch said. 'And why string a raven up anyway? What does it all mean, Rob?'

'We need to check the CCTV from the garage,' Murray said. 'I've sent Hartmann and Walton back up there already. As soon as we get that, maybe things will move along a bit further. Until then, I want to know why you want to speak to a vet.'

'We're thinking,' McCulloch said, 'that the ram might've been drugged before it was killed.'

'But until we get a toxicology report, there's nothing for us to go on,' Logan said. 'It's just a theory. Nothing concrete. And even if there is some kind of tranquilliser involved, we're still nowhere nearer to finding out why these animals have been killed like this.'

'What I don't get,' McCulloch said, 'is why this raven's been literally crucified at someone's front door. Could this thing even be connected to the ram, or could it be something completely separate? Just a coincidence?'

'Fair point,' said Murray. 'It's a mystery. Like when my bloody breakfast is going to turn up.'

'So, what's our next move?' McCulloch said. 'We can't really do much until we hear more from the lab, eh?'

Logan shrugged. He drank the last of his coffee and signalled over to the counter for a fresh one.

'Look, it could be a few days before we can proceed,' Murray said. 'I'm not writing it off just yet, but I've a feeling this is going nowhere fast. We'll see what comes back, but if there's no trace of any drugs, I don't see the point of taking it further.'

'But surely even you can see this is some weird shit,' Logan said. 'What if something else turns up?'

'We'll cross that bridge when we come to it,' Murray said. '*If* something comes up. In the meantime, we can keep you busy with something else.'

'Please,' McCulloch said. 'I've had enough burglaries to last me a lifetime.'

'No,' Murray said. 'It's a missing person. I just want you to go up to the house and have a chat with her partner. See what you can pick up, if anything. I'm told his employers have given him time off. As you can imagine, his head's probably in bits, but we can't rule him out.'

'Who's the missing person?'

'A woman. The guy's girlfriend. They've been together a while, or so I believe.'

'Name?'

'Kurt,' Murray said.

McCulloch nodded. 'Like Kurt Cobain, eh? Mum was probably a Nirvana fan.'

'I meant the name of the missing woman,' Logan said.

'Caitlin Slater,' Murray said. 'Boyfriend is Kurt Chadwick. This is totally out of character for her. All the usual stuff.'

McCulloch glanced at Logan. 'Probably run off with another man, eh?'

'Address?' Logan said.

'It's up near Peel Brow,' Murray said. 'On the little housing estate there. Lime Grove. He's been told to expect a visit from us, so pop by when you can and have a chat.'

'We may as well head up there now.'

'Here's a copy of the file,' Murray said, handing McCulloch the folder. 'In the meantime, I'll chase up those toxicology reports for you, but I can't promise anything. Don't say I never do anything for you.'

'So, Kurt Chadwick,' McCulloch said. 'Thirty-eight, truck driver, mostly works nights.'

'We might be lucky to find him awake,' Logan said.

Logan made a left down Peel Brow and turned right into the estate beside them. Lime Grove was easy enough to get to. They parked up beside the communal field and killed the engine, directly across from Kurt Chadwick's house. McCulloch had barely leafed through the report but there wasn't much of it, anyway. She'd picked up the basics: Caitlin Slater wasn't home when Chadwick had returned from work three days ago. He'd raised the alarm soon after, worried that this wasn't at all like her. All that. She wasn't answering her phone, none of her friends had seen her, and she hadn't been in touch with anyone else that he knew of. She'd also left her things at home so hadn't just upped and left him. In short, she'd disappeared.

'Come on,' Logan said. 'Let's go and see what he's got to say.'

The front door was somewhat ramshackle and in desperate need of a lick of paint. The refuse bins were overflowing, but that was no surprise, as these days, the council seemed to empty the bins whenever they felt like it. Logan pressed the bell, which gave a harsh, shrill ring, and a moment later they heard footfalls and the door unlatched and swung open. Kurt Chadwick looked shell-shocked and run down, like a man who hadn't slept for a week. He smelt like he hadn't showered for a week, either.

'Kurt Chadwick?' McCulloch said.

He paused and nodded. 'You found her?'

'I'm afraid not,' Logan said. 'I'm Detective Sergeant Rob Logan, this is Detective Sergeant Kelly McCulloch. Is it okay if we come in?'

Chadwick sighed and gestured for them to enter. 'I've been through all this already. As you probably know. None of it's bringing her back.'

It was clear he'd been spending most of his time in the living room. He moved some clothes and cushions off the couch and motioned for them to sit down. Offered them a cup of tea, which they declined.

'We'll try not to take up too much of your time,' McCulloch said. 'We know this must be difficult for you.'

'Shouldn't you be out there looking for her?'

'We do have a team currently working on it,' Logan said. 'And to be completely honest with you, Kurt, we're here because the senior investigating officer has asked us to go over some things with you, that's all.'

'I've already had two coppers round yesterday. Can't remember their names but I think they were detectives as well.'

Logan nodded. It was probably all in the report he hadn't really read over.

'So,' McCulloch said, 'I know you've been over this, Kurt, but would you mind talking through events for us again? I know this is hard but it's important and we need to be up to date with what's happening. Just so we're clear.'

Chadwick shook his head. He lit up a cigarette and sighed. The coffee table was littered with empty beer cans. Logan could forgive him for wanting a drink, though he hoped he hadn't been driving around town looking for her when he was half cut.

'I got a text message off her,' he said. 'About midnight-ish, I think. *On way home babe*. That's what it said. So I made a point of calling her because I'd just pulled into the services at Carnforth and I knew she'd still be awake.'

'You're in haulage, eh?' McCulloch said.

'Yeah. HGVs. I had to take my forty-five-minute break so thought I'd grab a coffee, you know?'

'And that's when you called her?' Logan said.

'Yeah. I'd just got myself a sandwich and a coffee and thought I'd give her a ring because she'd been at a party and her text said she was on her way home. You know how it is. It was late at night, and I wanted to speak to her, make sure she was okay, that sort of thing.'

McCulloch nodded. 'But there was no answer, eh?'

Chadwick shook his head and took a drag on his smoke. 'No. I just assumed she was asleep so didn't call back. I just sent her a text, as we always do, and went back on the road.'

'When did you finish your shift?' McCulloch said.

'About half-six. And that's when I called her again. But there was still no answer.'

'Was the phone ringing out or was it a dead line?'

'It was ringing out.'

'Is that when you called the police?' Logan said.

He turned to Logan. 'No, because it was still early and Caitlin sleeps like no one else, so I thought I'd leave her until I got home. I've been over all this with the other two coppers yesterday. When I got home, she wasn't here. The bed hadn't been slept in, so she hadn't been home at all.'

'And is that when you raised the alarm?' McCulloch said.

'No, I phoned her friend first. Lisa. She wasn't answering her phone until half-eight or thereabouts. I just assumed they were all a bit wrecked after the party, you know? Maybe Caitlin had slept on her couch or something. When I eventually managed to speak to her, she said Caitlin had left before midnight, probably around a quarter to. That was the last time she'd seen her.'

'And then you raised the alarm?' Logan said.

Chadwick nodded. 'I phoned the police, yeah. And then a couple of coppers came around. I spoke to them. Then yesterday, two plain-clothes guys came. Detectives, like you. I mean, there's a lot of talking and not much action, you know? Is anyone actually out looking for her? She could be anywhere. She could be dead.'

'Right now,' McCulloch said, 'it's being treated as a missing person case. We have a lot of people go missing all the time, Kurt.'

'So, she doesn't matter? Is that what you're saying?'

'That's not what we're saying,' Logan said. 'We have to give it a period of time before it becomes something else. Caitlin may get in touch yet. Has there been any sign she might've decided to leave? Has her mood been okay lately? I know these questions might be hard to hear, Kurt, but we have to consider these possibilities. You know, has your relationship been good in recent months?'

Chadwick almost laughed. 'So, now she's ran off with someone else? That what you're saying? She's had an affair and left me?'

'That's not what we're saying, Kurt,' McCulloch said. 'But it is a possibility.'

'We have a good relationship,' he said. 'We've been together eight years. She's always asking when I'm gonna marry her. She's not left me. If she had, she'd have taken her stuff, but it's all still here. Go and look for yourself.'

Logan nodded. He was probably right. 'So, how has she been lately? Have you noticed anything unusual about her? Could anything have changed?'

'Caitlin's Caitlin,' he said. 'She's got her routine that she sticks to. She always has Shredded Wheat for breakfast and absolutely has to have fish and chips on a Friday night. She barely sees the few mates she's got and takes ages to put her make-up on in the morning. I mean, for fuck's sake. This isn't like her.'

Logan and McCulloch exchanged a look.

'It's not unusual for people to just up and disappear for a while,' Logan said. 'Has her mental health been okay these past few weeks or months?'

'She's not depressed.'

'She talked about wanting a holiday, anything like that?'

'Look, she's not suicidal and she's not fucked off to bloody Benidorm. She's just missing, that's all. She went to a party, and she didn't come home. She's still out there somewhere, I know she is. She could've fallen in the river. Someone could've... could've raped her. Anything. Please. *Please* find her.'

Logan left McCulloch to try and comfort him. He cleared the beer cans from the coffee table and went through to the kitchen, where he could hear Chadwick sobbing and McCulloch telling him it was going to be okay, that they would find her. She shouldn't have been making those promises.

He picked up a framed photo of the two of them. Caitlin was pretty: a brunette with long locks flowing over her shoulders, dressed like an indie kid from 1995. Chadwick was clean shaven and a lot slimmer, with not a shred of grey in his hair. The photo was probably taken back at the beginning of their relationship. They looked happy and in love.

Logan found a half-full bin bag sitting idly by the sink. He tossed the cans in, followed by the remnants of a strange-looking takeaway. But he drew the line at washing the dishes, which were piling up on the side.

Logan doubted that Caitlin had just upped and left. There were no signs that she would've done that, particularly with all her clothes still here. The house still had her imprint on it. In his gut, Logan knew she hadn't run off.

But where was she?

And was she still alive?

'Rob?'

He turned to find McCulloch standing in the doorway. 'Yeah?'

'Time to go, eh? Poor guy's in bits. Says he's going out to look for her.'

'Can't blame him, I suppose.'

'Maybe we should go with him?'

Logan thought about it but not for long. 'No. Leave him to it. But we need a few more minutes.'

Kurt Chadwick was hovering in the back room, swinging his jacket on. 'What for?'

Logan shrugged.

Chadwick led them back into the front room with a sigh. They sat down in the silence before he spoke up again. 'I just want to look for her,' he said. 'You'd do the same. Wouldn't you? If it was your wife or whatever who'd gone missing.'

'Of course,' Logan said. 'We understand.'

'Totally,' McCulloch said. 'We don't blame you. But it's early days yet, Kurt. She may just turn up when you least expect it.'

'Like I said, I don't believe she's left, for whatever reason. She didn't even want to go to this stupid party, and I did try to talk her out of it, but she said she felt pressure to go. You know how it is. And now this. I'm telling you both right now, this doesn't feel right.'

Logan nodded. The guy had his reasons to believe what he believed. And maybe he was right. Maybe something really had happened to Caitlin. God knew there was enough weird shit happening around these parts lately.

'Okay, Kurt,' Logan said. 'I understand you want to look for her. You won't find us standing in your way.'

'You couldn't stop me.'

'We wouldn't want to,' McCulloch said. 'Honestly.'

'I just want to know what your plan is,' Logan said. 'If you have one.'

Chadwick sighed again. 'I don't. I'm just driving around in a daze, if I'm honest. I've been through the woods, I've been out on the hills. There's no trace of her, obviously. I feel so... so stupid. So bloody useless. I've thought about giving leaflets out or something but what good will that do? The more I think about stuff like that, the more pointless it feels, as if I'm just wasting time.'

'We do have a unit working hard on this, Kurt,' McCulloch said. 'And I'll make it my personal responsibility to keep you right up to date with what's happening.'

'In the meantime,' Logan said, 'this party. And this friend of hers. Lisa, right? Have you got her number? Or her address?'

'I gave it to another detective yesterday. I think she might've made a statement already.'

'Even so,' Logan said. 'I'd like to take it myself, if that's okay. Maybe we can go and speak to her this afternoon.'

Chadwick dug his phone from his jeans pocket and opened up his directory. Handed it to Logan, who made a quick note of both the mobile number and address. A few minutes later, Logan was at the wheel of the car as McCulloch stood on the pavement and dropped a comforting hand on Kurt's shoulder. He watched Chadwick get in his VW and drive away out of the estate.

'Poor guy, eh?' McCulloch said, as she got in the passenger seat.

'What do you reckon?'

'What do I reckon? What, you don't think he's got anything to do with her going missing, surely?'

Logan shook his head. 'Nah, course not. Don't think he's got it in him. He seems genuine enough to me.'

'Aye.'

'The thing is, though, where the hell is she? You think she's run off with someone else?'

'I don't think she's having an affair, no.'

'Then what? She got a long-lost father she's catching up with? It's a bit strange.'

McCulloch nodded. 'I hope nothing bad's happened to her.'

'But?'

'But I've got a feeling. I hate to say it, Rob, but I think we might be talking about the unthinkable here.'

'What? Murdered?'

'You said it, not me, eh?'

'We're a long way off from that, Kel.'

'That may be so, but he's right, isn't he? Where the hell is she?'

They drove in silence for a while until McCulloch broke it.

'It's not like murder's a common thing around here, eh? So, you know. I find it unlikely.'

Logan didn't believe her. 'I sense doubt, Kel.'

'Nah, don't be silly.' She held a hand up. 'I do find it unlikely. But you never know. I mean, there *are* some real weirdos about. Like that guy who killed that poor woman at the bus station, eh?'

Logan nodded. He was still in college at the time. 'That was a long time ago. And it was... well, let's just say it was unusual. It was a pretty bad mutilation. The kind of murder only a real psychopath could do.'

'Not many like that around.'

'No.'

But then, who was a psychopath? Could you walk past one in the street and truly know? Sociopaths and narcissists... Logan had known a few of those in his time. But a psychopath? Zero empathy? Not necessarily violent, but often the case. He had to admit they were few and far between, especially around here. Though it wasn't impossible. But then, you didn't have to be a psychopath to commit a murder. Under the right circumstances, anyone could do it. Just ask Kayleigh Matheson. Logan had no doubt that Ian MacNamara was far from a psychopath. And yet he'd been capable of murder. Of course, there was no conviction yet, but every man and his dog at HQ knew he was wielding that knife when Kayleigh went down to her death. And now, ironically, he was missing, too. And probably for very different reasons than Caitlin Slater.

Logan spotted something in the road, about fifty yards ahead, like a mound of snow that hadn't quite fully melted.

He had a sudden inkling that he needed to stop and remove it. 'You see that?'

'What?'

Logan slowed the car and pulled over just before the roadkill.

'Rob, what the fuck?'

An eighteen-wheeler rolled past as they left the car, all forty-odd tonnes of metal sending slews of mud into the gutter. Logan stumbled through the sludge and went directly to the dead animal. McCulloch hovered around him.

'Don't touch it, Rob. You don't know what kind of bloody diseases it might have, eh?'

'Of course I'm not going to touch it, Kel.'

'What is it?'

'Looks like a rabbit. Or a hare, maybe. Get me some of those gloves from the boot, will you? And I think there's some evidence bags as well.'

'What? You're not going to bring the bloody thing in, are you? It's obviously been hit by a car, eh?'

But Logan wasn't so sure. Yeah, of course there was a lot of roadkill around here, especially on this road: a direct route into Bury town centre. But this felt different. This one felt... otherworldly. The rabbit was snowy white, as if from a fairy tale, but dirty with rain and mud.

'Here you go.'

Logan pulled on the nitrile gloves while McCulloch held the large evidence bag open. He grabbed the animal by its hind legs and turned it over.

Both of its eyes were missing, as if they'd been cut out with expert precision using a sharp surgical knife.

'Jesus,' Logan said. 'Fucking hell.'

There was dried blood across its mouth, and its two front teeth stuck out like sharp needles. A hole gaped in its chest, where the heart had been removed. There was also a hole where its genitals should've been, the blood soaked into the fur.

Tied around its left foot was a black plastic name tag. Logan examined it up close. There was a sixteen-digit number and a QR code printed in white. It was obviously some kind of identification ring. The question was, where from? And why?

'This is some kind of weird, eh?' McCulloch said.

Logan held up the rabbit and dropped it in the evidence bag.

McCulloch sealed it quickly and put it out of sight in Logan's boot. 'What the fuck's going on, Rob?'

'Did you see its eyes?'

'I saw two holes where its eyes should've been.'

'This doesn't feel right.'

'Rob, this has absolutely nothing to do with our investigation. That's if you can call it a bloody investigation, eh? I mean, what? A ram with no head and feet and a bird with its heart plucked out.'

'And the ram's heart as well. And now a rabbit with no eyes. Come on, Kel. Something isn't right here.'

'That may be so, but I'll tell you what, Rob, if you were to spend half an hour walking across these fields you'd come across plenty of this stuff. I mean, all the wildlife around here and you're bound to find strange things, weird ways in which animals die.'

'Its eyes were cut out, Kel. And its heart. I mean, come on...'

'It was probably just hit by a car, Rob.'

'Kel, its genitals have been cut out. You're not telling me a bloody Toyota or a Ford Mondeo is capable of hitting a rabbit and slicing its eyes and balls out at the same time.'

'Now you're just being ridiculous, eh?'

'And that's not to mention the ID tag on its leg.'

'Could mean anything.'

But Logan wasn't listening. He went around to the boot and opened it back up. He unzipped the evidence bag and retrieved the ID tag from the rabbit's foot, prising it away over the muddy fur, and went back behind the wheel. McCulloch got back in the passenger seat and sighed.

'Come on, then. Let's get it back to HQ.'

'Hang on.'

'What're you doing?'

Logan held up his phone, still wearing the plastic gloves. 'I'm scanning the QR code.'

'What? For fuck's sake, eh?'

Logan scanned the code with the phone camera. It connected to a website: *followthewhiterabbit.net*. He clicked the link, and it took him to a blank white screen with a small icon of a bouncing white bunny in the middle.

As he watched, the figure of Alice walked across the top and a Cheshire Cat peeked its grinning head from the bottom corner. 'What the fuck is this shit?'

'I don't like it,' McCulloch said. 'This is creepy, Rob. Come off it, eh?'

Logan closed down the site and pocketed his phone before starting the car up and putting her into gear.

'Where to now?'

'Back to the station,' he said. 'We need to have a proper look at this site.'

'Is that really a good idea?'

'You got a better one?'

'How about helping to look for Caitlin Slater? You said you wanted to visit her friend, this Lisa.'

'It can wait,' Logan said.

'Oh, like this is more important?'

'Just half an hour, Kel. That's all.'

SEVEN

HQ was more quiet than normal for mid-morning. Logan and McCulloch headed upstairs and went straight to Logan's desk. McCulloch could see DI Murray through his office window, busy on a phone call.

'Is it too early for dinner?' McCulloch said.

'Kel, it's barely eleven o'clock. But a coffee would be good.'

McCulloch sloped off to the canteen while Logan fired up the desktop and waited for it to load up. *Follow the white rabbit*. As cryptic as it was enticing. Somehow he knew he was about to get involved in something he shouldn't.

He scanned the office, to make sure he was alone. But there were one or two coppers dotted about with their heads into paperwork. Besides, there was nothing to hide. He'd probably get a bollocking from IT if they knew he was about to explore a site without any prior permission, especially if it was a site he found through the corpse of a dead rabbit with its eyes cut out.

Speaking of which, he wasn't entirely sure DI Murray

would take kindly to another dismembered animal in the lab.

He clicked on the little Firefox icon and typed *'followthe-whiterabbit.net'* into the search bar. Waited for the white rabbit to dance across the middle of the screen. He hovered the mouse arrow over the little icon and saw it became clickable. When Alice walked across the top of the screen and the Cheshire Cat poked its grinning head from the bottom right corner, he found they were clickable too.

Then the Mad Hatter turned up, spinning into view from the left.

All clickable.

All inviting him in.

He wrestled with it for a moment. No doubt DI Murray would have a fit if he knew he was about to dive into a site they knew nothing about. A single click could send down the entire network. There could be all kinds of viruses and malware Logan was about to unleash. But it was a risk he was willing to take, for curiosity had now gotten the better of him. Wasn't that Alice's fatal flaw? Curiosity of the wonderland down that rabbit hole? And of course, she ended up in all kinds of trouble...

'Fuck it,' Logan said, and clicked on the white rabbit.

'Black coffee,' McCulloch said, plonking a paper cup on the desk. She pulled up a chair beside him. 'Not sure this is a great idea, Rob.'

He wasn't sure, either. But now there was no going back. The rabbit spun and then got bigger until it took up the entire screen and swallowed the other characters. The screen flashed red, yellow, purple, pink, then a kaleidoscope of colours became a mathematical fractal and zoomed in on one spot, getting faster and faster until it came to a sudden stop and a photograph appeared and filled the screen.

It took Logan a moment to fill in the blanks. 'What the fuck?'

'What is it?'

'It's my bloody car.'

To be more specific, Logan was looking at the rear end of his car, complete with registration plate to prove it. The photograph had been taken as the car was moving on a main road by a vehicle behind.

Someone had been watching them.

Logan felt woozy all of a sudden. He grabbed the coffee, hot and bitter, and sipped, trying to stay calm. Thinking. Had he just opened up a large can of worms? Now that he'd gone down the rabbit hole, could he even get out?

They sat in silence for a moment, mesmerised by the site's spell, trying to figure out where the photo could have been taken and what it all meant.

Logan looked up from the computer and saw Murray sauntering over. His apparent good mood would probably change pretty quickly when he discovered the mess his two coppers were getting into.

'So, how did it go with Kurt Chadwick?' he said. 'What do we reckon? Has he got blood on his hands?'

'I highly doubt it,' McCulloch said. 'Seemed a genuine enough guy to me.'

'Hang on,' Murray said, looking at the screen. 'I recognise that number plate.'

'It's mine.'

'Come again?'

'It's mine, sir.'

'Why's it on the ANPR? You been done for speeding again?'

'It's not the ANPR.'

'Well, what is it then?'

Logan and McCulloch exchanged a look and McCulloch shrugged.

'Well, what it is, sir,' Logan said, then trailed off, looking for the best way to explain without Murray losing his shit. 'See, there's this rabbit.'

'A what?'

'There was this rabbit at the side of the road.'

'A roadkill.'

'It's not just a roadkill, Kel,' Logan said.

'You're not making sense, Rob,' Murray said. 'What's a bloody rabbit got to do with this? Explain.'

'I'm trying if you'd just let me speak.'

'I'm all ears.'

A silence descended upon the room and logan felt all eyes upon him.

'We went to see Kurt Chadwick,' Logan said. 'We talked about the events leading up to him calling us in over his missing girlfriend. Seems a genuine enough guy. But he's adamant we aren't doing much to find her.'

'We're working on it,' Murray said. 'It's not like this is a murder enquiry. She's missing and that's all. I'm sure he's been made aware.'

'He reckons we're not doing enough, sir.'

'And I'm inclined to agree, eh?'

'And what about your number plate, Rob? Why are we looking at it on the computer screen?'

'Well, see, thing is, sir…'

'We came across this roadkill, this rabbit, on the way back from Kurt Chadwick's place,' McCulloch said. 'And Rob decided to check it out as it appeared to be mutilated, just like the raven, with its heart removed and…'

'And its eyes,' Logan said. 'And the rest.'

‘Still doesn’t explain why your car number plate’s on here.’

‘It had an ID ring on its leg,’ Logan said, ‘so I scanned the QR code and it brought me to this website and here we are.’

‘What the bloody hell do you mean, ‘here we are’?’

‘It seems that someone’s been following us, sir,’ Logan said.

Murray pulled up a chair. 'I can already see there are gaps in this story, Rob. Something tells me you're being somewhat economical with the truth.'

'Look, this is gonna sound weird but—'

'Try me.'

‘Like Kel said, we found this rabbit at the side of the road. Don’t ask me how it got there but it stood out and I felt like I just had to stop to have a look.’

‘You stopped to look at a roadkill? Seems a bit strange, to say the least.’

‘Well when I examined it, I found that its eyes had been cut out, sir,’ Logan said. ‘And its genitals. It’s bloody obvious it’s not just a roadkill. Someone put it there for us to find.’

‘Bollocks.’

‘Come on, sir.’

'So then you thought you'd just check out this website like it was bloody Facebook without the express permission of either me or the IT department? Am I right? Jesus, Rob, you absolute fuckwit.'

'I guess curiosity got the better of him, eh?' McCulloch said.

Murray took his head out of his hands. 'And what's your role in all this, Kel?'

'Sir, I tried to suggest that it wasn't a good idea.'

'No, you didn't,' Logan said.

'Yes, I bloody did!'

'Kel, come on...'

Murray picked up a nearby desk phone and dialled a number.

'Sir, what are you doing?'

'What does it bloody look like? I'm calling IT, which is something you should've done before you started messing with this shit, you absolute tit.'

'Hang on a minute,' Logan said. 'Hang on. With respect, sir, don't you find it strange that my car is on this site? And if my car is, what the hell else is on here?'

'I highly doubt this has anything to do with the investigation around those butchered animals.'

'Yet we find a white rabbit with its eyes, its heart, and its balls missing. Another butchered animal in the area and you're not seeing a connection? Come on, sir. You must surely admit that this is a bit fucked up.'

'What's fucked up, DS Logan,' Murray said, 'is your inability to see sense. You've jumped in here without any care or caution, straight onto this website without a single thought for what kind of malware or whatever the fuck else you want to call it that might be infecting every computer in the bloody building. Not a single thought for the consequences of your actions. And you expect me to take you seriously?'

'But we haven't seen what else is on the site yet, sir.'

'And we're not going to, Rob. Now I suggest you both disappear before you make it worse.'

'WHY DIDN'T you back me up, Kel?'

'Because you brought this on yourself, Rob.'

He knew she had a point. Of course she did. But he had

felt compelled to take action and look a bit more closely at the website. But there was very little chance of that now. The canteen was beginning to fill up, so McCulloch ordered them both some lunch while Logan stewed and thought about the next course of action. First, a decapitated ram, then a crucified raven. Now a mutilated rabbit. None of it made sense and, even worse, he half-expected something else to turn up.

Then there was Caitlin Slater. A missing woman nobody seemed to fear was in any kind of deep trouble. Just a woman who'd taken herself off from her partner for some good reason. Not that Kurt Chadwick seemed to think so, of course. If she'd been mentally unstable and taken her own life, she hadn't left a note. At least, nothing had been found yet.

He took his notebook from his jacket pocket and checked the address and number Kurt Chadwick had given them. *Lisa Kirkland*. The girl whose party Caitlin had attended the night she went missing. He guessed that if anyone might be able to give any insight, it would be her.

'Right, one jacket potato with chilli,' McCulloch said, putting a plate before him. 'So, what's the plan?'

Logan forked up a mouthful. 'We go and see this Lisa, a friend of Caitlin Slater. She might know something.'

'And if she doesn't, she might be able to point us in the right direction, eh?'

'Indeed.'

'But I was thinking more about this dead rabbit in the boot of your car. Murray said anything?'

'Kind of forgot to mention it was there.'

She sighed. 'Fuck's sake, Rob.'

'You saw what mood he was in. It didn't seem like the right time. What are you doing?'

'Giving him a call,' she said.

'You sure that's wise?'

'I ain't driving around with a dead rabbit in the car. It needs to go to the lab, eh? With the ram and the bloody raven.'

Logan knew she was right. And Murray was less inclined to give her a bollocking as she was currently flavour of the month. Besides, the rabbit really did need to go into the lab. He'd feel ten times better when it was out of his car.

Logan drifted away from listening to her conversation and ate. The potato was good, but the chilli wasn't up to its usual standard.

There was still no sign of the ram's head. And with no toxicology report, all of this was just dead animals. Strange and bizarre pranks that some sickos had carried out. But Logan felt there was something else to it. There had to be something else.

He had to check out the website further. For one thing, they had been followed. Murray wasn't exactly in the best of moods to pursue it right now, and not getting prior permission was a stupid thing to do, as it had now stalled things. He wondered if Vic still had that old laptop...

'Come on,' McCulloch said. 'He's still pissed off, but I managed to persuade him. We finish eating, then you bring the rabbit in. And there's at least some good news on toxicology. We might have a report by close of play tomorrow.'

'Do we know what IT said about the website?'

'They said you're a fucking idiot, eh? Now come on. Eat up.'

AFTER LOGAN HAD BOOKED the dead rabbit in, they hit the road.

'So, is Lisa home?'

'I don't know. I did call but there was no answer.'

'Could be another wasted journey. But at least it gets us out of the way, eh?'

Logan nodded. 'She's probably at work, to be fair.'

McCulloch clocked Logan eyeing the rear-view mirror. 'Look, don't worry about it. Whatever it is, or whoever it is, I hardly think they're gonna be on our tail all the time, eh?'

'There's got to be a reason, though, Kel,' Logan said. 'Which is why I need to see more of this website. If they're following us, why, and how often? All right, I shouldn't have bloody done anything on work premises. I admit it was stupid. But I've got to look into it further. There could be all sorts on that site. I mean, fuck me, it makes me want to leave my car at home every day and get the bloody bus into work.'

'And they're hardly reliable, eh?'

'The point is someone's out there trying to wind me up.'

'And it's working.'

'Yeah, it's working. I mean, forgive me for being paranoid, Kel. But what's next? You know what I mean?'

McCulloch sat back and sipped her coffee. It was almost one o'clock. She flicked onto Five Live. The radio was full of the joys of spring, too. Inflation through the roof, every man and his dog on strike, yet another Prime Minister. War, famine, pestilence...

'Shall we have some music for a change?' she said.

Logan shrugged. 'I like a bit of Smooth FM.'

It was better than nothing and infinitely better than the constant doom and gloom. McCulloch found the station and 'Red Light Spells Danger' by Billy Ocean chimed through the car. She turned the volume up.

'Do you ever feel middle-aged, Rob?'

'What?'

'You know, middle-aged. Like all the good stuff's gone and now all you have left is debts up to your eyeballs and bills coming out of your ears?'

Logan nodded. 'Something like that, yeah.'

McCulloch thought for a moment. 'It's even harder when you're single. Because you've got no one to share the burden with, you know?'

Logan nodded. 'I suppose so. You ready to tell us more about this date of yours yet?'

'There's nothing to tell. We've not even been out yet.'

'You must've spoken to the guy.'

'Only through the dating site, Rob. Bloody hell, how long is it since you last went on a date?'

Logan thought about it. His marriage had reached the stage where sex was out of the question, and the highlight of the weekend was picking out some garden furniture from B&Q. 'Me and Vic have been married nearly twenty years. So she was my last actual date. Before that, there was Caroline Ayers. We went out for eighteen months until she broke my heart.'

McCulloch scrunched up her nose. 'Sweet sixteen, eh?'

'Something like that, yeah.'

'Your first love?'

But Logan didn't answer. 'So. Lisa Kirkland. She's a dental nurse, apparently. Works locally. Just turned forty. She's relevant because it was her party that Caitlin Slater attended on the night she went missing.'

'She a good friend or just an acquaintance?'

Logan shrugged. 'No idea, but I guess we'll find out.'

'Where does she live?'

'Just down here.'

Logan turned left into a cul-de-sac just off the main Longsight Road. It was within walking distance from his own home, and he considered clocking off when this was done. Maybe dig out that old laptop of Vic's.

They found the house down the bottom end, just at the turning circle. Logan parked up out front and killed the engine. 'Let's see what this Lisa has to say, eh?'

It was a smart home: a semi-detached with well-maintained gardens. They stepped up and Logan dropped the heavy-duty knocker. A loud series of barks came from deep within the house and got louder as the dog approached the door in the hallway on the other side. The barks were accompanied by voices, and it seemed like they were in luck. The door opened and an athletic-looking guy stood beside a short and shapely woman holding back an Alsatian. The dog looked pissed off.

'Mrs Kirkland?'

'Yeah.'

'I'm DS Kelly McCulloch. This is DS Rob Logan. Is it okay if we come in?'

Lisa Kirkland stepped aside to allow them through as her husband, Paul, led the Alsatian into the kitchen. They followed as Lisa sat in the main armchair while Logan and McCulloch took the couch.

'I believe you might've had a visit from some of our colleagues,' Logan said. Lisa nodded. 'But we're here as a separate duo, if you like. Just to go over a few things. We're detectives, too, and we're involved in an investigation that may or may not be linked to the disappearance of Caitlin Slater.'

Lisa nodded. 'I understand. We've been over this already but it's not a problem. We all hope she's found safe and well, obviously, so whatever I can do to help...'

'Good,' McCulloch said. 'Right, well, as you know she's been missing since the night of your birthday. She never got home that night. So we're just trying to piece together events prior to her leaving here. Is there anything you can tell us about Caitlin?'

Lisa shrugged as her husband came in with a tray of tea and biscuits. He put it down on the coffee table and poured from a pot. 'I don't really know her that well, to be honest with you. We have a mutual friend in Louise. I think Caitlin works with her. Something like that. Anyway, she was nice enough.'

'So, you didn't know her,' Logan said, 'but she was invited to the party?'

'Well, Louise invited her and her boyfriend, I think. Which was fine. I'd asked Louise to invite whoever she liked as I wanted more people here. The more the merrier and all that. Her boyfriend was working but she turned up.'

Logan nodded and thanked Paul for the mug of tea. 'Did you speak to her that night?'

'Yeah,' she said. 'A few times.'

'You get on with her?' McCulloch said.

'Yeah. She seemed like a nice girl. A bit quiet.'

Logan frowned. 'What do you mean?'

'Well, you know. She was just a bit shy. Didn't have much to say unless you spoke to her.'

'Did she know anyone else apart from Louise?'

'I think so. But I think Louise was probably the one she knew most. You're probably better off speaking to her.'

'Can you give us her contact details?' McCulloch said.

Lisa grabbed her phone off the mantelpiece and found Louise McDonagh's number. McCulloch noted it down.

'I don't want this to feel like a cross examination,' Logan said. 'You're not under any kind of suspicion or anything like that. We're just trying to get to the bottom of why she's missing, that's all.'

'We understand,' Paul said. 'It's fine. I probably spoke to her more than Lisa, if I'm honest. She's a nice girl. I dread to think what might've happened to her.'

'What do you guys think could've happened to her?' McCulloch said. 'After she left here?'

Paul shrugged. Blew a gust of breath through his mouth and shook his head. 'God knows. I wasn't here when she left. I was upstairs. So I didn't say goodbye, you know. I just assumed she'd got an Uber, but apparently she walked.'

'Go on,' McCulloch said.

'Well, that's it, really. She left here on foot and walked up to Bolton Road West. It would've taken her probably half an hour to forty minutes to get home walking that way. So I suppose something must've happened to her between here and there. People don't just disappear, do they?'

No, Logan thought. They didn't. And Paul was probably right. Something must've happened to her. He didn't think she would take herself off somewhere or take her own life, either. There were plenty of woods around for her to go wandering in. Plenty of places she could've stumbled into and gotten lost. But Kurt Chadwick had said she wasn't depressed, wasn't suicidal. She could've been seeing someone else and left him, yet that didn't make any sense, either. She surely would've come forward by now. She would've come back to come clean to her partner and get her things.

Logan knew they needed more on her relationships with friends and family. He would check exactly where they were up to with the search, if indeed a search had even started.

'Are the police actually looking for her?' Lisa said. 'I mean, she's missing, yeah? Are they thinking the worst or... what? You know, people go missing and then they turn up, but it's been days now for her, hasn't it? I keep thinking of that poor woman in Lancashire and how she turned up in the water. Could the same thing have happened to Caitlin?'

'We're not ruling it out,' McCulloch said. 'All I can say is, at this stage, she's a missing person. Yes, she could be anywhere but it's really important not to speculate.'

'What if someone took her life,' Paul said. 'You know. I mean, it's a possibility. Isn't it?'

Logan nodded. 'It is. But we're not at that stage yet.'

'But when will you be at that stage?' Lisa said.

'It's really a question for the SIO on the case.'

'SIO?'

'Senior Investigating Officer,' McCulloch said. 'Look, we share your concern. She was quite well known in the community, I believe, so the investigation will ramp up soon enough. I'd expect a lot of door-to-door enquiries, media broadcasts, that kind of stuff.'

'Her boyfriend must be at his wits end,' Paul said. 'I feel for the guy, I really do.'

'We need to get a search party going,' Lisa said. 'Someone's got to do something.'

Wishful thinking, Logan thought. Half the town would be more bothered about where they were eating out on Saturday night than they were about a missing local woman who really could be anywhere. Leave it to the professionals. That would be their attitude, and, really, who could blame them? What could anyone really do?

'There's got to be some CCTV or something,' Lisa said. 'I mean, there are plenty of businesses around here that would have it. Plenty of houses, come to think of it.'

'I'm sure it's being looked into already,' Logan said. He sipped the tea now that it had cooled a little. 'But you're right. There's the Co-op for a start. Then the pub and the wine bar.'

'Isn't there an accountant's place around here somewhere?'

'There's the tearoom,' Paul said. 'And the travel agents. Loads of places further up the road. More pubs, shops, that kind of thing.'

'There's bound to be something,' Lisa said.

Paul shook his head. 'Poor girl. She was nice.'

'I hate to think what might've happened to her,' Lisa said. 'I really hope she's just decided to leave of her own accord. It's really weird because she seemed absolutely fine on my birthday.'

They were silent for a moment. Logan and McCulloch sipped their tea. Logan wondered if these two were the type to use party drugs like coke or ecstasy, or even ketamine, but he doubted it. He threw it in, anyway.

'Look, this is not an accusation or anything, and we're not about to search your house, but I need to ask. Was there anyone using any recreational drugs on your birthday, Lisa?'

Her face flushed slightly, and she looked to Paul for reassurance.

'Not that we're aware of,' Paul said. 'We certainly wouldn't, anyway. I hate all that shit. Can't stand it, if I'm honest.'

'Are you saying she might've been drugged?' Lisa said. 'At my party?'

'It's something we might have to consider,' McCulloch said. 'If somebody drugged her without her knowledge or if she'd taken something herself.'

'Particularly with something like ketamine or spice,' Logan said. 'Something that may have acted as a tranquilliser as she walked home. Maybe she took a fall or something like that. These are all possibilities.'

'I'm sure,' Paul said. 'I guess you can't rule out this kind of stuff. But from our point of view, drugs were out of the question. I'm strictly beer and wine these days, and Lisa only drinks vodka. Maybe Louise will know more if you speak to her.'

'These days?' Logan said.

Paul shrugged. 'It was a long time ago. Weed. A bit of coke. Worst time of my life, if I'm honest.'

Logan nodded. Drank the tea.

'Well, I think we're done here, eh?' McCulloch said.

'I think so.' Logan got to his feet. He retrieved a business card and handed it to Paul. 'Give me a ring if anything else jogs your memory.'

'Will do.'

'And thanks for your time,' McCulloch said. 'We know these things can be difficult.'

'It's just horrible,' Lisa said. 'You know, to think that her last moments could've been spent in our house. You know, among her friends and then... Whatever happened to her.'

'Her last moments?' McCulloch said. 'You seem pretty convinced she's not alive anymore.'

Lisa shrugged. Swallowed. 'Well, you just... assume, don't you? Listen, if there's anything else we can do, let us know. I'd hate to think we're not helping your investigation in any way. We just hope she's found safe and well, like anyone else around here.'

'Of course,' McCulloch said. 'In the meantime, we've a few things to look into. Thanks again for your time.'

The Kirklands waved them off at the front door. 'Coming Around Again' by Carly Simon was in full swing on the radio by the time they pulled away.

EIGHT

'Vic? You still got that old laptop?'

She was upstairs dealing with Izzy, who had taken to throwing water out of the bath.

Logan went up and repeated the question and found Vic drying Izzy off and getting her into her pyjamas. 'Well?'

'What old laptop? Didn't we get rid of a load of stuff?'

'Yeah, but I think we kept the laptop. Is it under the bed or something?'

'Think it might be in the office.'

Logan found it—an old Dell—in the bottom drawer of the desk. The battery was missing but it still had the cable. He took it down to the kitchen table and plugged it in at the wall. Got himself a can of Stella from the fridge and popped it open. Drank while he waited for the laptop to fire up.

He went over a few things in his mind as he drank and watched the screen gradually come to life. It had been a few years since the machine had been used, and it was near enough on its last legs back then, so it would be a while before it got to the point of trying to connect it to the Internet.

Logan sat by the radiator, a bit dazed, and let the events of recent days come in and out of his head. The ram, the raven, the rabbit. The three Rs. Maybe a rat would be the next one, although he didn't really believe there was any connection in any way. It was just a weird coincidence if anything.

Then there was Caitlin Slater and her mysterious disappearance. Her long-term partner, Kurt Chadwick, walking the streets alone, desperate to find her. It was hard to believe she was still alive, but if she was, she surely didn't want to be found. She'd have come forward by now. The fact that she hadn't, left only two options: she was alive and had indeed disappeared intentionally, or she was lying in a shallow grave.

Or there was another option.

She'd been kidnapped. Was being kept against her will.

Nah. As if...

'Where's *my* beer?'

Vic had crept downstairs in her dressing gown after Izzy had finally nodded off.

'Still a few in the fridge.'

She grabbed one and cracked it open. Being ever the sophisticated type, she poured hers into a fancy glass while Logan was content, as ever, with the can.

'What do you want the laptop for, anyway?' she said.

He'd thought about keeping it from her. She would only worry and make things worse. But then, two heads were better than one. And he guessed she'd find out, anyway.

So he told her. Starting from when they found the rabbit and finishing with DI Murray's bollocking about accessing the website.

'Well, I agree with him,' Vic said. 'It is pretty fucked up, love.'

'You mean I fucked up?'

'Well, you do have a tendency to act before thinking. I mean, it's basic, I would've thought, to go and ask someone in the IT department first.'

She was right, of course. She always was. She'd probably make a better detective than him.

'But I'm not sure it's a good idea to go looking around on this website,' she continued. 'I don't have a good feeling about it, and you shouldn't, either.'

'I know, but I feel like I've got to do something, Vic. I mean, what if it's all connected?'

'What, the dead animals?'

'Yeah.'

'The ram's head turned up yet?'

'No. But we're waiting on a toxicology report from the lab. To see if it was drugged before it was killed.'

'Which would mean...?'

'Depends. Same for the raven. And now the rabbit. If they were all drugged, there's a connection.'

'Yeah, but it could be just a coincidence, love. It might not mean anything.'

Logan grimaced. 'I don't believe in coincidences. It has to mean something. There has to be a reason for all this.'

'But still, I'm not sure it's a great idea to go on this site. Especially on our computer.'

'But we don't use it anymore,' he said. 'Do we? That's why I wanted this one specifically. So if there's malware or whatever it is, it doesn't infect our Mac. I need to know what's going on, babe.'

She wrinkled her nose in the way she always did and kissed his forehead. 'You'll figure it out. Oh, by the way. Did you hear about that woman? A woman's gone missing?'

Logan told her what he knew, briefly, and left out the

confidential parts. In a town like this, word could get around quickly. Before you knew it, the rumours would kick in and the truth would dissolve.

'As it stands at the minute,' Logan said, 'she's just a missing person, nothing more. We don't want conjecture turning into truth.'

'But what if she's... you know... been killed? What if her husband's done it?'

'She's not married. And besides, I highly doubt it. We're not talking about one of your crime dramas, love.'

'But it happens...'

'Yeah, it happens. On rare occasions. She's probably just left him, as sad as that may be for him. She could be on the other side of the world by now.'

'Come on, love,' she said. 'Who does that?'

She had a point. And like being murdered by your husband, he guessed it probably did happen on very rare occasions. Kayleigh Matheson was probably an exception. In this case, he had to admit the more likely scenario was that a stranger had something to do with her sudden disappearance. But he didn't want Vic to know he was thinking that. For one thing, he already knew that Caitlin Slater had left her passport at home, along with her clothes. She hadn't taken anything. Everything pointed to the obvious, and the obvious was that she'd simply vanished.

Logan turned to the laptop, which had finally stopped whirring and fired into life. He connected it to the house Wi-Fi. The machine was slow but workable. He resisted the temptation to switch to the Mac and stuck it out, watching the little wheel icon turn for far longer than he should need to, while it connected to Google. He typed in '*followthewhiterabbit.net*' and let the search engine do its work. A few minutes later, the site came up, just like before, and all the characters from *Alice in Wonderland* danced across the screen.

This time, he hovered the cursor over the Mad Hatter.

He waited. Was this really a good idea? What kind of mess was he really about to get himself into?

He clicked.

It did the same thing as before. The Mad Hatter icon spun like a pinwheel and the whole screen lit up and flashed a kaleidoscope of colours until it finally settled on one more image: a colour photograph that filled the whole screen.

'Fuck...'

The ram's head was sitting on a pole, a totem even, as if it had been hollowed out and dumped on a spike in the ground. Logan sat open-mouthed and studied the image. Was he looking at some kind of sacrifice? Some weird ritualistic pagan shit that went back thousands of years? Perhaps whoever had put it here was using it as shooting practice? The ram's horns were beautiful, spiralling out in perfect symmetry. Its eyes were round and glassy, like marbles. Its fur was black, brown, and white. The totem was in the foreground, but the background was blurry and out of focus. Logan guessed this was deliberate.

There was the possibility, of course, that this ram's head wasn't the one they'd been looking for, but Logan found that unlikely, given the circumstances.

It seemed to be looking straight at him.

Why go to these lengths? Whoever had taken this photograph, then gone to the trouble of uploading it to this weird website, must've had a good reason for doing so. Or maybe not.

Logan hovered the cursor over the photograph, wondering if he could zoom in somehow. He couldn't. But the cursor changed to another little finger somewhere in the background blur, inviting him to click. He took a drink and did just that.

The image on the screen changed once more. Now he was looking at a murky pond of dank water, and beyond it, a copse of trees that had succumbed to the ravages of winter, their leaves stripped bare, their limbs bitten by the wind. He was no tree expert, but they looked like birch, and he only came to this conclusion because he had a wood basket full of logs beside the wood burner in the living room and the bark looked similar.

But what the fuck?

What was this all about?

He pressed the *ESCAPE* button, figuring this would take him back to where he started. But then there they were again: all the characters from *Alice in Wonderland*. He watched Alice herself walk across the top of the screen, then stop. She turned her face towards him, blinking, inviting him to click.

He was reluctant at first, and slightly anxious at what he'd see next.

He was right to be anxious.

A new image filled the screen: sitting in a small white saucer on a steel kitchen draining rack next to a sink, were a pair of small, beady eyes, their tendrils of connecting tissue trailing off the actual eyeballs like bloody flames. Were they human eyes? No. Too small. Then the white rabbit came into his mind. The white rabbit with its eyes and heart and genitals missing.

It was a strange photograph, and weirdly beautiful, like a painting. Beyond the sink was a large window with long strips of what looked like fur and feathers hanging down from the top pane. Outside, another field, this one coated in a pale white frost. The light of a sunrise far beyond the hills cast daylight upon the world.

But those eyes...

Logan snapped out of it and left the table, draining the beer before getting himself a new one. He picked up his phone and found DI Murray's number. Hesitated before hitting the call button. It was still only just gone half-eight and Logan knew he'd be up. Whether he'd want to speak to him was a different matter, but he expected his boss to have calmed down by now.

Logan cracked open the beer and hit the call button.

'You've got a nerve.'

'Look, sir, I made a mistake. I'm sorry. I shouldn't have done what I did without asking permission.'

'Well, luckily for you, Rob, there's no harm done,' he said. 'Though Chris from IT has asked to send you on a one-day course on the dangers and pitfalls of computer viruses and the history and purpose of anti-virus software. I've booked you in for next Monday.'

'Shit, you're joking.'

'Yes, I'm joking,' he said. 'But he did say to tell you to not be such a dick again.'

'Understood.'

'Consider this a slap on the wrist.'

'Sir...'

'Now what can I do for you?'

Logan took a swig from the can. 'Well, two things. We went to see Lisa Kirkland, the girl whose party Caitlin Slater attended the night she went missing.'

'Go on.'

'Nothing unusual. Just a regular couple who seemed concerned about Miss Slater's welfare.'

'As most people are. And the other thing?'

'Well, I decided to look a bit further into this site, sir.'

'I guessed you would. Find anything?'

'Sir, it's fucking weird. But I think we've found the ram's head.'

This had Murray intrigued so Logan filled in the details. The fact that there was a photograph of the ram's head, but the location was somewhat problematic, didn't seem to faze him.

'Any thoughts on where this photo was taken?'

'None,' Logan said. 'Could really be absolutely anywhere. If I'm honest, it could be impossible to determine a location.'

'Any further photos of your car?'

'No. At least, I haven't come across any yet.'

Logan could almost hear the cogs turning in Murray's head down the other end of the line.

'What computer are you using?'

'An old laptop of ours.'

'Bring it in tomorrow. I want to see for myself. Maybe we can get IT onto it. See what they have to say.'

'Don't think they'll do anything, sir.'

'Well we can at least get their thoughts.'

'I think it's gonna take some old-school detective work. Get our heads together on this.'

Murray paused. 'The thing is, I'm not sure there's much point. After all, we're talking about a dead animal. It's hardly important in the grand scheme of things, is it?'

'Try telling that to Frank Morton.'

'I meant the resources we have to work with, Rob. You know as well as I do that the Chief will hardly take kindly to us pulling out all the stops to find this bloody ram's head.'

'Maybe not. But what if the toxicology shows something up? And don't forget the raven. And the rabbit. And there's this other photograph, sir. Looks like eyes in a saucer.'

Another pause. 'Have you been drinking?'

'What? Just a few cans. Hey, why don't we get Frank Morton in? He might be able to identify the head.'

'Well, if nothing else, at least it would put an end to all this nonsense. Listen, don't forget you're on duty tomorrow. Don't be turning up hungover.'

'Hardly,' Logan said. 'But anyway, is there any news on that toxicology report?'

'Maybe tomorrow but it's not a priority.'

'So, what is?'

Murray gave a long sigh. 'You know how busy we are. This Caitlin Slater thing's reaching a point of no return.'

'So, she's not just a missing person anymore?'

'I didn't say that,' he said. 'But it's Wednesday tomorrow. That would mean she's been missing four days. Still no sign of her. She's not returned home, and Kurt Chadwick's been in having a rant, pissed up.'

'You can hardly blame him.'

'No. He's clearly not coping.'

'I guess he wants action,' Logan said. 'And results.'

'Don't we all? Right, is there anything else you wanted from me? Because shit's about to go down if I don't order this takeaway. Jean's almost foaming at the mouth here.'

Logan said he would see him tomorrow and hung up before returning to the laptop.

He'd be a liar if he didn't think a part of him wanted to close the laptop down and never look at this site again. He really did want to close it down, more than anything. But now he was deep into it and wished he'd never looked at it in the first place. And he had to admit that the circumstances in which he came across it were somewhat troublesome. He'd never really asked himself the question: *what made him stop on that road?*

What made him stop at what he thought was a roadkill and leave the car?

His phone pinged and he checked the text. Kel McCulloch, asking if he'd gotten anywhere with the site. He dialled her up.

'I wasn't expecting you to phone, Rob. You could've just sent me a message, eh?'

'Better to just ring you,' he said. 'And yes, I have been on the site, in fact I'm on it right now. I'm bringing it in tomorrow. Already spoken with Murray. You can see for yourself just how fucked up this is.'

'Any more photos of the car?'

'Not come across any yet, but there is plenty of other weird shit.'

'Any people?'

'No. Not yet.'

Vic came in to get another beer, then left quickly to carry on with whatever she was watching on Netflix.

'Do you think there will be?' McCulloch said.

'I hope so. Maybe it'll point us in the direction of the twat following us around. Anyway, that's that. What are you up to? Don't tell me if it involves anything to do with women's stuff.'

'Er, like what, exactly?'

'You know...'

'No, Rob. I don't. You're a funny bugger, eh? If you must know, I'm trying to pick out something I can wear for my date on Saturday.'

'Ah, so you're definitely going out with this guy. What's his name again? Did you even mention it?'

'He's called Alex. And he's supposed to be phoning me anytime so if there's nothing else...?'

Logan laughed. 'Fair enough. I'll leave you to it. I'm

gonna see what else is on this thing. Oh, did you hear about Kurt Chadwick? He's been in the station, drunk. No more details.'

'He'll be bloody frantic, eh?'

'Not surprised. Murray reckons things are about to step up.'

'Good,' she said. 'About bloody time, eh? Look, I'll have to go. I'm expecting this call.'

'See you tomorrow. I'll look forward to all the juicy details.'

She scoffed. 'You'll be waiting a long time.'

McCulloch hung up and he returned to the laptop. The screen had gone blank, and he could hear it turning over and wheezing, like a geriatric. With Vic settled in the living room, her head stuck into a courtroom drama, he saw this as an opportunity to sneak himself a few more beers and an extra-large bag of Doritos. He kicked the machine into life again and waited for the site to come back. He was willing to accept that he could be in for a long night.

SAM AND CAITLIN

Colin had made it pretty clear that he wasn't happy about the raven's heart. But it was about time he sucked it up. His turn would come around again. Maybe, if he was prepared to wait, he could have the woman's heart instead. Or at least some of it. It was always better to share, he knew that. Course it was. That way, everyone could get a true experience and it would mean things would work out better in the end. Besides, he wouldn't have truly appreciated the raven heart anyway. That shit was fucking unreal. But it had been his turn this time and it was so worth it. Some part of him knew it was all fucked up. But so be it. He could handle that. Wouldn't want it any other way.

Sam took the keys that were hanging on the hook beside the kitchen door and stepped out into the cold night. It was a good job he was layered up because he would be out here for quite a while, and he had a few things to do. He'd slung the rucksack on with everything he needed safely tucked away in it. Checking in on the woman was one thing. A good smoke was another, but that was something he liked to keep to himself. The others, if they had chance, would be on to him like a shot if they knew he was stashing the weed in his room. Pollen was strong stuff, and he had a golf ball-sized lump of it hiding in his drawer.

He wandered out with the torch guiding the way and reached the quad bike that was parked up with a cover over it beside the Toyota pick-up. He pulled the cover off and mounted it. Put the key in the ignition and fired her up. He had to rev it hard a few times and let the engine warm up.

Sam pocketed the torch and flicked on the bike headlights. Thankfully, there was no snow, but what had already fallen was still lying frozen on the fields as far as he could see. It was bloody freezing. He was looking forward to getting it all done with and coming back to the living room and the fire. Darren had the cushy job of keeping it burning. No doubt he'd be pouring a whisky about now.

He pulled away from the house and went out onto the gravel path that ran past the farm. Except now it was more like sheet ice. He felt the tyres lose their grip and skid and he had to take it slow before he reached the dirt track that led out onto the open field. The bike moved much better once he was off the path and out in wide space, it was like child's play. The machine was made for this kind of terrain. The beam from the headlights was strong and he could see the totem with the ram's head impaled on top pretty clearly, even from here.

But that was not where he was going.

Instead, he banked away and drove the bike to the left and up towards the top end of the field. Colin had given specific instructions on where to put the damn thing and they'd spent the previous afternoon digging the hole for it. Now his job was to finish it off and erect the totem. Not so easy in this kind of light. It was also not so easy to get a firm grip of the head in this cold. Although the gloves would offer some protection from the conditions, it was difficult to actually manoeuvre due to the dexterity required. But fuck it. Didn't have to be perfect. As long as it went on the spike and stayed on, that was all that mattered. The cold would soon have it frozen, anyway. And it was about to get colder if the weather forecast was to be believed. Well below freezing, they said. At least minus ten. Possibly even colder out in the countryside. And up here, high above the city, they usually took the worst of the winter.

Sam came to a stop near to the site. He shut the quad down and stepped off. Dropped the rucksack off his back and stomped through the field with the torch to find where he needed to be. The pole was lying where they'd left it, one end of it sharp and spiky. It looked like a massive pencil. He grabbed it and pulled it over to the hole, which was about two metres deep. Dropped the blunt end in, where it stayed pretty secure. He filled it in around the sides with the earth that lay in a pile beside it and packed it down with his boots. He guessed it was a bit like planting a tree. Not that he ever had. Yet this was a tree that didn't grow. Instead, it decayed, out here in the elements. Animals and birds would feed on the flesh, stripping it down to the bone. In the summer, the skull would be bleached by the sun.

Once the totem was in place, Sam stepped back and took a seat on the quad. He retrieved the fat joint he'd already rolled and lit up, his chapped hands barely feeling anything but the sting of the winter night. Drew in a deep lungful and let the drug seep into his bloodstream. He turned his gaze to the night sky, that Milky Way stretching across the pure black. Looked down into the city, its lights twinkling. Were there other worlds up there? Probably. Maybe even millions of them. In the grand scheme of things, what they were doing didn't really matter. None of it did. Even existence itself. Everything would die eventually. There was no denying it. When it really came down to it, anyone could do anything they wanted. To take another's life, however that would be done, was pure power. The point of existence was to exercise that power, that pure potential, that ability to choose whatever you wanted without the limitations of society's expectations. The sheep down there didn't know that.

But they did. Sam, Darren, and Colin.

To kill brought a certain kind of ecstasy.

He took another drag and turned his gaze down to the barn. He knew she was getting weaker. Had probably lost weight. Had probably lost her mind a little bit, too. Was she asleep? Was she wishing she was dead? Was she hoping for someone to come and rescue her? She would certainly have a long wait.

Sam opened the rucksack. It was time to do what he came here to do. Then he would check on her. Maybe he would have some fun while he was there. He knew the others would probably do the same too if they were with her alone. She was a very good-looking woman. Sexy, even.

The rucksack was big, and it needed to be. He retrieved the heavy-duty plastic bag and dumped it on the snow. It was leaking blood, which was no surprise. He got to his knees and tasted it with a quick dip of his finger that he dashed on his tongue. It sent a shiver through him, though that could've been the cold.

He opened the bag up and reached inside. Grabbed one of the ears and pulled it out that way. There was no mistaking it: this was a mean-looking fucker.

Except it wasn't anymore.

Now it was nothing but a huge head that couldn't function, its powerful jaws useless and immobile. Colin had removed the eyes, leaving the sockets just like two black holes in space. For a moment, Sam got lost in that emptiness as he held the Rottweiler's massive head with both hands, his arms holding it as far away from him as he could. Blood dripped out from the dog's neck, and the smell of rotting flesh made his stomach turn.

Sam wanted rid of the damn thing and quickly did what he had to do: dropping the bowling ball sized head onto the sharp spike. It squelched into the flesh and all the other shit that was in there, and he had to twist it down so it was fully on the totem and held in place.

Not a pleasant job.

He'd had to disassociate himself from the gruesome task as best he could, which was far from easy, and avoided looking directly at the thing until it was done and he'd stepped back to observe from a distance. The totem was painted in its blood, and it continued to drip, as if from a leaky valve, onto the icy snow, turning it pink.

Sam wiped his hands on his jeans, sticky with the beast's blood, and retreated back to the quad after he'd zipped up the rucksack and put it on his back again.

There he sat, the bike's headlights firmly fixed on the totem. He lit up the joint again and took a hit, deep into his lungs. Blew a cloud that floated away and vanished, like she had done when they'd picked her up.

He turned his gaze back to the barn and imagined her in there, asleep under that massive blanket. Sleeping to escape what was happening in her little world.

Sam sat a few moments and smoked, a warm and fuzzy high enveloping him as he looked out across the farm and the fields and city beyond. Had he found his purpose? He thought so. And now he'd given in to it, gave himself to it, and would allow whatever he truly wanted in his heart to happen. Anything less and he would be denying himself the richness life had to offer.

He finished the joint, feeling utterly stoned already, and flicked the roach away. Pointed the headlights at his handiwork one final time before starting up, then revved and revved the machine until he could feel its power and he was ready to move off. This kind of thing, what he'd just done, always made him hard. He couldn't explain it but there was always a thrill he would have to relieve somehow.

Maybe she was still awake.

Caitlin could just hear the faint rev of an engine. A motorbike, maybe. Or even a small tractor. Out here, she guessed there were plenty of those. She knew she was on or near a farm somewhere because of how it smelled in here. Of animals, and horse shit. Hay bales and fertiliser. There was very little noise at night-time but then things would start early in the morning. Lights would go on, illuminating narrow beams under the barn door. She would hear voices and laughter. All kinds of movement. And that fucking cockerel would kick it all off about four in the bloody morning.

Sleep came and went. She was happy when it came, to escape what was happening, because that meant it was temporarily over. But then she'd wake again, even if she was exhausted, and the bad thoughts would run through her head at a hundred miles an hour.

When would it happen?

What did they want with her?

She thought of Kurt going crazy in the house. He wouldn't cope with this, no chance. No doubt he'd be drinking, starting a fight down the local if he let frustration get the better of him. All the things she'd tried hard to protect him from for all the years they'd been together. She'd only ever seen him cry once and wondered if he'd cried for her too now.

She knew, though, that he had more than enough sense to raise the alarm. He'd have called the police, got them to look for her. But if they were looking for her, it didn't seem like they were doing a great job.

How many days had it been now? She'd lost count. It had all just blended into one. Light and dark, but the light was still faint. She could see the daylight coming under the barn door, could smell the cold air, but it was only a little bit and nowhere near enough for her to be able to even see, let alone find a way out.

When the night came, it was really dark. She imagined she was floating in empty space, out there in the cosmos, conscious of nothing yet aware of something. And sooner or later, something would come to illuminate the black, like a star or a distant galaxy or a gaseous cloud of space dust.

But it never did.

All that ever came was a blast of cold. And then voices, or the footfalls of someone outside, or the massive heavy-duty latch sliding across the door. The thud of iron on wood and big leather boots.

The floor was hard and cold, and she'd been lying or sitting or hunched in a really uncomfortable position on it for many days and nights, her muscles and limbs aching like fuck, her back like lead, and her shoulders feeling like they were carrying ten-kilo weights either side. She'd lost the feeling in her legs more than once, had to constantly shift her position as best she could thanks to the chain around her waist and the one around her right ankle, digging into the flesh and bone because they'd put it on too tight.

It was hard to tell where those chains went, because of the darkness in here, but she knew they trailed off somewhere to her right and behind her. Of course she'd tried to wrestle her way out of them, to no avail. These fuckers had made sure she couldn't get away. But why? What the hell did they want with her?

That engine again. Getting nearer. They'd come into the barn a few times now, always after dark. She guessed someone was coming here now. She knew she would have to pretend to be asleep again. She couldn't look at them. Could hardly see them anyway as they were either shining a torch in her face or it was pitch black.

It was horrible to admit it, but she felt like a baby, lay there in her own piss and shit. In a weird way, she could accept her death. Was almost ready, even, to make peace with it. In fact, the sooner the better now.

But she wasn't ready to be found covered in her own shit and piss. It was completely degrading. The only thing worse than being abducted like this, of being held against her will, was that she had to do her toilet stuff—her private stuff—right here.

They'd leave food for her. In a bowl, as if it was for a dog. And that's how they saw her. That was certainly how they viewed her. Yet even that was a stretch, because dogs were treated better.

But that's how she felt. And that's how she now behaved, really. Like a dog. Tied up, on all fours, curled into a ball, sleeping for long periods and shitting where she slept.

It was almost funny, this end she'd come to.

But if they wanted her dead, for whatever reason, surely they'd have killed her by now. And maybe that was the ultimate humiliation. Maybe all they really wanted to do was degrade her so much that she would beg for the end, would plead with them to get it over and done with.

So she'd begun to pray. Not for her release or her rescue or salvation, but for the end to come quickly.

The engine had grown louder and had come to a stop outside the barn, turning over out there in the cold night before it shut down completely. She heard someone walking around outside, his boots crunching in what sounded like snow. There was a thud and a clunk and then that massive bolt and latch creaked, metal on metal, iron on wood and heavy as hell, and it slammed across the barn door with a loud, echoey clunk.

The massive door opened, and an Arctic blast rushed in. She could see him standing at the threshold, all lit up because of the headlight on the bike behind him. He marched in and she suddenly stopped breathing. He came right up close to her, and she had to pretend she was asleep but hoped that he'd come to swing a blade onto her neck or something so she wouldn't have to do this anymore.

She was aware he'd crouched down beside her, somewhere to

her right, close enough to reach out and touch her, which he did, with thick fingers that smelled of weed and damp, like the way a dog smells after a long walk in the rain.

Caitlin was shaking. She couldn't help it. She couldn't see him and didn't want to. She daren't open her eyes, anyway. She knew that whatever he was doing now, fumbling around in the dark and making grunting noises and breathing heavy over her, the air smelling of putrid flowers and gut rot, he was enjoying it at her expense.

She saw Kurt then. Saw his face in her mind.

Imagined herself running home.

NINE

The temperature had dropped considerably through the night. Logan hung about in the living room while Vic kept herself busy getting Izzy ready for school. He was already on his second coffee. He knew he needed it with the fog of alcohol still around him. He had a mild headache, though not from the remnants of the drink in his system. It was a stress headache, he was sure. He took two paracetamol and sank into the couch with the breakfast TV talking heads on mute.

He'd already packed the laptop away. He was keen for Kel and Murray to get a good look at it, too, if only to confirm he wasn't going a little bit crazy. It was already clear that whoever had built the site was fond of playing games and creating puzzles. *Catch me if you can*, they were saying.

He tried to think back to the time when he was driving his car up Brandlesholme Road, and the vehicles that shared the road with them that day. There was no way he could have clearly identified the vehicle behind them, the car from which the photo of the back of his own had been taken.

And he thought of that ram's head, out there on a pole in some bloody field, of which there were thousands within a ten-mile radius. Here, on the edge of the city and the gateway to the Lancashire countryside, it was green in every direction as far as you could see. Rolling hills for miles and miles. Barren moorland with boggy ditches and towering wind turbines. A vast landscape with pretty much nothing else other than the wildlife that inhabited it and the odd satellite town dotted here and there. There was no way of finding the head, unless there was something glaringly obvious he had missed.

Also, what the hell would anyone want with a raven's heart?

He cleared up the empty beer cans and threw them in the recycling bin out the front. It was going to be another cold one. An Arctic blast had blown in from way up north, and the clouds on the horizon promised more snow.

He spent the next ten minutes clearing the frost from his windscreen as the world came to life, keeping his engine running to warm the windows up. Then he rummaged around inside to dig out his police-issue overcoat. He caught the tail end of the forecast as Izzy found the remote and switched over to the Disney channel. The whole country was heading for minus twelve, minimum.

Then Caitlin Slater came into his mind. Caitlin Slater, presumed missing. He hoped beyond all hope that she was shacked up with another man by a cosy fire. But all he saw was her frozen face, the lips blue, her skin porcelain-white like some dreadful Victorian doll.

'Babe, have you sorted Izzy's breakfast?'

He called back that he was on it, though it was the furthest thing from his mind. 'What do you want, Iz?'

'Chucky eggs with soldiers.'

'Coming up...'

'And you know how I like my eggs, Dad...'

Just as the eggs were coming to the boil, his phone rang. It was DI Murray.

'Early for you, isn't it?' Logan said.

'There's another one,' he said. 'I'm standing in the middle of the road just outside the big Tesco in Bury. Peel Way.'

'What, near the station?'

'Within spitting distance, which is some audacity. We've had to close the road. Bloody bedlam right now, as you can imagine. It won't be light for another hour at least, so it's tricky. What a time to be alive, eh?'

Logan stopped for a moment, his head throbbing. He could hear the chaos of the building traffic down the phone, irate voices shouting in road rage, the sound of a hundred commuters pissed off. It was a major route out of town, and it was rush hour. It would be gridlock everywhere. 'You telling me there's another animal?'

'Yeah, it's a bloody dog,' he said. 'And I emphasise bloody. It's a mess. A Rottweiler, we think. Just get down here when you can. Hopefully we can clear it soon so traffic can get moving again.'

'Jesus.'

'The head is missing. Another decapitation. And the heart's gone, too. I'm beginning to think we might have to start taking this seriously, Rob.'

About time. 'Kel there?'

'No. Can you call her? I've called a meeting for ten o'clock. And make sure you bring that laptop of yours.'

Logan was about to say he would, but Dave Murray had hung up. A Rottweiler? Another 'R'? Someone really was taking the piss. And to dump it within two hundred metres of HQ was like rubbing salt into the wounds. Why such a public display? In what sick fuck's world was this shit considered normal?

'Dad, is my breakfast ready?'

'In a minute. And come into the kitchen, Iz. You want some juice?'

Izzy came skipping in, full of the joys of spring, clutching an iPad with some kids' YouTube nonsense blaring away. Logan often regretted allowing her to watch such garbage, but it was a good way to keep her quiet while he gathered his thoughts and got on with stuff. Now he felt like slinging it out of the window.

He dealt with her breakfast—the eggs were overdone for Izzy's liking, and she told him so—then went upstairs to find Vic still putting her face on.

'There's another one. A dog. A Rottweiler, apparently.'

'Jesus,' she said. 'What the hell's going on? Do you think it might be connected to that missing woman?'

'What?'

'You know. That missing woman. What if she turns up next, Rob?'

And the horrible thought hit him square in the eyes and sobered him up in an instant. A vision of Caitlin Slater's body splayed out and dismembered. A headless corpse dumped in the local park.

'God, don't be ridiculous,' he said. But he knew it had legs. 'That kind of shit only happens on the telly. You've been watching too many crime dramas, love.'

She gave him a look that said nothing was impossible. 'Just a thought. Don't tell me you coppers haven't considered it.'

It sounded outlandish enough to be rejected outright. 'This isn't *Luther*, Vic.'

'Just a thought...'

'Listen, you need to get a move on. I've got to get to work.'

'You just go,' she said, applying mascara. 'I'll walk Iz to school. Let me know what time you're home.'

He kissed her and Izzy goodbye, then left the house in a daze to join the traffic.

HE TURNED the heating on full and tuned in to Five Live and caught the news at eight o'clock. The roads were in a shocking state. Despite the gritting lorries having been out overnight, the side roads were treacherous. And the main routes into town weren't much better. Logan often wondered what he paid his council tax for.

The darkness was fading, with a touch of light coming in from the east. By ten o'clock, the traffic would be gone too. The news was dreadful but apparently the economy was improving, and we were expected to come out of recession by this time next year. Yeah, right.

He was about to call Kel, but she beat him to it. He answered and her voice filled the car on loudspeaker.

'What the hell's going on? Traffic's bloody awful, eh?'

'I was just about to phone you. There's been another one. A decapitated Rottweiler. Right outside Tesco.'

'A what?'

'Yeah, now even Murray's taking it seriously. Which is a good thing.'

'I should think so. Bloody hell, Rob.'

'That's why the traffic's so shit. Peel Way's closed until they can clear it.'

She sighed. 'Could be a while, then, eh?'

'They'll want to get it in the lab as well. Murray's called a meeting for ten.'

'Jesus, he must be taking it seriously.'

'With any luck, we get a few more coppers involved.'

'Did you find anything else on the website?'

'I'll fill you in at HQ. If we can get a few more eyes on it as well, all the better.'

'God, a bloody Rottweiler,' she said. 'What about its owner?'

‘I doubt they even know yet. Things are starting to move at a pace, Kel. And Vic's just said something that got my attention.'

'Go on.'

He took a deep breath, not even sure that this made any sense. 'What if she turns up next?'

'Who?'

'Caitlin Slater. What if whoever's doing this to the animals is about to do it to a human being? What if we wake up one morning and she's been found? A body in the park or something.'

'That's a lot of what-ifs, Rob. I can't see it.'

'Yeah, I suppose. It’s like something from a horror film, though, isn’t it?'

'Exactly. But this is real life, Rob. Shit like that just doesn't happen. Especially around these parts, eh? As far as I'm aware, we're not even treating her disappearance as suspicious, so it's some leap to get to that.'

'But it's coming, isn't it?'

'What?'

'Her case being treated as suspicious. Apparently, Kurt Chadwick's not best pleased with the way things are progressing.'

McCulloch thought for a moment. 'Can't blame him, though, eh? So, I take it Tesco's shut?'

'I think they might've closed it off, yeah.'

'It's bad enough in there at the best of times. It'll be chaos all day now. Think I'll do my shopping somewhere else after work, eh?'

'And they never have anyone on the bloody checkout, either. All automated, these days. Not only do they want you to buy your food from there, they want you to scan it yourself.'

'Keeping people out of work, eh?'

'Cheeky bastards.'

Logan pulled out of a traffic queue and took a detour through a freshly cleared side road.

'Speaking of cheeky wee bastards,' McCulloch said, 'I believe Clarky's been at it again. Threatening to jump off The Rock car park if we don't arrest the local councillor. Says he caught him fly tipping near the Irwell.'

'To be fair, that wouldn't surprise me.'

'Yeah, but to threaten to jump to your death for it... Bit much, eh?'

The first flakes of the morning came drifting down. Logan re-joined his main route, where the traffic was moving at a snail's pace, nose to tail, as far as he could see. Warmer days seemed a very long way off and in a separate universe entirely.

'Rob?'

'Yeah?'

'Everything okay?'

'Yeah, just... You know. This shit doesn't make any sense.'

'It rarely does, eh? It'll come together in the end. We'll find out who's chopping the heads off animals and they'll get sent down. Wouldn't even surprise me if Caitlin Slater turned up.'

'She's been missing since Saturday night, Kel. It's now Wednesday.'

'She's a big girl. I'm sure she can look after herself, eh?'

THE INCIDENT ROOM was filling up by the time Logan found a seat. He spotted Kel McCulloch minutes later, clutching two paper bags and weaving her way over. It was now 09:48. They'd cleared the Rottweiler's body about ten minutes after the phone call. Now it seemed the day was half over before it had even started. It was still chaos outside and not much better in here.

Kel took a seat beside him and handed him a paper bag. 'Managed to pick you up a bacon muffin.'

DI Murray and DCI Clayton arrived, taking the space out front. Clayton leaned against the desk beside the white board, all six foot four of him watching over proceedings like some kind of giant, his lanky frame long and narrow. The chatter and noise had gone up a notch again, the talk mainly being about the weather and this weekend's football fixtures. Logan guessed that half the office hadn't even been aware there had been mutilated animals dotted about the town in recent days. Most of the room would have been working on other things. Mainly trying to trace Ian McNamara thanks to DCI McKenna's fuck up. Maybe that was about to change now that Murray appeared to be taking it more seriously.

The DI raised his arms in an effort to settle things down, like a teacher trying to calm a disruptive class of fifteen-year-olds on a Monday morning.

'Can we settle down please?' he said over the noise. 'Can everyone please be quiet and start paying attention?'

The room fell silent, and Murray gave it a moment, his eyes scanning the room, arms folded, as he leaned against the desk beside DCI Clayton.

'Right then. As some of you may be aware, there's been a spate of animal mutilations in the area this past week. In the space of three days alone, we've had the displeasure to come across a ram, a raven and a rabbit, all with their hearts missing, the ram with its head and feet missing as well. And now, as you may have noted after this morning's absolute chaos, we have another one. Some poor bastard's gonna find out this morning that their dog has died in truly awful circumstances. It's another decapitation. I got called out of bed at five o'clock and when I got down to the scene, it had already been sealed off and the road shut. It's probably taken you longer than usual to get into work because of it, and now we need to do something about it.

'I've got two PCs down at Tesco pulling the CCTV from the garage. I think they have a number of cameras on the forecourt but with any luck, they'll have one or two pointing at Peel Way as well and we might be able to get something. Traffic was very light at that time, and we suspect the animal had been lying there a few hours. So, it would have been dumped at around two or three this morning. I'm guessing it's been kicked out of the back of a van or something. McDonald's also has CCTV nearby so we might have to send someone down there as well. Clear so far?'

There were nods and whispers from the room and DI Murray called for the lights to go down and gave the cue for the PowerPoint to kick in. A hush descended as the first image appeared on the screen that the junior officer, young Jonny Cane, had pulled from the ceiling: the decapitated corpse of the Rottweiler lying in the road.

'As you can see,' Murray said, 'it's not pleasant. The amount of blood tells us that the killing is fairly fresh and very recent. I'm estimating that it's happened within the last twenty-four hours but I'm sure we'll get confirmation from the lab at some point today.'

Logan recognised the same clean-ish cut where the head had been removed, and the gaping black hole in the dog's chest where the heart had been taken out, the rib bones protruding from the flesh like some terrible monster's teeth.

'Looks fucking grim, eh?' McCulloch said.

It was almost enough to put Logan off his bacon muffin, but he persevered. It was cold but it would fill a hole.

'We've already identified the dog as Bruno, and he belongs to a woman in the Redvales area. We've managed to bring a local vet in to help us with our enquiries. DS Rob Logan and DS Kel McCulloch have already been deep in this, and it's thanks to them that we decided to bring Dr Stephen Moreland in to help us out. In fact, DS Logan, can you come up here and give us some more details on what you've found so far?'

Logan swallowed hard and fought back the urge to stay glued to his seat. This was clearly Murray's way of punishing him for his carelessness with the website yesterday. He handed McCulloch his half-eaten breakfast and stepped out from the crowd of coppers. He would get Murray back when the chance came up.

Logan stepped up to the desk and stood between Murray and DCI Clayton, the beam from the PowerPoint at the back of the room shining its spotlight right in his face.

'Okay,' Logan said. Coughed to clear his throat. 'Well... well, as DI Murray says, it's Kel and me, that is DS Kel McCulloch, who have been working on this the past few days and, to be totally honest with you, we're still just kind of piecing it together. Things are happening fast and it's becoming a bit of a minefield. We could certainly do with the help of a vet, that's for sure. Just to fill in the blanks, really.

'So, it started, we think, with a ram up on Holcombe Moor. A farmer up there asked us to look into why one of his animals was missing a head. It was found dead up on the moor, mutilated badly, as all of these animals have been. Have we got a photograph we can show?'

The image behind him changed to several images of the ram lying frozen in a ditch.

'So, as you can see, it has no head, no feet and its heart has been taken out. Frank Morton, the farmer, can provide no explanation as to why or when this happened. We don't know if the animal has been killed up on the moor or, more likely, taken away and killed somewhere else before being dumped back there. But then that brings up a whole host of other questions. Why has it been killed? How has it been killed? What purpose, if any, does it serve? And obviously, most importantly, who's killed it?

'So, then we had a report of a raven hanging outside someone's door up in Tottington, and its heart had also been removed. The bird had been displayed in a crucified fashion, nailed between two porch beams by its wings.' He turned behind him and saw images of the bird in question. 'Now, your gut instinct might tell you that this is the kind of bizarre prank carried out by a bunch of bored teenagers high on drugs and alcohol or whatever. But then you realise that this is so unlikely you really have to ask who else could've done it? And again, why? For what reason?'

'We got any CCTV from this?' someone called out.

Logan thought it was DS Callaghan from somewhere near the back of the room and he squinted through the light in his face to make sure. 'I'm glad you asked that because I believe a couple of PCs have been out to get that sorted. Sir?'

'We've got CCTV coming in from a local garage in the vicinity,' Murray said. 'I expect to be viewing that within the next hour or so. Rob, you want to tell them about the website?'

Logan nodded, swallowed, felt the back of his neck go clammy, and the urge to visit the toilet. Saw two dozen pairs of eyes firmly fixed upon him.

'DS McCulloch and I were on the way back from speaking with Kurt Chadwick on the Caitlin Slater missing person case. And on the way down Bury Road up in Ramsbottom there was a roadkill that didn't quite look like a roadkill at the side of the road. When we stopped, I found it was a rabbit missing its eyes, heart and genitals. They appeared to have been surgically removed. Attached to the rabbit's ankle was an identification ring with a QR code on it. I brought the animal in, which is now in the lab, I believe?' DI Murray nodded for him to continue. 'So, I guess we're still waiting on the lab results from the rabbit and the other two. When I scanned the QR code with my phone, it took me to a website called *followthewhiterabbit.net* and this is where things get really weird. I don't know if we can pull up the site right now but...'

'Maybe later,' Murray said. 'Go on.'

Logan continued. 'I had a look at this site yesterday and last night and there's some very strange shit on it, especially some bizarre photographs and stuff, but I've only really just touched the surface with it. We could do with the IT department getting onto it because I really do believe this site is connected to these animal mutilations. One of the photos I came across appears to be the missing head of the ram and another, which is a bit of a concern, shows the rear of my car, including the number plate. This image would indicate that DS McCulloch and I were followed just a few days ago by whoever took that photograph and, if that's true, then that would be the person or persons responsible for the site in question and, probably, the animal mutilations. I think that brings us up to speed, sir?'

DI Murray drained his coffee and asked Logan to return to his seat.

'Very good, Rob,' Murray said. 'So, now, following on from all that, we have this poor Rottweiler. I believe we've made contact with the owner already and apparently, the dog's been missing for almost a week. Now that would suggest it was taken by someone, somehow, and if that's true then the same might be said of the others. I guess the question we have to ask here is why? Why is this happening? How can we put a stop to it? And what, perish the bloody thought, could turn up next?'

'I'm gonna come in here, Dave,' DCI Clayton said. 'Just to say a few things.'

'Sir.'

'Thanks, DS Logan and DI Murray.' He scanned the room, his gaze falling on every single copper. 'Okay, everyone. There's a lot of work to do on this so it's imperative we get onto it straight away and in a timely fashion. I want all hands on deck in some regard and DI Murray will be giving instructions on how we proceed from here. I don't think we've had a case quite like it, so it's a bit of a strange one to say the least. Perhaps, during our investigations, we might be thinking of where to turn and we don't have the experience to anticipate or predict what might happen next, but I do think we need to be extra vigilant. From my end, I'll be in contact with other forces around the country to see if there are any similar cases, and I'll be reporting back on that when necessary. Needless to say, it's essential we work closely as a team and, if we do that and commit to our vocation as police officers, we'll have this sorted and the person or persons responsible will inevitably be brought to justice. Before you all leave and load up on coffee, can I just say that I'm really happy with your commitment to the cause and trust that everybody will be taking this case very seriously. Thank you.'

'Just finally,' Murray said, 'before you all get busy, I'm gonna hand out some work for some of you and, in the meantime, the rest of you should continue with your current jobs. So, listen up. DS Logan and DS McCulloch, I want you both to continue with this and I want another briefing in my office immediately, so don't disappear. DS Hussein and DS Bennett, I want you both to join me in my office for a further briefing and to provide support to DS Logan and DS McCulloch going forward. The rest of you, look busy and stand by for further updates as and when. Right, dismissed.'

LOGAN PLUGGED the laptop in and waited for it to fire up. DS Shaun Bennett and DS Asif Hussein hogged the kettle in Murray's office and brewed five strong coffees while McCulloch pulled up four chairs around Murray's desk and Logan finished what was left of his cold bacon muffin as the old laptop came to life.

'Takes one sick bastard to chop animals up,' Hussein said, in his Bradford drawl. 'I mean, it might as well be someone's kid. Rottweilers have a good temperament, you know. My brother used to have one until he had to give it up. Couldn't handle the shit in the backyard and all that.'

'They're a real handful, eh?' McCulloch said.

Hussein nodded. 'Can't be nice finding out that's how your dog's died. Poor woman.'

'You'd better bring us up to speed, Rob,' Bennett said, handing out the mugs of coffee. 'Just so we don't go over ground you two have covered already.'

McCulloch filled them both in on the trip to the abattoir, the original meeting with Frank Morton, and the whole debacle with the white rabbit.

'Weird how it had its balls cut out,' Hussein said. 'What would anyone want with them?'

'What would anyone want with any of it?' Logan said. 'What's the point? What's the connection?'

'Sounds to me like more than one person's involved,' Bennett said, his Mancunian accent turned up to eleven and his shiny bald head illuminated by the light above him. Outside, the already grey skies had darkened some more, and the snow continued to fall steadily. 'I mean, surely it would take at least two people to hold the dog down while the other... you know... did the rest.'

'Which is why we think they might've been drugged first,' Logan said. 'Though we'll only know more on that when we finally get a bloody toxicology report from the lab.'

'But, yeah,' McCulloch said, 'when you take into account the size of these animals, it makes sense to assume that whoever's involved has probably snatched these things somehow. Probably after dark, eh? Then taken them away to wherever to carry out the necessary.'

'Before dumping them in plain view,' Logan said. 'Putting them on public display. It's as if they want to be caught out, which I'm trying to wrap my head around.'

'This rabbit,' said Bennett. 'You said you found it at the side of the road, yeah? What made you pull over? Any other roadkill and you'd just carry on, wouldn't you?'

Logan shrugged. He had a point and it had occurred to him, too. 'The fact that it was white. It stood out.'

'It would suggest, though,' Hussein said, 'that someone knew you were going to pull over and find it. Like it was put there just so you could be the one to come across it.'

'Like you were being followed,' Bennett said. 'Like someone knew you were going to go down that particular road at that particular time.'

A shiver ran through him and his stomach began to lurch. Already, the thought of someone following them—as was evident on the photo he'd found on the weird website —was enough to keep him looking over his shoulder. But what if Shaun Bennett was right? Was someone deliberately trying to fuck his head up? Were his thoughts even his own?

The laptop had stopped whirring and had settled on the home screen. Logan readied the machine for a Wi-Fi connection, knowing he would need to ask Murray first. Better to be safe than sorry this time.

Murray came in and took his seat. 'Right. The report from the lab is due in a few hours. It'll include, I'm told, a fairly detailed analysis of each animal. I'm also going to be spending some time in the CCTV suite with Martin Hobbs as we now have CCTV from both garages where the raven was found and the forecourt out the front of Tesco from this morning. Hopefully, something will come up because so far, all we have are a bunch of mutilated animals and a lot of conjecture.'

Logan nodded. Things were now beginning to move. 'And a website, sir. Is it okay I connect to the station Wi-Fi? I mean, I thought it better to ask given yesterday's issue.'

'Glad you have the common sense to explore permission this time,' Murray said. 'I've already cleared it with IT so go ahead.'

Logan entered the website URL into the search bar and

waited. A moment later, Alice came walking across the screen and turned her head, blinking.

'Reminds me of one of those arcade games from the eighties,' Hussein said. 'Proper shite graphics and all that.'

'Who's built it?' McCulloch said. 'That's what I want to know.'

'I want to get down to the meat and bones of all this,' Murray said. 'What's the motivation?'

'Sacrifice?' McCulloch said. 'For whatever reason.'

Murray scowled. 'If we're talking sacrifice, that puts it firmly in the realm of the weird, doesn't it? Satanists, secret societies, complete nutters...'

'Fanatics,' Hussein said. 'Been a few cases of animals being sacrificed over the years, no doubt.'

'Are you suggesting these are ritual killings, sir?' Bennett said.

'Could be, yeah. There are hearts missing from every one. What are they trying to say? What are they getting at?'

'Do you think,' McCulloch said, 'that it could be about power? Gaining strength, somehow, from the poor animals?'

'What, like whoever's doing this is taking on, somehow, the... I don't know... power of the animal?' Logan said.

Bennett nodded. 'The spirit of the animal, maybe?'

They all exchanged a look, like they needed to keep their voices down in case anyone else could hear what they were discussing.

'It's the kind of thing a serial killer does, innit?' Hussein said. 'Come on, I'm sure we've all seen those documentaries.'

'They usually start with animals and then move onto people,' Logan said.

'Yeah,' he said. 'Exactly. We got any missing people lately, sir?'

He'd said it half-jokingly, Logan knew. But he could see that it had piqued Murray's interest.

'Let's just see what kind of stuff we can get from the CCTV and this toxicology report before we jump to any silly conclusions,' Murray said. 'And in the meantime, Rob, you can bring us all up to speed on this bloody website.'

They gathered around to make room so each could see what was happening on the screen. Logan tried to remember what he'd clicked on as he sat at the kitchen table last night, several beers in. And then moments later, once again, he went down the rabbit hole.

COLIN

Colin closed the door behind him and went over to the desk: a black lacquered thing that weighed a tonne but was solid and well made. The unit itself was about ten feet long and covered the back wall of the basement. The computer tower sat beneath the desk, the fan whirring to keep everything cool and in perfect order. The machine gave out a constant hum.

There were two monitors. He used one for gaming and the other for web design and internet browsing, though Colin's browser was somewhat unconventional. Google had been out of the question for some time.

Beside the monitors was a landline phone, which Colin hardly ever used. He had often thought of binning it. Two speakers were placed at either end of the desk and an expensive high-backed leather chair completed the set-up. There were two digital SLR cameras that Colin would usually leave on the desk when they weren't in use, and at the opposite side of the room stood two tripods, one with a camcorder fixed on it and the other he would use for the SLRs. On the shelf behind it were several lenses and other photographic equipment, a steel case, and a pair of binoculars.

Standing in front of the tripods was a huge telescope that needed at least two people to manoeuvre. Below the photography equipment was a bookshelf full of sci-fi and fantasy novels, graphic novels and pornography. There were also several grimoires that were at least eighty years old. Much older than him.

The shelves were dusty, and the paperbacks smelt ancient and well thumbed. With no windows in the room, the air was dank and carried a level of heaviness and dread, which he put down to the many restless spirits he was sure were still hanging around.

The carpet was granite-grey, and the room stank of cigarette smoke and stale brandy. The heavy-duty porcelain ashtray he'd bought one rainy afternoon on a weekend trip to York sat beside him, full of cigarette butts, and there were several bottles of alcohol within reach. Brandy, absinthe and vodka. There was also a fridge half full of beer humming in the corner. On the far wall hung a samurai sword and a few daggers. The blades were strictly for display only.

There was another shelf lined with skulls. Mainly small animals and birds, which had bleached over time.

The other skulls were kept in a cabinet in another room nearby.

Colin sat at the desk and fired up the computer. The secondary monitor—the one for browsing—kicked in almost immediately. He waited a moment before going in to update the White Rabbit with more photographs he'd taken this morning at first light. He grabbed the Nikon beside him and connected its Wi-Fi to the computer. Then he uploaded the shots to the desktop and organised them into a subfolder titled RotDog, which made him giggle, and uploaded some select photos from this folder into the back end of the White Rabbit site. He spent half an hour going through the motions of repurposing and cropping the images he wanted before putting them in place so that the coppers could come across them easily. It was important to stay one step ahead of the game and one step ahead of them if they were to keep this thing going, but he also wanted to put it right in their face. Colin knew that all of this was really putting it to the test, and it was a big risk. But the thrill of it was helping to keep him alive. It was like a particularly potent drug, and though he knew they could be leaving themselves wide open, part of him accepted that, and he'd take whatever fate brought him.

He was dying, so it didn't matter if he was caught. But if he could go right to the end of it all without being found out, all the better. He could go out with a bang and leave this world happy in the knowledge he'd taken them on and made them look like complete idiots. That was enough for him, really, but if he could get his kicks along the way...

He was surprised they hadn't drawn conclusions already and found them. He supposed he'd done a much better job than he ever thought he would. In a way, he wished he could be around to see the aftermath when it was all done, but he knew he'd be gone by then. It was almost time, perhaps only a matter of months, so if he was to reach the ultimate conclusion, it would have to be done soon.

He wanted to be gone, though. His body and mind had taken a massive hit over the years and the pain was bad. It was killing him. Sometimes, it was very difficult—almost impossible—to breathe. Darren and Sam had tried to persuade him to give up smoking, but it was way too late for that. It was almost laughable, really. A bit like putting a plaster on a fatal wound. The damage had been done. He wasn't making it any better, but he was past caring now.

For the past few years, Colin had needed oxygen cylinders because there wasn't enough oxygen in his blood. He'd paid for their delivery privately. They usually came every ten days, so he had a constant supply and would never run out. He spent hours and hours with a mask over his mouth, sucking that air in as best he could, until he couldn't stand it any longer. Sucking it in like his life depended on it, which it very much did. The cocktail of drugs he was ingesting—both prescription and illegal—left him high most of the time.

But there were other things that sustained him.

And he'd become certain that without these things, he would've been gone a long time ago.

He left the chair again, his legs aching. He had to be careful about how much he did these days in terms of physical activity, but he always made sure he was the one to do the important necessaries. Darren and Sam handled the dirty work, the heavy-duty stuff. The stuff that made a mess. Physically, he couldn't handle it now. Not only was he too ill, he was too old. There were some men who remained sprightly and fit well into their sixties, but he wasn't one of them. Now approaching sixty-six, he wouldn't make it far beyond that. So he would go out his way and be done with it. What little time he had left, he would make sure it was at least fun.

He made his way into the adjacent room. The basement itself was big enough to house several large rooms and some smaller ones that were hidden away beneath the farm via a narrow tunnel. His own private computer space was where he liked to spend most of his time, and then directly next door was the room where the magic happened. Perhaps Crowley himself would've approved. Not that Colin cared about such approval. Though he'd conducted many experiments over the years and had proved certain things to himself as completely real, the black arts were not to be taken lightly. So, he had always made sure he conducted things accordingly, especially ceremony and rituals. High magic was his calling, his purpose.

And killing was his true will.

Beyond next door were more rooms. The farmhouse itself was massive, built in 1725, and had kept most of its original features, including the spaces down here. Colin had occupied the house since the early 1980s, inheriting it from his grandfather, Albert, who had run the original farm since the mid 1930s. There was plenty of history within its walls, most of it unpleasant. There were even plenty of things Colin couldn't explain or account for.

He shuffled into the next room. He always felt a certain thrill whenever he went through the black curtain, and it was no different now. The subtle red lighting on the other side was in stark contrast to his computer room, which was as normal as you could get. Darren had rigged up the lighting in here on his request. He was a good lad, really. Never had any problem with whatever was asked of him, even the things most people would run from. Sam was the same, perhaps even more so. Neither had ever complained about their duties. He must've done something right while raising them. They always knew, he guessed, that they were different to other boys. And now they were men, free to explore their own true will, he was delighted when they decided to stay and continue his legacy.

Their biggest test, though, would come when they decided to take the woman from this world. Colin didn't doubt their loyalty. But they were reckless enough to leave traces of their dirty work and he didn't want any such carelessness to bring an end to it all before the work was done. He had to watch them carefully and proceed with caution. It was easier said than done, especially where his health was concerned.

He let the dark wash over him and moved into the middle of the room. He always felt a surge of energy run through him whenever he stood upon the pentacle painted on the floor. It had been here as long as he could remember, from well before he ever occupied the house. It had been here well before his grandfather had lived here too. The paint, he knew, was not actually paint but something else entirely. This was part of what gave it energy and power. A triangle of evocation captured the circle within it forever. It was all ultimately symbolism, yet important for ritual, and ceremonial magic required it. His cloak, made of red velvet, also had a pentacle embroidered on the chest. He felt great power whenever he wore it. He grabbed it from the hook at the wall and flung it over him.

The altar was pure symbolism, too, but important. Upon it were a male skull and a female skull, both human. Both had been there from the beginning of his time here at the farm. Probably well before that, too, perhaps for as long as the pentacle, or even longer. On the wall behind the altar itself was a hexagram.

Colin stood in silence in the middle of the room, upon the pentacle, and let the energy of it run through him. He always felt a surge of great power. He was re-energised every single time he did it, feeling the oxygen in his blood course through his veins like a life force. He remained there a few moments before approaching the black door on the right, which was reinforced with steel. He pushed it open, which took some effort as it was so heavy, and moved inside.

He flicked the switch just beyond the threshold and the bright LEDs in the ceiling illuminated the room in white light. The stainless-steel cupboards that lined the room on the western side were filled with bones and skulls. On the eastern side was a refrigerator, where he kept the blood. Directly above that: the sink and a work surface. In the middle of the room, which Colin considered a different kind of altar, was a stainless-steel table where he did the work. There was a drainage well around the perimeter, and it was slightly sloped at the edges, so that blood could run off freely. Without that, the messy business he conducted would be a whole lot worse. Directly below the table were a series of stainless-steel drawers where he kept his tools.

There was a black-and-white domestic cat upon the table

now. The animal's colour was important and symbolic. Sam had done what was asked of him efficiently and without drama. He was good at that kind of thing.

Colin moved over to the fridge and opened it, removing a small glass bottle, like a kiddie's milk bottle, from the shelf in the door. He unscrewed the cap and brought the rim to his lips, drinking deeply and without hesitation. A moment later, the bottle was empty, and he ran his fingers across his mouth to remove what was left of the blood. He gasped at the air and drew it in deeply. He knew he would need oxygen soon.

He went over to the table and stroked the cat. The animal was in a very deep sleep, its light body already having left this realm. He watched it breathing for a moment before removing the blade from the drawer at his waist.

Then he went to work once more.

TEN

'Bloody hell,' DI Murray said. 'Must be some kind of nutcase running this thing.'

'You can say that again, eh?' McCulloch said.

Logan drained his coffee and watched his colleagues navigate the website as he had done last night. He stood behind them as all four—Murray, McCulloch, Hussein and Bennett—hunched together around the laptop.

'The thing I don't get,' Hussein said, 'is why the bloody thing exists at all. You know what I mean? Why even go to the trouble of making this website and for what purpose?'

'Yeah, what's the point of it all?' Bennett said. 'With you there.'

Murray handled the mouse, clicking away on everything clickable. Logan had already showed them the images of his car, the woodland trees, the ram's head, the eyes in a saucer beside a kitchen sink. But now Murray had found more photographs which were equally weird.

'Go back,' McCulloch said. 'I want to see that again.'

Murray did as she asked and there it was: a totem bearing the head of a goat. The animal's skin and flesh had been ripped to the bone by the elements, but some of it remained. The eyes were missing, perhaps gouged out by birds. Some crooked teeth were still in its mouth, though most had gone.

'Crackpots,' Logan said. 'Whoever's doing this.'

'Some weird shit, this,' agreed Hussein.

'You know,' said Murray, 'I'm gonna have to get IT onto it. Maybe speak with Chris and see if we can go deeper and find out where this thing's being hosted.'

'They'll probably be able to pinpoint a location,' Bennett said.

'Yeah, but whoever's doing it would probably be taking great care to keep themselves hidden.'

'Yet it's like it's been shoved in our faces, eh?' McCulloch said. 'You know. A fuck-you kind of thing.'

'Let's see how far the rabbit hole goes,' Murray said. He picked up the phone and dialled internally. 'And I think we're gonna need something much more powerful than this machine, Rob. No offence.'

'None taken.'

McCulloch took the mouse while Murray waited on the line, pacing up and down his office. Outside, the weather had turned some more, the darkening sky casting a deep gloom.

'There we go,' McCulloch said. 'A raven. But is it the same one?'

They studied the image on screen. It was impossible to tell if this was the same bird, but it was likely. The creature was lying on a steel table, photographed and illuminated from above. Its wings had been opened and a hand on either side held them at the tips. The hands clearly belonged to two different people as there was no way it would be possible for one person to do so. The bird's bloody organ—the missing heart—sat on the steel table beside the creature like some kind of removed tumour. Its beady eyes were glassy and dead. The hole in its chest was neat enough to suggest that someone had taken a sharp scalpel to it. Logan guessed that whoever the hands in the image belonged to could also be on the CCTV from the garage near to the house where the bird had been crucified.

Murray burst into chatter down the phone as McCulloch clicked back out of the image and landed on the previous page with the image of the goat's head on a totem.

She had to leave the laptop, the image on screen giving her the creeps, and handed over to Hussein so she could instead gaze out of the window. 'Jesus, it's like bloody Siberia, eh?'

'Not seen it this heavy in a long time,' Logan said.

Bennett nodded. 'They'll be closing the schools any time now.'

'Here you go,' Hussein said. 'Some right fucking characters, these people. Come and look at this one and tell me we aren't dealing with some bombastic clowns. Fucking hell.'

They turned back to see what he'd found.

Two hooded figures stood side by side, facing the camera, their sackcloth cloaks heavy and baggy and covering their faces, like a pair of demonic monks out in the broad-daylight countryside. In this image, it was a hot day, the grass around them dry and sunburnt, the trees beyond full and green. Kneeling between them, naked and pale, was the ageing and wrinkled body of a female, her long grey hair all the way down to her waist, her sagging breasts like deflated balloons. Her head was covered in a sack, her arms bound behind her back. Each of the demonic-looking figures had a hand on either shoulder.

No faces.

No names.

'This is fucking nuts,' Logan said. 'Look at the state of it.'

Although it wasn't graphic, it was disturbing. Either this woman was a part of some kind of weird sexual game between them or a daft pagan ritual to take advantage of the waning moon, or she was a victim.

'I think I need another coffee,' McCulloch said. 'Maybe throw some whisky in it as well, eh?'

Bennett did the honours as Murray continued to chatter down the phone to IT.

'If she's a victim,' Logan said, 'maybe this photo was taken before she was killed. I mean, right before. To capture her last waking moments or something. We won't know until her body turns up. But it would make her the first human.'

'Could we be looking at the killers?' Hussein said. 'You know, right after this was taken, they go and slaughter a goat...'

Murray returned to the desk and they showed him what he'd missed.

'Bloody hell,' he said. 'Am I gonna have to go further here and get more units involved? What the fuck is this shit?'

'What did IT say?'

'They said to stop what we're doing immediately and wait. Which means they want to take your laptop, Rob. They also want to isolate this site and talked a lot of bloody gobbledygook about browsers and servers and the dark bloody web. Chris from IT is on the way up right now.'

'Hang on a minute,' McCulloch said. 'Before you shut it down. What's that?' She pointed to something in the image, just visible beyond the trees.

'It's a church spire,' Logan said. 'Though which one is anyone's guess.'

'But if we can identify it,' Hussein said, 'that puts us in the right ballpark, doesn't it? The field where this picture was taken has got to be within spitting distance of this church.'

'Any ideas, sir?'

Bennett leaned in. 'I know where that is. You can tell by the crucifix on top of the spire. It lights up at night. St Michael's. I think it's in Ainsworth Village.'

'Loads of farmland around there as well,' Logan said. 'So, that would make sense. We'll need to check it out.'

'If that's the case,' Murray said, 'looks like this field is west of that spire. We'll have to cross reference it with other photographs, maybe check it on Google Maps. I want all four of you up there this afternoon. See what you can find. And we could do with identifying this woman.'

'Reckon that'll be impossible, sir,' Bennett said. 'Unless we chase up death records, missing persons, that kind of thing.'

'We don't even know if she's dead. But I tell you what, why don't you get onto it, Shaun?'

Bennett winced. 'It'll be like trying to find—'

'A needle in a haystack? Best get started straight away, then. But before any of that, we've got some CCTV to look at. I'm told there's plenty of it. I want everyone down to the viewing room in ten minutes. Martin Hobbs has got it all set up and ready to go.'

CUSTODY SERGEANT MARTIN HOBBS ushered them into the CCTV viewing suite, a room that was usually out of bounds for the average copper. He dimmed the lights and asked everyone to take a seat around the bank of large monitors.

'Bloody parky out there, eh?' he said. 'Not seen it like this since 1963.'

'Didn't realise you were that old, Sarge,' Hussein said.

'I was born in 1962,' Hobbs said. 'So, technically, I was there.'

'You'll be ready for retirement soon, eh?'

'You can say that again. Right, are we sitting comfortably? Anyone need popcorn?'

They all sat down as Martin took the controls and brought the CCTV to life.

'So, this first one,' Hobbs said, 'is from the Tesco garage. They have a number of cameras trained on the forecourt itself, several in the shop, and two on the outside facing Peel Way. All in full colour. It might take us a while to check everything but what we have checked, I think you might be interested in.'

He played the first files, time stamped at 02:28. An empty road, cold with frost and a little snow and illuminated from the high street lights and the nearby McDonald's. Both the garage forecourt and the fast-food place were open twenty-four hours but were expected to be quiet at this time of the morning, perhaps even totally dead except for the odd taxi driver hanging around.

'Watch,' Hobbs said. 'You'll see it any second.'

A large white transit van, probably a Ford, went by from west to east, heading past the McDonald's, which Logan knew was on the right of the screen.

'White van man strikes again, eh?' McCulloch said.

A moment later, it came back in the other direction after presumably pulling a U-turn at the traffic lights and coming down the opposite carriageway.

'Check Camera Two,' Hobbs said. 'You'll see the number plate's missing.'

'Just a rusty white van,' Logan said. 'Like the worst plasterers in the world.'

'Back to Camera One and you'll see the back doors open and the animal flung out. *There.*'

'Jesus,' Logan said.

'I'll slow it down and you'll see it better because if you blink, you'll miss it.'

They watched again as, in slow motion, the white van drove at a normal speed for the road. The double doors opened and the Rottweiler fell out from the back. Then the van picked up speed and disappeared from view.

'I'll chase up CCTV from the other premises in the area,' Murray said. 'The little retail park up the road will no doubt have plenty.'

'Could take a few days, eh?' McCulloch said.

'But we might get a better look at the driver. Did we not get a decent image of the guy behind the wheel, Martin?'

'Not really, I'm afraid. Camera Two shows the figure in the front but he's all in black. Probably masked up. We've checked it through and there's no other appearance of the van, not on this footage anyway. Checking the CCTV from the other places nearby might yield better results.'

'At least we know we're after a van,' Hussein said. 'Narrows it down a bit.'

'Probably thousands of them in the city, though,' Bennett said.

Logan edged his chair closer. 'Can we zoom in?'

'We can,' said Hobbs, playing around with the joystick to get a closer look, 'but it won't bring any joy, I'm afraid. You can see for yourself. A black figure, no licence plate. It's the same at the back. I'll show you the McDonald's footage as well, just so we're clear.'

Logan's phone buzzed in his pocket. It was Izzy's school app. Probably a message about yet another non-uniform day to raise money for the school, which was dying on its arse. Vic could deal with it.

'Okay,' Hobbs said. 'Moving on to the next feature. Not much different from the first, I'm afraid, but you get a closer look and a better angle of the rear of the van.'

Once again, he manipulated the joystick and played the footage back at full speed from the same timestamp: 02:28. The van came into view again, driving past the McDonald's at thirty mph from west to east. Then a moment later, where it must've pinned around at the next junction, it came back in the opposite direction. As it passed the restaurant, the body of the dog fell from the open door. It was a slightly clearer image, but the detectives were still none the wiser. There was no visible figure from the inside and the licence plate had been removed. The van continued to move off after the body had been dumped in the road. There was no other traffic.

'So, there we have it,' Hobbs said. 'That's the best we can do so far on this one. Which then brings us to...'

'The raven,' Logan said. 'Right?'

'I'm glad you're paying attention, Rob,' Hobbs said. 'But this time, there's no van. Are we strapped in for the third feature in our movie marathon? Anyone need more popcorn?'

'Could do with another coffee, eh?' McCulloch said.

But Hobbs wasn't listening. Instead, he messed around with the machines and brought up another tape, this one from the MOT garage down the bottom end of the Braithwaite's house where the raven was found. The timestamp on this was 06:08.

Two figures dressed in black, their faces covered with hoods, walked along the pavement on the main Tottington Road from south to north. One of the men—their build was obviously male, their height a good estimate at just short of six feet—was carrying a large black rucksack. The other held what looked from this angle like an iron bar. It was dark, with very little light from the nearby shops and street-lamps illuminating the high street. But there was enough light to get a good image of the two figures. Again, though, there were no faces. Just silhouettes with secrets. They could've been anyone, of course, but then they came back ten minutes later after Hobbs had fast-forwarded the tape, this time from north to south, their faces obscured by their dark and heavy hoods. They could have passed as shadows.

'I reckon,' Hobbs said, 'that they were having a good look at where they wanted to put this bird. They'd decided on something in those minutes. They don't appear again on this CCTV, but they do show up a bit later on, when they actually reappear with the bird. I'll show you.'

He brought up another tape, this time from a haber-dashery on the opposite side of the high street. Its front directly looked over the little side road with the garages and the Braithwaite's property. Beyond the property itself was a mid-height wall that separated the buildings from the field and trees beyond.

'If you watch now,' Hobbs said, 'you'll see them climb over this wall with the bag. The Braithwaite house is just there on the right of the screen, right next to the wall. The house is on their left.'

It was snowing, though not heavily. The time stamp was 11:33. They watched as the two figures once more came into view, climbing over the wall from the field side, each dressed in black clothing, and this time with balaclavas. They looked around before ducking behind some bushes beside the wall and then coming into view again right outside the Braithwaite house. One of the figures removed the raven from the rucksack and the other quickly hammered in the nails on each wing. The whole thing was over in less than a minute and they each clambered over the wall again and disappeared, not two fucks given.

And with no one else around—the nearby garage mechanics no doubt busy inside—they could get away with it right under everyone's noses, and in broad daylight, too.

McCulloch shook her head. 'Cheeky bastards, eh?'

'You sure there's no sign of a white van?' Hussein said.

Hobbs shut down the machine. 'Not *the* white van, at least.'

'Probably half a dozen gone up and down that road,' Bennett said. 'Plumbers, sparks...'

'Deliveries,' Logan said. 'Wish we had that number plate.'

Hobbs nodded. 'You saw yourself. Both plates had been removed.'

'Because they were obviously up to no bloody good, eh?' McCulloch said. 'So, what now?'

Murray sighed. 'I'll keep trying to trace further CCTV. See if we can get a decent image of any faces. But for now, we'll have a quick break, then back up to the boardroom. There should be a toxicology report winging our way right about now. And I believe Dr Stephen Moreland will also be there to brief us. I hope you're all ready, because we're about to go deep. Martin, thanks for your time and keep me updated if anything else comes up.'

. . .

KEL MCCULLOCH OPENED the dating app—*Heart Suite*—and found the direct message in her inbox. Although she'd already arranged a date with Alex, the copper from Merseyside CID, it didn't hurt to keep things ticking along with one or two others. There was a part of her that knew she was being silly, was perhaps pushing it more than she'd like, but she was having fun, and she was an adult, for fuck's sake.

She'd do what she liked.

If she really wanted to find that man—that one guy who'd sweep her off her feet, someone she could build something with, maybe even have kids with while there was still time—she would have to push a few boundaries. Kiss a few frogs along the way. Maybe one frog would turn into a prince.

She clicked on the little envelope icon and opened up the message.

HEY KELLY.

Is that your real name?? Lol

I'm not normally this forward but... fancy a drink?

Mark

FOR A MOMENT, she considered deleting it straight away. He was probably some weirdo pervert out for what he could get, but then she clicked on his bio and... he wasn't actually that bad. Despite the boring name and the average looks—like a primary school teacher who was into jogging and trains—he was the type who could be full of surprises. She clicked through his handful of photographs. He was pretty good-looking, actually. Athletic. Not entirely what she'd normally go for but enough to warrant a date, especially if it was somewhere local and he was paying.

Okay, maybe he was just another guy after a shag, and she'd seen plenty of those types, but she could always let him down gently if she wasn't feeling it and she could have her friend Jenny in a nearby pub if things went really tits-up.

What the hell. Maybe he wasn't that bad a catch. And she wouldn't ever know unless she found out for herself.

She chose her words carefully and replied.

THEY GATHERED IN THE BOARDROOM. Dr Stephen Moreland, a veterinary pathologist from one of the local big surgeries, sat beside Dr Janine Graham, one of the forensic pathologists with GMP, at the head of the table. DCI Clayton had taken up a chair on the right. DS Kelly McCulloch sat beside him while Logan and DI Murray took the opposite side. There was a folder between the two pathologists that looked pretty ominous.

Murray had sent Hussein and Bennett off to see if they could shed any light on the location in the photograph near St Michael's church, with both complaining about having to trudge through the snow. But they'd cheered a little after Logan managed to persuade Murray that he needed to sign off the use of two Land Rovers for the week.

Chris from IT had taken Logan's laptop, saying they should be able to trace a location based on the IP address and this would be dependent on the user's VPN—Virtual Private Network—settings. He promised to return the laptop as soon as they'd finished. Logan told him not to bother.

'Right, then,' DCI Clayton said, 'we'd better get this meeting started.'

He made the introductions and kept them brief. Everyone knew each other except for Dr Moreland, who made a short introduction himself. He was a specialist in veterinary pathology but had spent the last three years running his own surgery practice in Bury. He rarely did any work for the police, though had done in the past, and he usually wasn't required for such gruesome investigations. This case was a rare one indeed, he said, but something he'd been keen to get his teeth into. Logan had him down as early fifties, well-educated and respected, and with money to burn.

Dr Janine Graham, on the other hand, gave a different vibe. She was younger, mid-forties, very pretty and curvaceous and, if the rumours in the station were true, fronted a goth rock band at weekends. Beneath the standard office attire and neat, pinned brown hair, was a pale white body oozing sex and tattoos. Logan had to admit that he quite fancied her, and he guessed he wouldn't be the only one around HQ. But it was well known she was married to the guitarist in her band, a six-foot-three clone of Eddie Van Halen. Even if Logan was single, he'd have stood no chance.

Dr Graham kicked off proceedings as Murray poured coffee for everyone from a glass decanter on the table.

'So,' she said, her local accent loud and colourful as she removed the paperwork from the folder, 'we have a toxicology report and a breakdown of some of the procedures we went through upon our examinations of the animals involved. I'm sorry it's taken a while. Longer than I would've liked, to be honest with you, but there were a few factors involved. We had to send tissue and bloods down to London for testing and of course wait for the results. But you'll be pleased to know we now have them. Dr Moreland has written his report, and you will all have a copy in front of you.'

Right on cue, DCI Clayton handed out a report to each from the bundle of paper in front of him.

'And now I'll hand over to Stephen,' said Graham, 'who will give a breakdown of everything we know.'

'Afternoon, everyone,' Moreland said. He took a sip of hot coffee and opened the report, urging everyone to do the same. 'So, as Janine said, we had to send tissue and bloods to London to ascertain a toxicology report on the animal cadavers involved. We carried out an autopsy on each one—'

'You carried out the autopsies, Stephen. I just watched.'

'Ignore Janine,' he said. 'She was very helpful and professional throughout. We carried out the work here in the GMP Mortuary at Bury HQ and in liaison with the Royal London School of Pathology, which is where our samples were sent. Toxicology tests were carried out on tissue and bloods from all specimens and subsequently, our results were returned to us.

'There are several things I want to go over so that we're all clear on the scientific method involved. Autopsy was carried out on all animals. This involved strict examination of the wounds, surgical examination of the muscles, tissue, bones and organs of each specimen, and as already stated, both tissue and blood samples were taken and sent for toxicology. To keep it brief, and I would urge you all to read the report in full when you can for further detail, each animal has had organs and limbs removed, including the head on several of the animals, prior to examination postmortem. I should stress that we haven't yet had sufficient time to conduct autopsy on the Rottweiler.'

'Bastards, eh?' McCulloch said.

'Indeed,' Moreland said. 'So, let's try and reach a

conclusion on how these poor beautiful creatures were killed. We'll start with the Ovis species. That's the ram to you. It was an elderly male sheep, approximately fifteen years old, which is very good in farming terms. Cause of death is decapitation, but according to the toxicology feedback we have, this animal was probably helped along as a result of a combination of very high doses of the analgesia and anaesthesia drugs xylazine and ketamine, both of which are commonly used for cattle and sheep.'

'So, you're saying it was the drugs that killed it?' Logan said. 'Not the actual blade.'

Moreland nodded. 'The animal was probably injected with very high doses of xylazine and ketamine, which more than likely incapacitated it. We found evidence of intravenous needle marks in the jugular vein. The head was then properly removed. Everything else is just dressing up. Why the head and hooves were removed is another question, but it would've been the drugs that helped it along. The removal of the heart would've sealed its fate, but it would've been long dead by then, anyway.'

'So why remove it at all?' McCulloch said.

Moreland shrugged. 'Who knows? But I can tell you that the head, the hooves and the heart were all removed with several surgical blades, including large scalpels and probably a saw.'

'In your opinion,' Logan asked, 'were they... well, were they removed in a professional manner? Or has someone just gone and ripped the heart out and chopped the head off? I don't mean to be so crude but—'

'No, you're right,' Graham said. 'You'd think it would be easier for them to swing an axe at it and chop it off, but no. This was most certainly a surgical procedure.'

Murray spoke up. 'Could the animal have been injected with this stuff...'

'Xylazine and ketamine.'

'Xylazine and ketamine. Could it have been injected when the animal was out in the field somehow, and then taken somewhere else to be killed?'

'That's quite possible, yes,' Moreland said. 'In fact, I'd say that was likely.'

'Were the same drugs used for the others?' asked DCI Clayton.

Moreland nodded. 'Examinations haven't yet been carried out on the dog, but yes. Xylazine and ketamine were both found in both the raven's and rabbit's blood.'

'Which points to what?' Logan said. 'Could it be we're dealing with someone who knows about this stuff? You know, these kinds of anaesthetic drugs, surgery on animals, all that stuff?'

'Possibly,' Graham said. 'Certainly where the surgery's concerned. It wouldn't take much for someone to understand the drug and administer it, but surgery's a whole different skill set. It seems, from our examinations, that whoever's done this was highly trained in the procedures.'

'Do you mean to say we could be looking for a surgeon or doctor?' McCulloch asked.

Moreland shrugged. 'That's a possibility. A surgeon... Veterinary surgeon, maybe. Certainly someone who has a very good knowledge of anatomy.'

'A butcher?' Logan said. He exchanged a look with McCulloch. The visit to the abattoir was fresh in his mind. 'Could that be a possibility?'

'Someone who's proficient with handling surgical instruments would be my best guess,' Moreland said. 'Though I wouldn't rule out a butcher, no.'

'But unlikely?' Murray asked.

'You wouldn't expect a butcher to have the same expertise, if you like, as a surgeon. But they could certainly remove body parts from an animal of this size. I can't speculate on why the body parts were removed but I can say, with a degree of authority, that they were removed with some precision.'

'And that's not all,' said Graham. 'Each of the animals have had an incision in the carotid artery, to drain it of blood. A considerable amount of blood was removed from the ram, and we think that was probably done prior to removing the head. Same for the others.'

'Jesus. This is fucked up, eh?' McCulloch said.

'Do you think it'll happen again?' Logan said. 'In your opinion? I mean, going off what you've found, does anything point to this happening again?'

'Who knows?' Moreland said. 'Your guess is as good as mine. I think we have to be open to that, though, yes. Especially given that embalming fluid has been found in the bodies of these animals. Which would indicate the killer might want to do more.'

'Embalming fluid?' McCulloch said. 'So, what, the killer's tried to preserve them as well as destroy them? Doesn't make sense to me.'

'I would have to agree,' Moreland said. 'And it seems a real clumsy affair, if I'm completely honest, as if whoever's done this really didn't know what they were doing. The bodies are almost half blood, half embalming fluid. They're a bit of a mess.'

'Could they have tried to preserve them and failed?' DCI Clayton asked.

'And then decided to just forget it,' Logan said. 'For whatever reason.'

'Should we be adding a taxidermist to our list of potentials?' Murray said.

'Not quite,' Graham said. 'Taxidermists don't embalm bodies. It's a different discipline. Embalming would fit with someone who is very familiar with anatomy. Regarding preservation, yes it's possible they tried and failed and decided to just dump them.'

'But in relation to the bird,' Logan said, 'it was displayed rather than dumped. In a way, you could say they were all displayed. Are you able to carry out an autopsy on the dog today? See if you can find more of the same.'

Moreland nodded. 'We're booked in for six o'clock this evening. I believe the owner wants us to do it quickly so she can cremate the dog.'

'Can I just ask about the rabbit?' McCulloch said. 'A few things, really. Did you find any evidence of a microchip, you know, something to identify any ownership? And what, in your opinion, happened to its genitals and eyes?'

'It's a good question,' Graham said. 'Firstly, yes, a microchip was found under the rabbit's skin. It was called Bobby. A male. The owner has been informed and their address added to file. Stephen, do you want to cover the other part of the question?'

'Of course.' Moreland took a sip of coffee before continuing. 'Well, the eyes were completely hollowed out. Everything was removed with a small scalpel and the sockets drained of blood. The whole of the eye was removed. The cornea, the retina, the lens, the nerves, all the connecting tissue. We found the same with the genitalia. The whole reproductive system was extracted, as was the anus.'

Logan glanced across at McCulloch, who was squirming. 'But why?'

Moreland shrugged again. 'I can't answer that, I'm afraid. That's a question for you guys.'

There seemed little else to go on and little point in hearing more. Logan leafed through the report, which he thought might make for interesting bedtime reading. At least all the jargon Moreland had written would no doubt send him to sleep quicker than one of his anaesthetics. The bottom line: they were looking for someone who knew about anatomy, was proficient with a surgeon's knife, and was familiar with the science behind body preservation. Piecing the rest of the puzzle together meant getting to grips with the reasons for it all. Heads removed, hearts removed, blood taken. None of it made any sense. But then what kind of killing did? And perhaps there really was no reason.

Logan's thoughts turned to Caitlin Slater. He couldn't quite explain his fear around her disappearance, but it was there. Could it be really possible that whoever had taken these animals had taken her, too? The thought of it caused a wave of anxiety. There was still no sign of her. Not even the tiniest clue.

'If there's anything else...?' DCI Clayton said.

'That pretty much covers everything so far,' Graham said. 'As Stephen confirmed, we'll be carrying out an autopsy on the dog, Bruno, at six o'clock this evening. If we have anything else to show, we'll make everyone aware.'

'You'll find detailed elements in the written report,' Moreland said. 'I recommend you go through it. For now, though, that's everything we can give you. Let's hope nothing else turns up.'

'I've got one more question.' Logan left his seat, still carrying his warm coffee, feeling that moving around would make what he was about to say that little bit easier. 'Could the same surgical instruments be used on a human body?

The scalpel, the saw, all that. And could these drugs also be used to anaesthetise a woman?'

'What are you getting at, Rob?' Murray said.

'Just putting it out there.'

'For what reason?'

'We have a missing woman, sir,' he said. 'Caitlin Slater. What if the same thing's happened to her? What if she's been taken somehow? Just pulled from her house.'

'There's no evidence or sign of any tampering with her property—'

'Pulled off the street then.'

'DS Logan,' Clayton said, 'the Caitlin Slater disappearance likely has nothing to do with these animal mutilations.'

'I beg to differ, sir.'

'Oh, really? And can you provide us with some evidence for that?'

This stopped Logan in his tracks around the boardroom table. 'Admittedly, sir, no. No, I can't. But the pattern of these animals disappearing and now Caitlin Slater disappearing... It's similar, isn't it?'

'Not really, no,' Murray said.

'But how long has she been missing now, sir?' McCulloch said. 'She can't just remain missing forever, eh?'

'Of course she can,' Clayton said.

'But when does her missing status become something else?'

'Kelly,' Murray said, 'you know full well a missing persons case stays that way until we have evidence to the contrary.'

'Have we checked CCTV near to where she was last seen?'

'As far as I'm aware, it's not a priority.'

'Then what the bloody hell is?' Logan said.

The comment brought a stony silence around the table.

DCI Clayton pursed his lips. 'The Senior Investigating Officer, DCI Warburton, will be holding a briefing tomorrow morning on the Caitlin Slater disappearance. DI Sanderson, I believe, is leading the enquiry. I suggest you attend if you believe there are any discrepancies in the investigation and perhaps you'd like to put forward your theory then?'

Logan nodded, paced over to the window. 'Okay, sir. I will.' He gazed out blankly, at the ever-falling snow. Was Caitlin Slater still out there or had she been taken from this world already? 'At the very least, I'd expect to hear that CCTV has been pulled from all the nearby premises from where she was last seen.'

DCI Clayton stood, clutching the report. It was everyone's cue to follow. 'I think this meeting is concluded. Dr Graham, I'm sure we'd all appreciate any updates should anything immediately alert you. Thanks everyone.'

Logan watched him leave the room.

McCulloch joined him at the window. 'Arsehole, eh?'

'Can't see the wood for the trees.'

Pretty soon, the room had emptied except for Moreland and Graham, who were both poring over some significant page in the report.

Logan had one final question. 'Do you guys think I'm jumping to wild speculation?'

Moreland met his gaze. 'I didn't get to answer your question.'

'Was rudely interrupted, eh?' McCulloch said.

He nodded. 'Well, the answer would be yes on both parts. The drugs and surgical implements could be used on a human. The dosage wouldn't be that much different to a cattle or a horse.'

'Ketamine,' McCulloch said, 'as we know, is a street drug. Crazy, I know.'

'Kids are using it down the pub, these days,' Graham said. 'They know how to have a good time, don't they?'

'Really dangerous,' Moreland said. 'Could easily cause major damage, especially if overdosing.'

'But it's widely available,' Logan said. 'In drug dealing circles, I mean.'

'Nothing like a bit of horse tranquilliser to get the party started,' Graham said. 'And no, Rob, I don't think you're wildly speculating. The sad thing is, though, that you'll only be proven right if a body turns up and we come to the same conclusions at autopsy. Good luck with finding her.'

'We're not even on the case, really,' McCulloch said. 'Not officially.'

Logan scowled. 'But I'm gonna push for it. Because something doesn't add up.'

DARREN SANK into the couch and lit up a smoke, the ashtray balanced on the armrest beside him. He opened up the *Heart Suite* app on his phone and went straight to the messages. She'd replied already, which surprised him. She must be one of those types: desperate for a man and kids, probably involved in a few dating sites. Different ones for different circumstances. *Tinder* for casual sex. *Soulmates* for a life partner. *Heart Suite* for romance and fun and potentials...

He reckoned she fell into all of those categories. She was probably craving a real man. Someone who could give her a good seeing to after a night out. Someone who could take her for a slap-up meal, the works, lots of wine and a few cheeky cocktails, then back to hers for fun and games.

He'd found her pretty quickly, after a bit of detective work—ha!—and had matched the *Heart Suite* bio with her Facebook profile. For a copper, she was a bit lax with her privacy settings. Her Facebook photographs had shown it was definitely her: Detective Sergeant Kelly McCulloch. How the hell she'd made a detective, he didn't know. She was dumb as fuck, leaving herself wide open like this. A little bit prim and proper. The kind of girl who loved knitted jumpers and herbal tea. She even had an Instagram account where she posted photos of her jigsaw puzzles, for fuck's sake.

But she wasn't much of a puzzle herself. It was easy to see why she was on these dating sites. She needed someone to combat her loneliness. Someone who could show her a different side of life, away from the stresses of her job.

Could he play that role? Undoubtedly.

Could he charm her? Absolutely.

He opened the message.

Hey Mark,

Sometimes being a bit forward works wonders eh?

I don't mind.

Is Friday ok with you?

Could meet for a drink in Bury?

Kel x

THE DAFT BITCH had fallen for it already. He left the couch and threw another log on the fire. Colin was busy down in his fucking dungeon and Sam was out chopping more wood.

He reckoned Friday was good. Sooner than he would've

liked but still, with any luck he could get her into bed and fuck her little brains out.

She had a tidy rack.

Pretty fit, really.

He finished his smoke and hovered his thumb over the cursor to reply.

KURT HADN'T BEEN SLEEPING WELL. He'd been racked with worry ever since he'd come home to an empty house. He knew this wasn't like Caitlin, to just up and disappear. She'd always made a point of telling him what she was up to, no matter what. Always sent a text update or phoned every three or four hours, wherever she was. Had always, always told him of her plans.

The party was the problem. That's what he knew for certain. If she hadn't gone to that stupid fucking party, she'd still be here now, with him, where she belonged. Yet the police didn't seem interested in what had happened there. He knew what people got up to at house parties. It wasn't just booze they were into these days. He knew that Caitlin wasn't into any drugs. Not since their early twenties when they'd had a spell smoking weed for a while. Back then they'd both kid themselves they were enjoying it, but they never really did. Caitlin was always into wine, had never taken any chemicals, hated clubbing and all that shite. Pills and bloody Es or whatever it was now. And Kurt hated all that stuff too. Much preferred a beer. But even that was tailing off. Driving trucks for a living required careful alcohol consumption so he'd trained himself to avoid it.

But he did like a beer. It helped him to relax. Work had allowed him to take some leave while he got to grips with Caitlin's disappearance, but they expected updates every few days, wanted to know when he'd be back at work. As if his mind was up to driving a fucking truck. Laughable, really.

He knew he should be avoiding it. Alcohol. But for fuck's sake, the lack of action from the police was tearing him in two. He felt like someone had taken something and sliced it through the middle of his body. Just pulled his heart right out. She was gone. *Gone*. And no fucker seemed to want to do anything about it.

Those coppers who'd come to the house, questioning him, as if he'd done her in. Ridiculous. He loved her more than anything. So why couldn't they see that? They'd said he wasn't a suspect, but he reckoned they were full of shit. Of course he was. He'd been expecting a knock at the door again, this time to arrest him. That woman copper came across as nice and all that, the Scottish one, but he reckoned that was just a way of building trust, so he'd let his guard down. Trick him into slipping up and making a mistake.

Well, they were wrong. As if he'd killed the woman he loved. It was crazy to think that.

He went to the fridge and opened it up. There were ten cans sitting there, just waiting to be drunk. He knew that once he opened one, the rest would follow. It was the taste. Just went down so easily. And it helped to block out the worry. God knows he felt so useless, but it wasn't as if he hadn't been out looking for her. He'd been *everywhere*. Had called her phone a million times but it always rang out. What if she was still alive somewhere? What if some nutter had taken her and had locked her up in a house or something?

They'd wanted to try again for a baby. Losing the first one almost killed her. It had hurt him, too. He'd just started getting his head around the idea of being a dad and then it was gone suddenly in the night. She'd woken him up in tears, with a pool of blood on the bedsheets. It had taken them a while to come to terms with it, and they were just coming around to the idea of giving it another go. He was going to marry her, really wanted to. He was getting ready to ask her.

And now this.

He took a can from the fridge and popped it open. Drank half of it in one and went back into the living room. It was getting a bit out of control. He knew it, of course. He could handle the mess, but it surrounded him, and he couldn't make the effort to clean up. It just seemed so pointless without her here.

He sat in silence and drank, keeping one eye on the window, just in case he saw her walking down the path. But deep down, he knew she wasn't coming home.

So he tried to think of ways to find her, to bring her home himself.

ELEVEN

Logan and McCulloch found the Land Rover parked in the undercroft, in an annexed section directly beneath the boardroom they'd left over an hour ago. After signing the relevant paperwork for the vehicle, which included instructions to return it to the same parking bay every day after use, Logan took the driver's side while McCulloch loaded the back seats up with heavy winter coats and boots, and carefully placed two hot takeaway coffees in the holders on the dashboard.

'Lucky to get this, eh?'

'It's the least they can do,' Logan said. 'If Murray wants us to go traipsing through those fields up there, then we need decent gear, and that includes the vehicle.'

'But it's bloody brand new, Rob. I'm not sure I trust your driving in this thing.'

'Bollocks. This is no problem. Always wanted one of these, to be honest.'

'Aye, well don't go screwing it around town like a boy racer, eh?'

He glared at her. 'I spent nearly two years on the traffic unit. I think I know what I'm doing. Right, how do you start this bloody thing?'

He found a *START* button beside the handbrake. These brand new 4x4s were as modern as they come, which was a good thing. But he'd never liked automatics. It was infinitely better than his own VW, though, and more suited to the terrain and weather.

The afternoon had become darker than they would've liked, the town overcast with a massive black cloud and an ethereal whiteish glow from the fallen snow, which had now reached at least two feet deep and was still falling. If they were in a country that had these conditions regularly, it wouldn't be a problem. But the British infrastructure couldn't cope. Countless roads hadn't been gritted, trains and trams had come to a halt, water pipes had frozen and gritting lorries were out all day and night.

'It's beautiful, eh?' McCulloch said. 'Just not so pleasant when you have to travel around in it.'

Logan had taken them out of HQ and up towards Ainsworth. He knew where St Michael's was, and half expected to see its illuminated crucifix atop the spire even at this time. It was pushing towards two o'clock and the local schools would be kicking out soon if they hadn't already. The weather had caused a lot of early closures this side of the city for one reason or another. The side streets and local fields would be filled soon enough with kids playing in the snow.

'So, what did you make of all that?' McCulloch said. 'DCI Clayton's a bit of an arse, eh?'

Logan shook his head. 'I know. I don't know what he was trying to achieve in there.'

'Mustn't like being challenged by an underling.'

'They never do.'

'You were right, though. You'd think it would be a priority to check CCTV. Makes me think Warburton and Sanderson haven't a clue. So, are you going to attend this briefing tomorrow?'

He nodded. 'Yeah. And you can come with me. I'll probably need the moral support.'

'Will be interesting to see what they have to say. That's if we can even get in to work, eh?'

'It's apparently gonna snow through the night. Could be a real nightmare tomorrow.'

'Yeah, well, it had better bloody improve by Friday.'

'You meeting this Alex guy or something?'

'Not Alex. He's Saturday. We're going for a coffee in town.'

'So who's the lucky fella, then?'

McCulloch stared out of the window. 'He's called Mark. Seems a nice guy. Meeting for a drink. And before you say anything, I'm gonna rope Jenny into it. She can hover around in the curry house up the road, eh? Her and her fella or something. I'll probably meet her afterwards.'

'And how long have you been chatting to this Mark? You've got to be careful, you know. You don't know who you might be getting involved with.'

'I think I can handle it, Rob. He seems a lovely guy.'

'What does he do for a living?'

'You know, I don't think it says in his bio. I'll have to check.'

By the time they'd reached The Black Bull, both of them were tempted to just fuck it all off and dive inside for a pint beside the fire.

The kids swarmed the snowy pavements like ants. A

snowball hit the windscreen and Logan gave a dirty look to a gang of twelve-year-olds who ran off laughing. Logan had to laugh, too, knowing it was something he'd have probably done back when he was at school.

He watched them go. 'Bet the little tykes are buzzing their tits off, eh?'

They carried on for a further mile until they came to St Michael's, standing Gothic and gloomy on the left side of the road. DS Hussein and DS Bennett were nowhere in sight, but they'd left their vehicle—an identical Land Rover—parked just beyond the church gates. Logan pulled up behind it and killed the engine while McCulloch dialled them up.

Hussein answered straight away. 'Please tell me you've brought us a flask of Bovril. Bloody freezing out here.'

'No such luck, Asif.' McCulloch warmed her hands on the takeaway coffee while Logan got to grips with the winter gear in the back.

'Bloody typical, that is. Might have to just call in the pub instead.'

'You found anything up here while we've been busy?'

'Not really. But how did it go for you guys? Toxicology bring us any closer to finding out what these nutcases have been up to?'

McCulloch filled him in while Logan retrieved the police-issue black winter coat and slung it on. He exchanged his own shoes for a pair of Caterpillar boots.

McCulloch followed, switching the phone between ears as she changed. 'So, that's pretty much it so far. All animals, except for the Rottweiler as they haven't done it yet, were injected with these drugs. Xylazine and ketamine. The vet reckons they were given very high doses.'

'Probably someone who has access to these drugs quite

easily,' Hussein said. 'Hey, hang on, I can see you both from here. Turn around.'

McCulloch did so and spotted the two coppers hanging around through the woods behind the church. Hussein waved and beckoned them over.

They joined up moments later, both Bennett and Hussein catching a quick smoke while they could.

'So,' Logan said. 'Where are we?'

'Well,' Bennett said, 'we thought we'd try and pinpoint exactly where that photo was taken. You know, the one with the old crone in it.'

'God, you don't think she was a real witch, eh?' McCulloch said.

'She looks nothing like my wife,' Hussein said. 'So, probably not, no.'

The joke brought a small chuckle.

Logan looked around, trying to ascertain exactly where they were in relation to the image from the white rabbit website. It had been a schoolboy error to not bring a copy of the image with them, but it was easy to be careless when all the other shit was clouding his mind. He spun a three-sixty and took it all in. With the church so close by and the image marking it at some distance away, beyond the trees, he calculated the photograph had been taken from the opposite side of the road, at a different angle. The church spire had been to the left of the frame, so Logan guessed they were currently standing at a point to the right of the church from the photo's vantage point.

He pointed. 'I think we need to be over the other side. On the other side of the road.'

'There's a kid's park over that way,' Bennett said.

'Beyond that, I mean. There's a big copse of trees over there, as well. I reckon it's behind that.'

As they walked, they went over the morning's events, with the CCTV they'd viewed as the main focus of conversation. The two figures in the footage involving the raven were surely involved with the ram and the Rottweiler. Probably the rabbit, too. And although they had no clear picture and no clear evidence of the people involved, it was becoming pretty obvious that this was all the work of the same individuals.

'Do you think with this toxicology report,' Bennett said, 'that they could've picked the drugs up on the street market? And if they did, where from? Or from whom?'

'That's if they did,' McCulloch said. 'I guess they could've got them from a number of places. Perhaps they stole them? Or got them from the Dark Web?'

Logan nodded. 'It'll be interesting to see if IT can find anything we can't. There's got to be something hidden away on that site.'

'If anyone can dig into that kind of stuff, Chris can,' Hussein said. 'He's one of these weird Asperger's types, you know. Computer-obsessed. In our case, that's a good thing. He knows where things will be hidden.'

'Is this from experience?' Logan said.

Hussein nodded. 'We needed his input a while back on a fraud case. Some of the shit he found out was incredible.'

'Sounds a lot better than me fumbling around after a few beers,' Logan said.

They moved way past the houses behind the kid's park, and the hidden pub beyond, and into the scrub past the trees. Possibly farmland. Perhaps a map would've been a good idea, but they'd overlooked this as well. For a first reconnaissance mission to scope the area, they were failing miserably.

They eventually came to a spot that satisfied Logan. But

standing in a small field beyond a copse of trees, surrounded by snow, seemed utterly pointless. For a start, it was a completely different season to the photograph. Such a weird photo it was, too. It reminded him of some strange painting he couldn't recall. It was the way the figures posed with the sacks over their heads. Fucking weird, basically. He turned another three-sixty to try and get a feel for it.

There was definitely something about the spot they were standing in.

Something familiar.

'I don't think we'll ever know the point of the photo,' McCulloch said, now having to raise her voice over the wind that was blowing in hard from the east. 'Not in this weather. The conditions are bloody awful, eh? It's practically a fucking blizzard.'

All four stood with their coats fully fastened and their hoods on, turning blindly this way and that, looking for any sign that they were standing where they, or rather Logan, thought they should be.

And then he had a thought.

'Do me a favour and let's recreate the photo,' he said, retrieving his phone. 'It's the least we can do while we're here.'

'But we don't even know if we *are* bloody here, man,' Hussein said.

'All the more reason to recreate the photo so that we can compare it. Come on. It won't take two minutes.'

They shuffled around. McCulloch reluctantly dropped to her knees, then Bennett and Hussein flanked her, each with a hand on a shoulder.

'Shaun, put your hood up,' Logan said. 'Kel, can you let your hair out? And everyone, heads down.'

He got them into frame and could just about spot the

church spire in the background, blurred by the falling snow. He took several shots from a few different angles until he was as satisfied as he could be given the conditions, then told them they could now relax.

'When I get married,' Bennett said, 'remind me to not hire you as the photographer.'

'Knees are bloody soaked now, eh?' McCulloch said, wiping herself down.

'Well?' Hussein said. 'It look anything like the original?'

Logan scrolled through the shots, his hands beginning to chap, as they all gathered around. There was one that stood out as similar to the original. It might at least help with a location, to have at least something to go off.

'God, we look like three big kids out to build a snowman, eh?' McCulloch said.

Bennett squinted through the snow. 'Let's have a quick look around. Just for anything strange we might come across.'

'What, like rat skulls and dismembered cat paws?' Hussein said. 'Likely to be buried under all the bloody snow.'

As Logan went to put his phone back in his pocket, he caught sight of a figure far beyond, across an adjacent field. It was a man, moving slowly, ducking out of sight as he descended a slope. He pointed the figure out to the others and they moved over towards the edge of their field, but there was no sign of the man. But as Logan reached the ancient stone wall that divided the land, he saw the figure again. Definitely a male.

He was up to something.

'Could be anyone, Rob,' McCulloch said. 'Maybe a farmer or something.'

'Yeah,' Hussein said. 'Or a golfer. Isn't there one of those fucking golf clubs up here?'

Logan nodded. 'Yeah, but not in this weather. The course won't be open, for a start. And anyway, I think that's a bit further away.'

'There's two courses,' Bennett said. 'But I doubt anyone will be out playing golf in this.'

'I don't know,' McCulloch said. 'I've seen those twats play in a fucking hurricane, eh?'

There was a gunshot, loud and echoing, from across the field. The guy came into view again, this time with a shotgun slung over his shoulder.

'Probably one of the gentrified folk out shooting pheasant,' Hussein said. 'Make himself a nice roast dinner later.'

'You fucking idiot,' Bennett said. 'There's no pheasant around here.'

'There's bloody loads, you bell end.'

An engine fired up. A motorbike or a jeep or something else suited to the terrain. It revved hard and kicked in and then they saw it: a red quad bike, racing across the field and over the hill, a massive bloom of snow and fumes billowing out from the back of it.

'You can tell he loves riding it, eh?' McCulloch said.

'Did anyone bring any binoculars?' Logan said.

Bennett shrugged. 'There might be some in the car.'

'Nah, he's gone now anyway. There's a lesson here, though. Fail to prepare, prepare to fail.'

'God, you sound like my old PE teacher, Rob,' McCulloch said. 'Come on, I've had enough of this shite. I need a bath and a good bottle of wine, eh?'

Another gunshot rang out, the echo loud and booming off the hills.

'Let's hope he has a licence for that firearm,' Hussein said. 'Otherwise we might have to give him a knock.'

'Is there a farm down there?' Logan said. 'Anyone know?'

'Wouldn't surprise me,' McCulloch said. 'There's a few around here, I think.'

He nodded. 'Could do with having a good look at a map of the area.'

'You want to go orienteering?' Hussein said. 'We could rig you up with all the gear.'

Logan laughed. 'Fuck off.'

He looked out across the fields, white and frozen. Wondered if Caitlin Slater could be out there somewhere.

Waiting to be buried.

THERE WAS a steak pie waiting for him when he got home that Vic had spent the afternoon making. The house was warm, with the burner crackling away and the aroma of onions and baked pastry hanging in the air.

'Busy day?'

Logan crashed onto the couch and shuffled off his boots. The toasty blast of the fire surrounded him, the red glowing coals mesmerising. Outside, the snow billowed and blew, a billion flakes clouding the grey sky, the night as black as mud.

'You could say that,' he said. 'The roads were chaos this morning. It's almost as bad now.'

'So, what happened to the dog?'

'It had been dumped. The head had been taken off. Heart taken out.'

'Fuck!'

'I know.'

'So, what happens now? Is it connected to that missing woman, you think?'

'I hope not,' he said. He kicked his socks off as she handed him a mug of hot tea. 'There's a briefing tomorrow morning. I'm going along. DCI Clayton thinks I'm pushing my nose into the Caitlin Slater case, clutching at straws, all that. So I want to see what they've got to say.'

'I've heard her boyfriend's been seen stumbling about town, drunk. Poor bloke. He must be really struggling.'

Logan nodded. 'As you can imagine. I don't know how I'd cope if you went missing.'

And he wasn't surprised Kurt had been seen. In a small town like this one, everybody knew everybody's business. Gossip whirled across the local Facebook pages like the snow outside.

'Not much chance of that,' she said. 'Not intentionally anyway.'

He drank the tea and flicked through the channels. Not a single thing piqued his interest. Although he felt like switching off and trying to escape the activities of the day, his mind was clouded, overwhelmed. The images from the CCTV kept coming back to him. Those two figures. Could they be the same men who had kicked the Rottweiler from the back of the white van? Probably. He just wished they had more to go on.

His thoughts also kept turning to the drugs that were found. Xylazine and ketamine. Maybe Kel was right. Maybe they had been stolen, which would logically link to a veterinary surgery where such chemicals were stored. Or maybe they'd been acquired from the Dark Web.

'Tea's out,' Vic said.

He joined his wife and Izzy at the table. The food looked amazing and when he got stuck in, he was transported back in time. Vic had done a great job. As they ate, she updated him on her latest news: the bank had approved the money for her street food truck. It was good news, but he was only half listening, and nodding in all the right places.

'Rob?'

'Yeah?'

'I said I'm going to order it. What do you think? Are you actually even listening to me?'

He met her eyes. 'Sorry, babe. Yeah, I think it's a great idea. Would be really good for you. Sorry. I'm just full-on with this case. I'm getting easily distracted.'

'I can forgive you,' she said. 'But at least try and be present for once. And I need to remind you that Izzy's got a birthday party on Saturday afternoon. From one o'clock until about three. And I'm going out with Mel in the evening.'

'I could be working,' he said.

'But you never work Saturdays.'

'I know, but things are a bit mad at the minute, you know. I could easily be called in, put some overtime in.'

'Your daughter comes first.'

'Can't you take her?'

'No, this is your job,' she said. 'I've got a hair appointment in the afternoon. I did tell you this.'

But he certainly didn't recall it. A two-hour gap in his Saturday amounted to very little in the grand scheme of things, but oh, how he hated kids' birthday parties. It was all bouncy play centres and chicken nuggets and parents you had to make conversation with, as if you didn't get enough of them at the bloody school gates.

He sighed. 'Okay, I'll take her. But you can do the next one.'

'I don't know about that...'

After he'd eaten, he went to the office—more commonly known as the spare room—and fired up the Mac. He needed a good aerial view of the farmland up in Ainsworth, just to get his head around what he might be looking for, which he didn't even know himself. He spent a few minutes trying to pinpoint exactly where he needed to be and found St. Michael's pretty easily. Although the cartography on Google Maps was pretty basic, he could see there were a few farms dotted around, and two golf clubs. Dividing the land between the farms and the golf clubs was a major B-road and a country lane heading north. Technically, there were three farms aligned beside the lane on either side, each with plenty of acres of land, though the boundaries were unclear.

He switched to Google Earth, figuring he'd have a much better perspective on things if he could actually see the places he was trying to visualise on the map. He put in the coordinates and watched as the software did its work, zooming in on the area. He dropped down onto the country lane—Harwood Road—and virtually walked along it, trying to pinpoint exactly where the field was in relation to St Michael's. He knew he was in the right zone, just not the exact place. And there was only so far you could see with Google Earth. He knew he would have to get down there in person to have a better understanding. Nevertheless, he moved along the road northwards, right up to the next intersection of Bradshaw Road and back again, turning three-sixty degrees so he could peer into every direction. Looking for... what? Something. Anything that might catch his eye.

As he made the return walk south, he turned to view the entrance to what looked like a stone yard filled with rocks and pallets of farming materials. There was a Toyota pick-up truck parked out front and what looked like a quad bike beyond that. Instantly, the quad bike they saw from this afternoon came back to him, and he pictured it tearing across the snowy landscape.

Heard those gunshots again in his mind.

He tried to move further into the yard, but it wouldn't budge. He was blocked from entering. Google Earth had gone as far as it could go without trespassing on someone's territory.

Logan sat and studied the vehicles on-screen, wondering if he could catch a number plate on the pick-up. It was faint and blurry and ultimately impossible to define, but maybe there was a way to enhance it.

He returned to the kitchen and found Izzy at the table playing with her braiding toy. He grabbed a Coke from the fridge and found Vic in the living room, deep into another crime drama. Or was it the same one?

'I might have a bath and get an early night,' he said. 'I feel like I need to catch up on some sleep.'

'Okay, love. What are you doing up there?'

'Work thing. Nothing interesting.'

'You've had a missed call,' she said. 'Phone's on the mantelpiece. I meant to bring it up to you but forgot... sorry.'

DI Murray had called over an hour ago. It was now approaching eight o'clock and he was ready for sleep, but he also knew Murray wouldn't call unless it was important. He returned to the office room and called Murray back, bracing himself. Whatever it was he wanted, he wasn't about to leave the house any time soon, no matter what it was.

'Rob,' said Murray. 'I have an update. Hope this isn't a bad time.'

'I wouldn't bother calling you back unless it was,' he said. 'But before the update, what was all that about this afternoon?'

'All what?'

'You know what. Clayton. What is his fucking problem?'

A sigh. 'I think he took umbrage with the way you addressed him. That's all. Look, he's my boss just like I'm yours. Yes, I know he can be a bit of a prick, but that's just the way he is sometimes.'

'But don't you think that what I had to say today had some relevance? That this Caitlin Slater thing might just be a missing woman at this stage, but it could be linked to our dead animals. I don't know where bloody Warburton and Sanderson are up to with her disappearance, but I tell you what, Dave, surely one of the first things you look at when someone goes missing is re-tracing their steps. So, why hasn't there been CCTV of her? There's plenty to go on, for fuck's sake.'

'Well, that's partly why I wanted to speak to you,' he said. 'There have been some developments. Yes, there is some CCTV. You'll be briefed on that in more detail tomorrow morning, if you're still attending.'

'I said I would.'

'Good. But, look, I believe it's been more of a legal thing as to why they've failed on CCTV up to this point. Something to do with confidentiality with the school.'

'School?'

'Just one of the CCTV sources. And what I'm hearing is that they believe it's her.'

'Is this a last whereabouts thing? The last time she's been seen?'

Murray hesitated. 'I think so. But look, I'm just the messenger. I guess we'll all find out more tomorrow.'

'I'll be there. Was there something else?'

'As a matter of fact, yeah. I just had a call from Chris in IT. He didn't go into a lot of detail, but they've found another website through the white rabbit one.'

'Another website?'

'That's what he said. He went on to talk about encryptions and firewalls and all that shite, so don't ask me anymore. But we have a meeting with him tomorrow, right after the Miss Slater briefing. He sounded keen to get more involvement on it, anyway. So, looks like your instincts have paid off. Well done.'

Was he hearing this right? Was DI Dave Murray actually praising him?

'Er, thanks,' he said. 'Okay, well that's good news I suppose. Well, not good news but you know what I mean.'

'Yeah,' he said. 'So I'll see you in the morning. Bright and early. Briefing's at nine.'

He hung up and started running the bath. Called in on Izzy, who had fallen asleep with her gang of teddies scattered around her. He lifted her gently and put her under the covers before crashing on the bed as the water filled. The sound took him away for a few moments, but not far enough to forget what was happening at work. Saturday was supposed to be his day off, and he could really do with it, but then taking Izzy to a birthday party always felt like work anyway so he figured he may as well go in. Besides, things were beginning to get interesting. He wondered about the quad bike they'd seen this afternoon. And that gunshot. Shotguns could be acceptable in the area, especially on farms. And after looking at the map, he was pretty sure that the field they were standing next to was a farm. He would have to take a closer look in person, to ensure he was in the right geographical location. And though there was nothing to really pin them down to this place, no real need to be there other than try and ascertain the location of the photo on the white rabbit website, he felt an inkling, a conviction, that something wasn't quite right about it.

Vic snapped him out of his reverie and suggested he get in the bath before it flooded the bathroom. He was so tired now, he didn't think he had the energy to get in. But when he finally did, taking his phone with him to play the audiobook he'd been dipping in and out of, he stayed there, his thoughts far away from here, until the water began to bring a chill like the ever-falling snow outside the window.

TWELVE

Kurt had woken early. Although he hadn't really slept, not properly. There was too much going through his head. He'd drank until he fell asleep on the couch, then took himself up to bed when he awoke at around 2am, cold, in the darkness of the living room. The blinds had been left open and the light from the streetlamp outside was shining in. He'd also heard voices outside, probably a couple of kids on the way home from the pub, though it was a bit late for that. Maybe a house party. A house party like the one his Caitlin had gone to when she should've been at home, would've been better off at home, waiting for him to come back from work.

Though a house party on a Wednesday night was unlikely. Or was it Tuesday? In all honesty, he'd lost track of the time. Minutes became hours, and hours blended into days. All fragments of disappearing time when daylight turned to night and back again. It didn't really matter what day it was. With every moment that passed, every agonising second, like a clock ticking slowly by, it was another moment without Caitlin, the woman he was going to marry.

It was 5am when he stirred. He lay there motionless for a while, drifting in and out of sleep, until he finally left his bed an hour later and dragged on the clothes he wore the day before without showering. The bed felt so empty now. Like his heart. It was a crushing emptiness. He knew that any moment, he could explode in a flood of tears. He was always so close to it, enveloped by a desperation he'd never felt before. It was such a debilitating loneliness, an aching feeling of being so utterly useless, that he couldn't actually think straight. There was a strange feeling of detachment, as if he wasn't really here at all, that he was somehow occupying a separate world to everyone around him.

They'd sent a woman copper round to see him. A liaison officer. She made him tea and a sandwich and talked to him, then left him alone for a while, then talked some more before leaving. Said she would call again, every day, until they had some better news for him other than the black nothing he was living in on a daily basis. It had only been four days since she'd gone but those days were long. The longest he'd ever lived. And he was beginning to wish he wouldn't wake up again.

He made himself a coffee and wandered from room to room, trying to think of a way, any way, to find Caitlin. It was the only thing he could do, since no one else seemed to be doing anything. The police weren't interested, the community wasn't interested. Seemed all anyone really thought was that she'd gone and left of her own accord.

But he knew her. He knew her like nobody else did and he knew she would never do that. She loved him. She really loved him, and he loved her. So, he would go to the ends of the earth if he had to. He knew she would do the same for him.

He put his heavy coat on and fastened it up. Put his work

boots on and laced them tight. Found his gloves in the bedroom. Finished the coffee and went into the kitchen drawer to grab what he needed. He put his wallet, full of cash, in his coat's side pocket and zipped it up. Took his car keys from the mantelpiece and unplugged his fully charged phone at the living room wall. He checked for missed calls, just in case. She hadn't called.

He went out to the car and cleared the snow and frost from the windscreen. Got the engine running to heat the windows. Back inside, he closed the blinds upstairs and downstairs and locked the back door. Found his favourite woolly hat and put it on. Packed a few essential things in a rucksack. And once he was sure he had everything he needed, he left the house and locked the door behind him.

She was out there, and he would find her.

Even if it killed him.

THURSDAY MORNING BROUGHT chaos at HQ. Logan met McCulloch on the steps, and they made their way inside. The roads had been treated overnight but were still treacherous, especially in the side streets. The snow had continued to fall and was a foot deep in places, but the main routes in and out of town had been gritted and cleared enough to at least keep the traffic moving. There was a lot of commotion at the main desk. The owner of the Rottweiler, a fortysomething woman in combat pants, was demanding the release of her dog's body.

On top of that, a young man in his early twenties had been brought in for an assault with a screwdriver on a local shopkeeper. And an elderly gent was wandering aimlessly around the waiting area, telling anyone who would listen that his cat had gone missing, and he wanted the police to find it.

Just another normal morning, really.

Dave Murray met them as they ascended the stairs, suggesting they skip breakfast and head straight into the Caitlin Slater briefing. There was just enough time for McCulloch to grab them a coffee. Logan said he'd save her a place.

'Chris from IT wants to see us as soon as we're finished here,' Murray said, as they made their way to a section of seats near the back of the incident room. 'Says he's got something to show us.'

'This'll be that new website, I expect.'

'Right. Hopefully he'll have something more we can go on. You have a plan for today?'

'I'm taking the Land Rover back up to Ainsworth. Do a bit of scouting around.

He didn't bother to mention the guy with the shotgun, feeling there was little point given that it was pretty normal to see and hear such stuff on local farmland. He didn't mention the quad bike, either, for much the same reason.

The incident room gradually filled up and soon McCulloch weaved her way through with two canteen coffees in takeaway cups. The conversation rumbled away as Murray complained about his missing mug of tea before dropping the bombshell that he wanted Logan out on patrol this Friday with the StreetSafe team, a regular crew that parked themselves in the town centre of a Friday and Saturday night to keep the weekend punters under check.

'What?'

'Come on, Rob,' he said. 'Don't say you didn't know about it. It's on your rota.'

'Yeah, but not until next month.'

'I've had to bring it forward. Did I not mention it?'

'No, you bloody didn't. Well I can't do it.'

'Why not?'

'I've got to take Izzy to a birthday party.'

'I thought you said that was Saturday?' McCulloch said.

Logan scowled at her. 'It's my night off,' he said. 'You can't just spring this on me, Dave.'

'Like I said, I thought I'd told you I had to bring it forward. Bloody good job I mentioned it.'

'Well, it's too late,' Logan said. 'You'll just have to find someone else.'

'Look, it was supposed to be DS Carmichael but as you probably know, his wife's about to give birth. I said I'd let him swap.'

'So, when's the baby due?' McCulloch said.

'I believe she's going in for a C-section Friday afternoon. You were the only one available, Rob. Sorry.'

'Can't Kel do it?'

'She's got the day off.'

'Off all weekend, actually,' she said. 'Back in on Monday, eh?'

Logan held his head in his hands. 'For fuck's sake. Do I have to? Can't someone else do it?'

'It won't go unnoticed, Rob,' Murray said. 'Stepping in for your colleagues like that can do wonders for your chances of promotion.'

'I don't want a fucking promotion.'

'Aye-aye,' Murray said. 'Here's Warburton now.'

DCI Warburton raised his hands to calm the room as DI Sanderson sidled in beside him. A moment later, a silence fell. Warburton gave Martin Hobbs a cue to dim the lights and pull down the white screen for the projector.

'Good morning, everybody,' Warburton said. 'Well, at

least it was a bit easier to get into work today. Right, let's get down to business. As you probably all know, we've had a missing person since last Saturday. I shouldn't have to go into the backstory by now as it's common knowledge all over the station, but a Miss Caitlin Slater, thirty-one years old, never arrived home after her night out with friends. She'd been at a house gathering locally and left around midnight on Saturday, alone. She never turned up at home and her boyfriend, Mr Kurt Chadwick, had reported her missing when he couldn't reach her on her mobile.

'Her last whereabouts are known to have been at a house belonging to a Mr and Mrs Kirkland. The couple had thrown a party for Mrs Kirkland's fortieth birthday, to which Miss Slater had been invited. It was the last place she'd been seen, and a number of witnesses, including the Kirklands, have corroborated this.

'We think she would've made her way home on foot as there's no record of a taxi or an Uber. And given there's been a lot of noise about tracing her journey through the local CCTV, I can now hand over to Paul Sanderson, who will give a breakdown of what we've managed to get a hold of so far.'

'Is it just me,' McCulloch whispered, 'or does DCI Warburton look like big bird from Sesame Street?'

Logan sipped his coffee. Working Friday night... Exactly what had he done to deserve such a punishment?

'Right,' Sanderson said. 'We have a few pieces of CCTV footage to show you. But first I want to make you alaware that we are about to step up our investigation. A search party has been arranged with volunteers from the local community and will be coordinated in the coming days.'

'Bit late for that, eh?' McCulloch whispered.

'And so,' he continued, 'it'll be all hands on deck from tomorrow and we'll continue our search going forward. A specialist search unit will be deployed to cover the local woodland and moorland, and we'll be bringing specialist divers in from the North West Police Underwater Search and Marine Unit to scour the local rivers and reservoirs. As I've already said, volunteers from the local community, including friends of Miss Slater, will join the search in a coordinated effort to try and find some trace of her. I trust you all understand this is a complex logistical exercise, especially given the weather conditions, and that it's not without its challenges. Further instructions will be given later. If you are on leave or you have a rest day coming up, I would ask that you volunteer for overtime and help us in this search for Miss Slater.

'Okay, moving on now to the CCTV. As DCI Warburton has alluded to, we have found some CCTV of a female we believe to be Miss Slater. It's not much to go on, but we believe it highlights her journey from the Kirkland residence and the route she would've taken to get home.'

Martin Hobbs rolled the tape.

'Beginning with the first clip,' Sanderson continued, 'we can see this view of Longsight Road from the local Co-op. You can see a few cars moving by, a taxi and a motorcycle, then a woman we believe to be Miss Slater walks into view from the right and continues to walk northbound on this main road and goes out of view again.'

They watched as the woman walked on her journey home from the Kirklands' house. She looked tired and maybe a little bit drunk, but certainly didn't appear to be so intoxicated that she was stumbling or in a drug induced state. Something about the way she moved told Logan she was in perfectly good shape. She didn't appear fearful or worried, had not picked up her pace, and didn't seem in much of a rush to get home. She was wearing a large wraparound knee-length cardigan and high heels, and her gait was relaxed and confident, as if she knew the route she was going to take.

Sanderson went on. 'The next piece of footage is from one of the local pubs. The Hare & Hounds has a number of cameras out front, and we got some good footage of her walking up Bolton Road West. She must've crossed Longsight Road and turned right onto Bolton Road West to head home, which would've been quite a walk. You can see her here walking under the trees of the woodland at the opposite side to our vantage point here at the pub. She's clearly holding her phone and probably texting or browsing on social media or perhaps ordering an Uber or something like that. She appears a little bit unstable on her feet but we're putting that down to the conditions. It was quite frosty and there was a little bit of surface ice around. Foggy, too.'

The phone told Logan she was probably sending the text Kurt had mentioned when they'd gone to see him.

It was clear she was alone. The time stamp said it had just gone midnight.

'And then we see her again, about four minutes later, and this time the CCTV is from the local school, Woodfield Comprehensive. The CCTV is some distance away and it's coming from a high lamppost within the school grounds, but it catches her pretty clearly. You'll see a car speed past, followed by a white van. They're both going over forty which, for the conditions, is pretty silly. Miss Slater appears to turn to see them race away from her, heading back to where she came from. Then as we watch her continue her journey, the van pulls over and we think someone leaves the driver's side to speak with Miss Slater, but the view is obscured by a tree. She does not appear again on any footage in the area. Needless to say, we need to find whoever was driving this van.'

Logan stood up. 'Do we have any ANPR on the vehicle?'

Sanderson shook his head. 'Number plate's been removed, as far as we can tell.'

And then the questions came thick and fast.

Has she been abducted?

Can we trace the vehicle?

Have there been any other sightings of Caitlin Slater?

'Are you thinking what I'm thinking, Rob?' McCulloch said.

Logan turned to Murray. 'We need to trace that van. If it's the same as the one connected to these animal mutilations then it doesn't bode well for Caitlin.'

Murray stood to address Sanderson and Warburton. Told them what they were thinking. About the connection with the animals and of course, most recently, the Rottweiler. Turned to Martin Hobbs for corroboration. Hobbs nodded, said he was thinking the same.

'We need a more forensic analysis on this van,' Logan said. 'See if we can identify the make and model and the year it was made.'

'It won't give us much,' Murray said. 'Yeah, we could probably identify what it is, right down to the bloody components in the engine, but will it do us any good?'

'Time's running out, sir,' Logan said. 'We've got to do something. If Caitlin Slater was taken by the same people doing these animal mutilations, I don't need to point out that she could be next.'

'I understand your concern, DS Logan,' Warburton said. 'And we share that concern. Right now, we have a search party prepared to scour the area from tomorrow. We have a better chance of identifying the van and its location if we can identify the person behind the driver's wheel.'

'There's more than one involved,' Murray said. 'Look, why don't you come and review the CCTV we have in connection with the mutilations, and you'll see what we're talking about. You'll see the two suspects we think might be involved here. And like Rob says, if Miss Slater's been abducted by these people, the outcome doesn't look good.'

Logan could hear himself breathing, could feel his heart pounding. He turned to McCulloch and saw she'd gone pale. They both knew that Caitlin Slater could be gone already, and it would only be a matter of time before they found her body, dumped like all the rest, perhaps displayed in a crucified fashion, her head missing, her heart torn out.

'Fuck,' McCulloch said. 'Looks like tomorrow's gonna be a busy day, eh?'

'I bet you wish you were working now, don't you?'

She sighed. 'I'll come in. Sod my day off. I'm coming in to help.'

'We might've found her by then,' Logan said. 'We just need to look in the right place.'

'Are you certain this is the same van?' Sanderson said. 'The van with the mutilated Rottweiler from yesterday?'

'We can't be one hundred percent,' Murray said. 'But it's looking that way, yeah.'

There was an audible gasp from the room. Coppers from all directions turned to look at Logan and McCulloch.

'Is there anything else on this footage?' Logan said, standing. 'Anything at all? Like, what were the other vehicles? Are there any other people we can speak to in connection with this?'

'What about the taxi driver?' McCulloch said. 'There was a taxi driver, wasn't there?'

'And the car that was speeding in front of the van,' Logan said. 'We could identify that, couldn't we? I mean, why was it speeding? Was the van chasing it? Who was driving that car?'

'And the motorbike, eh?' McCulloch said.

Logan nodded. 'We need to speak with them all. There's someone out there that might've seen Miss Slater that night. Certainly the taxi driver...'

'And what if she'd been drugged?' McCulloch said. 'What if someone at that party had spiked her drink or something?'

'Have we spoken to everyone who attended?' Murray said. 'Have we really explored all avenues?'

Logan realised then that they hadn't spoken with the friend yet. Why had Louise McDonagh specifically invited Caitlin? Why did she let her leave the party alone?

'Right,' Warburton said. 'DI Sanderson and I will review all CCTV again with DI Murray. For everyone else, stand by for instruction. Let's trace all vehicles involved and get them in for questioning. We need to find this woman. Dead or alive, she's out there somewhere. Now let's do our bloody job.'

'ROB, I'M COMING WITH YOU,' McCulloch said. 'I'll grab us a coffee.'

Logan left the incident room and made his way upstairs, with three things clear in his mind. He would speak with Chris from IT, drive out to the farm he wanted a closer look at, then find Louise McDonagh. He'd need all the coffee he could get, not to mention a stiff drink. The weekend couldn't come soon enough, though he suspected it wouldn't be as relaxing as he'd have liked. Somehow, he knew there would be no Saturday night in front of *Match of the Day* with a few beers, as much as he deserved it.

Maybe the job really wasn't for him. He'd grown tired of living his life like this. Perhaps that *normal* job he was leaning towards was getting ever nearer. Once this case was over, he'd make some enquiries, take time out to come up with something.

He found Chris Kearney hiding away in a far corner of a room where computers went to die. The whole place was like a graveyard for hard drives, monitors, units and CPU's. There were a few other staff members dotted around, each working on something at a terminal. The whole place reeked of computer geeks: the kind of blokes who spent their weekends playing *Dungeons & Dragons* and watching American sitcoms. The room also smelled of strong coffee and some kind of chemical cleaning fluid.

'Chris?'

Kearney didn't look up. 'I wondered when you'd make an appearance. Where's Dave Murray?'

'He's here.' Murray walked in with McCulloch, clutching two A-grade canteen coffees.

'You'd better all gather around, then,' Kearney said.

He was a ponytail and goatee kind of guy, Logan saw. A proper computer expert. Probably earned about a quarter of a million a year and some on the side. He smelt of expensive aftershave.

'What have you got for us?' Murray said.

'Well,' Kearney said, 'as I said on the phone, you're probably not going to like it. But it's here. I've traced everything, right down to the model of PC being used to do this stuff. But it's pretty disturbing. You'll have to prepare yourselves. I've already booked myself in for counselling next week.'

'That bad, eh?'

'Worse,' he said. 'I hope you've not eaten this morning.'

'Let's get on with it,' Logan said, figuring it couldn't be any worse than what he'd witnessed this week already.

'Okay,' Kearney said, his fingers flying across the keyboard at a rate of knots. There were a number of windows open, and Kearney enlarged two of them. 'On the left, we can see your site. The one you found through that rabbit.'

'Follow the white rabbit,' Logan said. '*Alice in Wonderland.*'

'That's the one,' he said. 'We've had a good look at it all. We found plenty of images we managed to copy. I've filed it all for you. I can copy you all in an email with the content if you want?'

'Go ahead.'

'Right,' he said. 'So, I'll show you here. I want you to keep an eye on the window on the right of the screen because it's about to populate with material. It's another website but hidden.'

'The Dark Web, eh?' McCulloch said.

Kearney pointed. 'You've got it. It's not the kind of site you'll find with just a regular internet browser. You'll need a Tor browser to even get started with this. I suspect whoever's building these sites is using just that. The white rabbit site is simply a way in to the real stuff. The dark stuff. It's like a secret door, if you want to think of it that way.'

'As if that isn't dark enough,' Logan said. He sipped his coffee, hot and bitter.

'Yeah,' Kearney said. 'But you ain't seen nothing yet.'

He found an animation of a white rabbit and clicked on it. The window on the right began to populate. What seemed like a billion images and words flashed across the screen and filled it with incomprehensible data. The screen went black and an image of a five-pointed star appeared, burning in from the darkness.

'Is that a pentagram?' McCulloch said.

'It's a pentacle,' Kearney said. 'Because it's got a circle around it. But it's actually not even that, because it's inverted. Upside down. And watch now.'

A goat's head morphed into the shape of the inverted five-pointed star. Kearney enlarged the window, and it filled the whole screen. The symbol was red on black, the goat's head looking right through them.

'I've seen that image before,' Murray said. 'Somewhere.'

'You probably all have,' Kearney said. 'It's an image of Baphomet.'

'Isn't it Satanic?' McCulloch said. 'Or something like that.'

'Something like that,' Kearney said, nodding. 'But that's a whole other rabbit hole I'll let you explore in your own time. Needless to say, this isn't your average website.'

A series of words burned through the screen as the image of Baphomet faded, replaced with a line of text.

Do what thou wilt shall be the whole of the Law.

'WHAT THE FUCK?'

'What the fuck is right,' Kearney said. 'It comes from Crowley. Alistair Crowley. He was an occultist. He was into magic, among other things. Was probably involved in MI5. Secret societies and all that stuff. But yeah, what a welcome, eh? And if we highlight the words and click on them, we get this. You'll see that it's now opening up into the site proper. I should warn you, though. Some of this isn't pretty.'

Logan and McCulloch prepared themselves. Murray looked resigned to the inevitable. He'd seen many bad things before. In photographs, on tape, up close and personal. But this thing had gotten him to a point where he was beginning to expect the worst.

'Show us,' Murray said.

The screen was blank and deep black. Kearney hovered a mouse and the arrow moved across the screen. Weird symbols popped up here and there, like stars in a midnight sky.

'I don't know what these symbols are,' Kearney said. 'Maybe you guys can look into it. But when we click on them... *boom*.'

An image unfolded on the screen. It was the body of a woman, naked and face down, on what looked like a steel table in a dimly lit room. There was a cloaked figure beside her, looking into the camera. The figure was wearing a pig mask, the snout wide and fat, and holding a long knife that looked sharp enough to cut through solid wood. It wasn't clear if the woman was alive or dead, and why would it be? Nor was it clear who this person was or when the photo had been taken. It was in a sepia tone, so it looked aged, but it could've been made to look that way with a simple filter in Photoshop.

'Jesus,' McCulloch said. 'Is she dead?'

'Who knows?' Murray said. The pig mask stared out at them. 'But whatever this is, it's hardly tasteful. Do we know anything about where this is, Chris? I mean, do we know where this website's being run from?'

'We're working on it,' he said. 'But it's not straightforward, as you can imagine. These things aren't so easy to pinpoint.'

'Do you have a hint of a location?' Logan said. 'Anything at all?'

'Not from the data we've analysed so far, I'm afraid. But we do have another image. You might recognise something that's in it.'

Kearney navigated away from the naked woman. He hovered the mouse again and another weird-looking symbol in the midnight sky jumped out. He clicked on it, revealing another photo, this time of two figures, perhaps young teenage boys, fifteen or sixteen maybe, standing together in a field of dandelions. The sun was setting behind them, and it was clearly high summer, the light fading from the day. Each of the boys wore a papier-mâché mask. The taller one wore the face of a crow, the feathers jet black, the beak like shoe leather. The smaller boy bore the face an owl, its wise old eyes made of emerald-green stones, its feathers stuck on and made of fine tissue paper.

'Like some kind of pagan celebration, eh?' McCulloch said.

Logan frowned. 'Seems harmless enough. A bit bizarre, yeah, but—'

'You recognise anything?' Kearney said.

'No,' Logan shrugged. 'Should I?'

'Have a closer look,' he said. 'What can you see in the background? In the distance?'

Logan peered in, studying every aspect of the photo, but nothing jumped out.

'Oh, fuck,' McCulloch said. 'It's Holcombe Hill, Rob. That's Peel Tower.'

'You're kidding me...'

'I don't think she is,' Kearney said. 'You can see it. Right between the two of them. Right there on the hill.'

Peel Tower. Holcombe Hill. Right near where Frank Morton's ram was found decapitated, its heart ripped out.

'So,' Murray said. 'What are you suggesting? That this website is maintained right here in Bury?'

'Well, we can't be one hundred percent,' Kearney said. 'But there's a good chance, yeah. We'll have to do a bit more investigative work, but right now, going off this photo at least, it looks like they're building this stuff right under our noses.'

THIRTEEN

There was more. More photos of people in animal masks. Farm animals, birds, even mythical creatures. There was a grainy video of a frog dissection. Another of a rat. A video of some weird kind of black mass. A video of a stone-walled corridor full of skulls and bones. Hardcore pornography. Photographs of a figure dressed in black tied to a chair.

And then there were the totems. Skulls that had been sun-bleached and left out in the elements. Heads of what looked like wild rabbits left on spikes. Bodies of strange, deformed things stored in jars of formaldehyde. Weird videos of blood moving through tubes. And more of those strange symbols, pretty much everywhere.

There were also several live cameras. Direct links to live feeds in dark rooms where pretty much nothing was happening.

'This is fucking depraved,' Logan said. 'Absolutely sick.'

'I can't watch anymore,' McCulloch said, leaving the room.

'Chris, can we have someone monitoring this?' Murray said. 'I mean, like twenty-four-seven?'

'If anyone's got the stomach for it,' Kearney said. 'I don't see why not. We could set up a monitor in a separate room downstairs, maybe.'

'Let's get onto it.'

'Have you found anything on here that would suggest a black market in drugs?' Logan asked. 'I mean, like, medicines, veterinary drugs, anything like that?'

Kearney thought about it. 'Not yet. But then it's not as if we're looking for that. But now that you mention it, I'll get onto it.'

'I'm looking for anything to do with the acquisition of a drug called xylazine. Also ketamine.'

Kearney nodded. 'Well, you could probably get both on the Dark Web. Hard to say just yet if any of that can be found on this site as it doesn't appear like they're trading in anything. There'll be plenty of other sites where you can pick that kind of stuff up. Like Silk Road.'

'Like what?'

Kearney turned to Murray, as Logan spied McCulloch out on the landing, head stuck into her phone. 'Silk Road. It's a black-market trading site. Or was. The FBI shut it down in 2013. But there's plenty of others around just like it. The kind of place where you can get your drugs, your pirated and stolen goods, weapons. Pretty much all the dodgy shit.'

'Dave,' Logan said, 'have we had an update on the Rottweiler? Were the same drugs found?'

'Nothing yet, but I'm guessing Dr Graham will have an update soon enough. Doesn't matter, anyway. What's done is done. We have more pressing matters to attend to.'

'Chris,' Logan said. 'Can you do everything you can to trace where this site is being maintained from?'

'We're on it,' he said, indicating the others in the room. 'As soon as we know more, I'll update.'

Logan paused a moment, looking at all the shit on the screen in front of them. 'What kind of nutters are we dealing with here?'

Neither Murray or Kearney could answer.

LOGAN AND MCCULLOCH left DI Murray to organise the round-the-clock monitoring of the *dark site*, which they'd all agreed was the easiest way to describe it. Murray said he would rope in a couple of PCs and DS Becky Mortimer to oversee it. They would set up in a spare room adjacent to the CCTV viewing suite near the main desk where Martin Hobbs spent most of his time. Murray also insisted on forensic analysis of the photographs on the dark site. If they could find anything that would help identify a suspect, it was well worth the hassle. While Murray liaised with DCI Warburton and DI Sanderson on logistics around the search party across what would be a massive area with a range of terrains, Logan and McCulloch went down to the undercroft to get their Land Rover.

'So I had a look on Google Earth,' Logan said. 'There's a farm with several vehicles parked up. I reckon it's the place where that guy was firing that shotgun.'

'Was one of them the white van, by any chance?'

'No, but I want to a proper look.'

But going back there might be a different story in the weather conditions they would be contending with—the snow had stopped but had accumulated several feet deep and it would no doubt prove problematic getting there.

Nevertheless, he kept telling himself he needed to try, even just to satisfy his own curiosity. But it was more than that. It was a need. A need to know.

LOGAN STARTED the Land Rover up and moved towards the exit. He longed for some normality, so found Smooth FM on the radio. Anything to try and escape what was rattling around his head.

'You know what I wish?' McCulloch said.

'What do you wish?'

'I wish this was all over. It's the worst case I've ever been involved in. Not to mention the weirdest, eh?'

'It's fucked up,' Logan said. 'But I tell you something, Kel. It's helped me to make up my mind.'

'About what?'

'The job,' he said. 'I'm not cut out for it. And maybe I never was. It's time to knock it on the head. I can't do it anymore. All the fucking...death. It's not a healthy way to live.'

McCulloch was silent for a moment. 'No one ever said this was gonna be easy, eh?'

Logan shook his head. 'I don't know why I became a copper in the first place. I mean, what was I thinking?'

'It's that mid-life crisis talking, Rob,' she said. 'You're a good copper. One of the best I know. None of this is anyone's fault. These animals, these mutilations, that fucking website. None of it is anyone's fault but the absolute nut jobs doing this shit. We have to learn to separate ourselves from it. We have to learn to leave this stuff at work and be ourselves at home. I know it's hard. But we're only human, Rob. This shit's bound to get to us.'

'I know that,' he said. 'I know. It's probably been the

worst week of my career, if I'm honest. For dealing with stuff, you know? For having to deal with stuff, carry it around with me. You know what I mean?'

Kel was nodding. 'You sleeping okay?'

Logan shrugged. 'I think so. Probably because I feel knackered all the time.'

'I'm not,' she said. 'That's why I'm taking the weekend off. I know I said I was coming in to help tomorrow and I know they want all hands on deck, but come on. What bloody difference can I make, eh?'

'Probably none.'

'So, I'm going to go out, let my hair down, get myself a man and have a bloody good time. And you should, too.'

'I'm a married man, Kel. And one hundred percent heterosexual.'

'I meant the letting your hair down bit. It'll do you good.'

'You're full of good advice, aren't you?'

'But I'm right though, eh?'

'I suppose you are, yeah. And when this is all over, I might just do that. Could do with a good night out. But spare a thought for me. While you're out Friday night, painting the town, I'll be on duty, dealing with the pissheads. Not my idea of fun.'

'You won't be alone. And if you're good, I'll bring you a coffee.'

'And then I've got a bloody kids' birthday party to go to Saturday. Gonna be a proper shit weekend.'

They were silent a moment as Logan took the Land Rover up the Bury and Bolton Road.

'At least we can try to forget about it, though, eh?' McCulloch said. 'I mean, we can go home, put the job behind us if we really try, crack open a bottle and see our families and our friends. If Caitlin Slater's been taken by these... these fuckers, whoever they are, then what has she got, eh? That's if she's even still alive.'

LOGAN TOOK the Land Rover up Ainsworth Road, past Whitehead Park where a few hundred locals were having a snow day, their sledges dotting the landscape, their snowballs launching through the air, the littlest kids wrapped up in bubble coats and mittens. He longed to be there with them, to be free of this madness.

'So, tell me again,' McCulloch said.

'There was a quad bike,' he said. 'It looked like the same one we saw on the farmland yesterday. Where we saw the guy with the shotgun.'

'But is that anything to do with this?' she said. 'Or are we just going up there on a hunch?'

He was quiet a moment. Shrugged. 'Just a hunch, I suppose. A feeling. And I want to have a closer look around. See what Google Earth couldn't show me.'

'We've got to be careful, though, eh? Can't just go snooping around.'

'I wouldn't call it snooping,' he said. 'Okay, maybe I would. I'll give you that. But, you know. I feel like I have to do *something*.'

The road was thick with snow and most people had taken the sensible decision to stay at home. It was unnecessary to be out in these conditions if you could help it. Most of the schools in the district had closed indefinitely, which the kids, of course, were delighted about.

But even the Land Rover was struggling. Logan had put it into four-wheel drive so they could climb the hill. The grip on the heavy-duty tyres was thick and rigid, but it was more about keeping the vehicle on track. Maybe it was time to add bloody chains to the tyres as well.

They followed the road, avoiding the thickest patches in case even they got stuck, and eventually came to the Black Bull at the corner of Lowercroft. It was still a bit of a climb up to Arthur Lane, but they made steady progress. They passed the odd homeowner shovelling the snow from their drive in a useless effort to clear it. Madness, considering there was even more on the way.

'Do you think she ended up in that van?' McCulloch said.

'You saw the CCTV,' Logan said. 'Seemed pretty obvious to me.'

'She could be anywhere.'

'We need a better idea on where that fucking van is,' he said. 'There's got to be something more, some more CCTV tracking, whatever. Just to see if we can trace a route out of the area, give us at least some idea of where it went.'

'Convenient for the trees to block the view of her getting in it, eh?'

'She wouldn't have got in it of her own accord. No chance. She was obviously abducted. They took her like they took the animals.'

'Question is, what have they done with her?'

'Or what *haven't* they done...'

'God, don't. Doesn't bear thinking about, eh?'

Logan nodded. He didn't want to think about it, but there it was. He couldn't escape it if he tried. 'Have we heard anything about Kurt Chadwick?'

'Apart from him calling into the station drunk the other day, no,' McCulloch said. 'He can't be coping very well, though. Poor guy. I assume he's on the search party tomorrow.'

'You'd have thought so, but I suspect not. It's too much for him. They'll see him as more of a hindrance.'

'We got a family liaison officer down there?'

'What, with Chadwick? I don't know. I guess there should be. He seems to have been left to his own devices. And if he's turned up at the station drunk once, he probably will again.'

'Wouldn't like to be in his shoes, eh?'

But Logan didn't answer. The lights changed and he took the Land Rover straight ahead, making the hill climb steadily and warily. He could feel the tyres slipping in the sludge and ice. The temperature gauge on the dashboard read minus eight. With darkness only a few hours away, that would drop again, perhaps significantly. If they'd dumped her already, killed her and mutilated her body, it would be frozen solid by now, perhaps lying in a ditch somewhere nearby, or at the bottom of a frozen reservoir.

If they did have her, and they were keeping her alive... Going off the pattern so far, it didn't look good at all for Caitlin Slater.

'I wonder what she was like,' McCulloch said.

Logan glanced at McCulloch. 'So, you think she's gone.'

'I've had a bad feeling about her since the start,' she said. 'You know that.'

'Talking about her in the past tense,' Logan said. 'You sound like you don't give her a chance.'

'I just think she'd have turned up by now, eh?'

'It's only a matter of time until she does,' Logan said.

'Yeah, but in what state?'

'Dead or alive?'

McCulloch shrugged. 'If she's alive, no doubt there'll be a lot of trauma for her to deal with.'

The silence surrounded them for a moment. Logan felt

like the Land Rover had been swallowed by pure white. He battled with the wheel to try to keep it in a straight line. Perhaps a tractor would've been more appropriate. He considered he'd been somewhat naive in bringing this thing up here, but it was infinitely better than his VW and a lot warmer.

They reached the bend at the top of the road and followed it round into Arthur Lane. Going off what Logan had found on Google Earth last night, he knew that Harwood Road was somewhere up here. He swung the vehicle through the narrowing lane, caked with snow on either side, half expecting to see a couple of golfers in Farah slacks and bloody Pringle jumpers, wrestling a golf bag through the ice. He knew he was close to at least two of the fucking places nearby, and it was enough to make him want to throw up. Even they weren't mad enough to be out in this. Or were they?

Of course they were.

'Jesus,' McCulloch said. 'Look at that pair of wankers, eh?'

'Just out to get away from the wife,' Logan said. 'Straight into the nineteenth hole for an afternoon bender and a bit of swinging. Fucking threesomes over the bloody snooker table...'

McCulloch laughed out loud, conscious that this was probably the first time all week she'd let it out. 'Is that really what you think?'

'I've heard the stories...'

'From who?'

'Another time.'

They followed the road and made a right turn into Harwood Road, a narrow lane that had more twists and turns than a typical crime novel, some of them dangerous.

Logan knew that the farm he was looking for was somewhere up on the right-hand side, just where the road began to climb. At the summit of the hill further along, you could see for miles around, including down into the city. On a clear day, it was quite a sight. Now, though, with the sky being so heavy and grey with more impending snowfall, there was nothing but the whiteout of winter.

Logan pulled over into a narrow space and killed the engine. There was just enough room for other vehicles to pass. He looked out at the farmhouse beside them, hidden through the bushes behind a small incline. There was a stone wall that circled the building, and an iron gate that had been left open, presumably to allow the coming and going of the pick-up truck and the quad bike. As far as they could tell, there weren't any people around. It was deathly quiet, except for a raven perched on a nearby gate, cawing into the afternoon. He wasn't even certain if the place was a working farm at all. There was certainly no livestock in the area. So, what kind of farm was it? Maybe it had been a working farm in the past, though not anymore. But it was a large enough farmhouse to get lost in. The kind of place that would have plenty of rooms. It was clearly an old building with a fair bit of history, so it would be interesting to have a proper nose around.

'Shall we go in?' Logan said.

'Looks like there's nobody around, eh? And besides, we're the police.'

'We haven't got a search warrant.'

'We can just have a look. It's not as if we're searching for anything.'

The bitter chill hit them as soon as they'd left the Land Rover. Logan instinctively thought that this might be a bad idea. Leaving the warmth of the car behind felt like a sudden jolt. He wanted to get back in as soon as possible. They would have a quick look around then leave, head over to Louise McDonagh's place for a little chat. Try to understand more about Caitlin Slater.

McCulloch hugged herself. 'God, it's fucking freezing, eh?'

Logan took in a great breath of cold air. He could almost feel ice particles on his lungs. He was looking forward to a roaring fire when he got home tonight.

They trudged through the snow, making their way up the path out at the front of the house. The quad was parked up with a cover over it, beside the pick-up: a Toyota. Snowdrifts coated the walls of the farmhouse and black coal spilled out from a large bucket by a woodshed that was piled high with logs of ash and oak. A plume of smoke rose from the back of a field beyond the far side of the house. There was obviously some kind of small fire burning away out there, the acrid smell of smoke cutting through the afternoon.

Logan and McCulloch made their way slowly around the perimeter, not looking for anything in particular but keen to keep an observant eye on whatever they would come across.

There was a windowsill out front, beneath a large window which Logan assumed looked out from the kitchen. He stepped up and peered in, but it was difficult to see anything. There was a thick coating of frost that wouldn't budge when he ran his gloved hand over it.

A row of tiny bird skulls were laid out across the sill on the outside. One of them fell into the snow at his feet and he picked it up and examined it up close. It was probably from a starling or a blackbird, nothing bigger than that, and light as a feather. Who would keep such things outside their windows?

A wind chime made of bones rattled in the breeze nearby. It hung from the back door in a tangle of fishing wire. What looked like feathers and animal tails hung inside too. Although the windows were frosty, when they peered in, Logan thought he could see a small teddy bear sitting on the kitchen worktop by the Aga, which struck him as somewhat odd.

'This place is giving me the creeps, Rob. I think we should go.'

'Let's have a look around the back first.'

McCulloch followed. 'God, it's awfully quiet, eh?'

They continued along, keeping balance on the walls, occasionally stumbling into the icy snow, the cold biting. They came away from the farmhouse and into an adjacent field, where a small tractor was parked up and rusting. Beyond that: an untouched field of pure white, frozen hard as rock. There was more snowfall coming in, light and serene, over the hills, and a north wind was picking up fast. It wouldn't be long before the conditions turned for the worse.

They stood in the field, looking around. It seemed like they were the only people for miles.

'Just a quick look,' Logan said. 'Then we'll talk to Louise McDonagh and hopefully get ourselves a cup of tea. Christ, it's so fucking cold.'

'Can we call it a day after that? I'm thinking we leave this stuff to Warburton and Sanderson, eh? It's their bloody case.'

There was a gunshot again.

A loud echo across the winter afternoon.

'What the fuck was that?' McCulloch said.

Logan held her close, looking around for any sign of whoever was wielding the shotgun. At the far end of the field sat a large barn, like a scar of black in the white, imposing and caked with gloom. In front of it were a few trees stripped of leaves, down to the bare branches, like winter had taken all the life from them.

'Is that a barn?' Logan said.

'No shit, Sherlock.'

'Let's have a look.' He started to walk out into the field, but then the unmistakable sound of an engine firing up burst loud, near to where they'd come in. It revved hard, exhaust fumes pluming out. Seems like the house was occupied after all. As they stumbled their way back to the front, the Toyota pick-up pulled out of the drive and headed uphill away from them.

Another gunshot echoed off the bare woodland.

Now they found themselves running, or at least running as best they could, each footfall heavy as lead. The blizzard was blowing in, the wind biting, like sharp stabbing pains to Logan's face. And as they reached the Land Rover, they could just make out the back of the pick-up moving over the crest of the hill.

Logan caught his breath. 'So, there *was* someone home.'

'I think we need to just get out of here, Rob. I don't like those gunshots.'

'It's probably just someone shooting pheasant. Easy to get a bit paranoid in these conditions. The cold, the white out...'

'You think they knew we were snooping around?'

Logan shook his head. Shrugged. Stumbled back towards the front door. 'Who knows? But we can always just give them a knock. Have a little chat.'

'No, don't be silly, eh? I don't trust it. Got a funny feeling we should just go. Maybe come back another day.'

Logan stopped in his tracks and sighed. Fumbled for the key fob and buzzed the Land Rover to unlock it. 'Let's go and speak to Miss McDonagh. See what she's got to say.'

THEY FOUND Louise McDonagh at home. Lisa Kirkland had given them a number and Logan traced her address. It was on a council estate up in Edenfield, the kind of place where the bin men forgot to empty the bins and even the local rats stayed away. 37 Carbrook Drive still had the Christmas decorations up, even though it was approaching February. Maybe Louise was the kind of girl who just left them up all year round.

McDonagh seemed surprised to see them when she answered, but Logan put that down to the fact that she had guests, or rather one guest: a half-naked man who popped his head over the upstairs landing banister when they entered.

McDonagh blushed a little. 'You coppers have good timing, don't you?'

'We can come back another time,' McCulloch said. 'I can see you're probably busy.'

'Not busy enough, I can tell you. To be honest, you'd be doing me a favour. It's about time he left anyway.'

'If you're sure?' McCulloch said.

McDonagh ushered them into her home. 'Can I get you a tea?' she said. Her broad Lancashire accent was even stronger than Vic's. 'Or a coffee?'

'Coffee for me, eh?' McCulloch said.

'It's only instant.'

'Even better. No sugar.'

Logan went for a Yorkshire tea. The only sensible option.

McDonagh took them into the living room: a small, cold affair with a grey couch and shit wallpaper. McDonagh had attempted to brighten the place up with various prints and decor, but it was a lost cause. There was no warmth and no soul. It felt like a place that wasn't entirely lived in, and maybe it wasn't.

'So, Miss McDonagh,' Logan said, once they'd all taken a seat. 'I trust you understand why we're here?'

She nodded. Lit up a smoke and blew a cloud across the room. 'Cait.'

'Caitlin Slater,' McCulloch said. 'Yes. We just want to shed some light on a few things.'

'Isn't that what you all want?' McDonagh said, laughing. 'To shed some light.' Logan and McCulloch shared a glance. 'What do you want to know?'

'You joining the search party tomorrow?' Logan said.

McDonagh looked at Logan, then directed her gaze toward the corner of the room, to a pile of waterproofs and a filled rucksack. 'I am. Are you two joining us?'

'We'll do our best,' McCulloch said. 'But there'll be plenty of people out there, I'm sure.'

McDonagh nodded. Let the silence hang between them. 'So, how can I help?'

'This party,' Logan said. 'Tell me about that.'

McDonagh sighed. Took a drag on her smoke. 'It was my friend's fortieth,' she said. 'I invited Cait and Kurt along.'

'But only Caitlin went, right?' Logan said.

'That's right. I'm pretty sure Cait said he was working. She met me for a drink in the Hare & Hounds, then we went to the party at Lisa's house.'

This was the first either of them had heard about a drink at the Hare & Hounds before the party.

'Lisa Kirkland's house,' Logan said. 'Correct?'

'That's right.'

'The Hare & Hounds,' McCulloch said. 'Tell me about it.'

'It's a pub near Lisa's.'

'Yes, I know. But tell me about your evening. From the beginning.'

McDonagh took a final drag on her cigarette and put it out. 'She met me at half-seven. We had a couple of drinks in there, then walked to Lisa's house, which took about ten minutes. Then we stayed there until Cait left.'

'Was the pub busy?' Logan said.

'Yeah. Busy enough. But we got ourselves a seat for an hour and then left after two drinks. There's not much else to say.'

'Did you see anybody in there talking to Caitlin when you were at the bar? Anything like that?'

She turned to Logan. 'Can't say I did, if I'm honest. I mean, it's possible, but...'

'Any conversations with anyone you didn't know?' McCulloch said.

'Like I said, it's possible, but I don't think so.'

'Okay,' Logan said. 'Moving on to the Kirkland's party. How was it? In general, I mean.'

'Just what you'd expect, really. Plenty of people there, all having a good time.'

'How many's plenty?' Logan said.

McDonagh shrugged. 'I don't know. Thirty or forty.'

'Food laid on?' McCulloch said.

'A bit. The usual kind of stuff. Most people were just getting pissed. You know how it is.'

'Any drugs?'

McDonagh paused. 'Not that I know of. But I suppose there could've been. I don't do drugs. Never have. I'm strictly cigarettes and alcohol. Like that Oasis song.'

Logan could hear the guitar riff then blocked it out immediately. 'It's just that we're working on the possibility that Caitlin may have been drugged at the party.'

'What, like, spiked?'

'It's a possibility, eh?' McCulloch said.

She was silent a moment, thinking. 'I didn't see anyone taking anything. And everyone seemed cool, you know. No dickheads or anything like that. It wasn't the type of party where people get off their face on whatever... Caitlin would've hated that.'

'Why did you invite Caitlin?' Logan said. 'I'm led to believe she didn't even know Lisa Kirkland.'

'She didn't. I just thought she might fancy a night out, that's all. Both of them, really, though I know Kurt often works late shifts and stuff so I thought Cait might fancy letting her hair down for a change.'

Logan and McCulloch nodded in all the right places. Though Logan didn't have Caitlin down as the ultra-sociable type, especially since the Kirklands had said she came across as quiet. The party was probably her worst nightmare if she was an introvert.

'Did she enjoy the night?' McCulloch said.

'I think so, yeah.'

'But she left alone,' Logan said. 'Did you not think of maybe leaving with her?'

'I didn't even know she'd left. I was in the kitchen. When I came out, she'd gone.'

McCulloch nodded. 'We know she walked home. A pretty strange decision given it was late and cold.'

'If I'd have known she was doing that, I'd have gone with her.'

'But you didn't catch her up,' Logan said. 'Did you?'

'Well... no. By the time I realised she'd left, she was long gone. I probably couldn't have caught up with her, anyway. Look, it's not a crime to let your friend leave a party by herself. But I'm surprised she left without telling me, to be honest.'

'Well let's talk about that for a minute,' McCulloch said. 'About how she appeared that night.'

'What do you mean?'

'Her behaviour,' Logan said. 'How did she seem to you? You know her well enough to judge whether she was her usual self or not, I'm guessing?'

'God, you make it sound like she was mental or something.'

'That's not what we mean, Louise,' McCulloch said. 'We just want to know if she seemed herself, that's all. Did she talk about anything that brought her mood down? Anything like that?'

'Not really, no.'

'Did she say anything unusual?'

'No,' she said. 'Cait was just Cait. Like she always is. And you know something? I should be the one grilling you. Like, what are you even doing here? You know, you turn up out of the blue at my door and cross-examine me, as if I've got something to do with her disappearance. She's my friend. I want her here, with me, like she used to be, moaning about Kurt and how she wants a bloody kid and can't wait to get married. That's all I want. What's happened to her? You know, don't you? Is she dead? Please tell me.'

She had broken down a little. Not floods of tears, but a few. Enough to make the atmosphere just that little bit heavier than it was already. Logan let the silence remain for a few moments. McDonagh lit up another cigarette and stared out of the window at nothing.

'Tell me,' McDonagh said. 'What do you think happened to her? Seriously?'

Logan didn't want to share what they knew already, especially what they'd seen on the CCTV. There was little point in alarming Louise McDonagh any more. The search party was still required and going ahead as planned. Caitlin Slater really could be anywhere, but the dark site was worrying. And it was pretty obvious, having looked over some of the shit on there, that whoever was in control of it, and the animal mutilations, could be more than capable of the darkest, most depraved things. The white van that had possibly been used to abduct Caitlin seemed to be the very same vehicle the Rottweiler had been dumped from. His gut feeling was that the outcome didn't look positive. There was no point telling her anything and it was all confidential, anyway.

'We're hoping,' he said, 'that the search will bring us closer to knowing what's happened to her.'

'Do you think she's dead? You do, don't you?'

Logan and McCulloch fell silent, exchanging a look that said it all. Yes, they did. If they were completely honest, in their heart of hearts. Yes. They believed Caitlin Slater was dead. Perhaps her life had been taken in the most cruel and brutal circumstances imaginable. A person just disappearing raised all kinds of questions. The freezing cold conditions would've been catastrophic even if she hadn't been abducted by the kind of people driving that van.

'We're still hopeful of a positive outcome, Louise,' Logan said. 'As we always are in these kinds of circumstances. But we also have to be realistic. There is a good chance that

Caitlin has come into some trouble. We're doing our very best to find out.'

She was sobbing now. Trying her best at keeping it together but failing.

'It's all my fault,' she said. 'I shouldn't have invited her to the party, and I should've stayed with her. I shouldn't have let her leave on her own. Please bring her back.'

As they left the estate, Logan could still see her crying hard at the front door.

He dialled up Murray, who answered almost immediately. 'Where are we up to, sir?'

'Everything's in place and ready for tomorrow,' Murray said. 'Chris is hard at it, trying to pinpoint the bloody origin of the dark site. He's been talking bloody gobbledygook all day about IPs, VPNs, ISPs and fuck knows what else. The bottom line, Rob, is that we think we might have the bastards. We suspected it would come from somewhere up in the hills around here, just going off the photos and content on the site. But Chris tells me they should be able to geolocate it specifically within hours. The whole team's working flat out on it.'

'And what about the monitoring of the site? Is that sorted?'

'DS Becky Mortimer's been roped in. Says she's up for it through the night if it helps bring Caitlin Slater back.'

'Somehow, sir, I don't think she's coming back.'

'Until we find evidence to the contrary, Rob, I'm holding to the belief that she's still out there somewhere. Alive. The next forty-eight hours are going to be crucial. Don't bail out on me now.'

'I've no intention, sir. But just one thing. We're just

leaving Louise McDonagh's house. Caitlin's friend who went along to the Kirklands' party with her. She says they had a drink in the Hare & Hounds before going to the Kirkland house. Just wondered if any CCTV had been monitored from inside the pub. Hope it's not been overlooked because it might bring something up.'

'I'll get on to DI Sanderson. Is that everything for now?'

But before Logan could reply, Murray had hung up.

He watched the skies darken and the streetlights flicker on as McCulloch trained the steering wheel through the snow. She could handle the vehicle better than he could. The radio was on, but he could barely hear it over the thoughts in his head, so he turned it up. Smooth FM was gearing up for the rush hour drive time show and Elton John was banging out 'Saturday Night's Alright for Fighting'. He hoped it wasn't an omen.

CAITLIN

Was it day four or day five? She didn't know. Could hardly care anymore. She'd tried a few things to keep herself going in an effort to remind herself that she was a real person with real memories. She went right back to her childhood, tried to pick out the key moments and re-live them in her mind, just so she could feel something. Just so she could remind herself that she existed, that she was human in every way. Just to keep herself going from one moment to the next.

She thought about school. About the street she grew up in and the friends she had, now all grown up and gone, living their own lives. She wondered if anyone knew about her now, and if they did, would they even give a shit? Would anyone from her past know that she was slumped on the floor in a freezing barn, tied up in chains and waiting for the inevitable? Or was she being too negative?

That's a laugh. Negative. It was hard not to be when you'd been abducted off the street and made to lie in your own shit, starved and treated like an animal. Less than an animal.

Surely it was about time the heroes bashed down that bastard bloody door and rescued her. Or maybe that was never going to happen. Just wishful thinking. Just a wild dream.

She thought about many things. The simple little things we all take for granted, like having a cup of coffee in the morning or sitting down for tea of an evening. Watching her favourite TV shows at the weekend with a bar of chocolate or a glass of wine. Walking in the local woods, kicking up the leaves. Feeling the sunlight on her face and the wind in her hair. All the simple things. Sleeping in her own cosy bed and rolling over to Kurt in the middle of the night.

Now, she was resigned to never getting out of here. She had just about made her peace with that. Those men—if you could even call them that—would come and go, but they would never take her with them. She prayed they would, just so she could see something new and finally put an end to all this. Because she wasn't going to escape. There was no chance of that. She just didn't have the strength to run away, even if she tried.

And Kurt. She could only imagine what he was going through. She knew he wouldn't be looking after himself. Knew that he'd probably have let alcohol get the better of him. But she believed he was strong enough to hold it together. Strong enough to take the pain. But she did worry that he could let things get to him easily and let the cracks form. And once the cracks had him, it wouldn't be long until he fell to pieces.

Now, she could hear movement again outside. Voices in the cold air.

They were coming for her again.

FOURTEEN

Darren and Sam worked well together. They always had. Ever since Colin had taken them in and raised them as his own sons. It was a strange upbringing: completely devoid of any normality. They didn't realise this until later, much later, when the other kids at school had bullied them and made fun of them and called them all the names under the sun. They were the weird kids. Darren knew it first, as he was two years older than Sam, but Sam soon caught on. Darren had realised he wasn't exactly the same as other boys his age when he spent the lunch break trying to cut his arms in the toilets. One day he bled so badly that they had to get him an ambulance and he was off school for months after that, going to various care programs and seeing a shrink. Colin had taken him out of school and had informed the authorities he was home schooling them from now on.

Darren was thirteen then. Sam would've been eleven. He lasted a few more years until Colin took him out of school permanently, too. He'd been killing birds with an air pistol he'd nicked from one of Colin's secret drawers. There had been several social workers involved over the years, but the visits eventually tailed off.

Colin had schooled them well. They had become well-rounded young men who worked on the farm and kept themselves out of trouble. Their past behaviours were to be expected given that they'd left care at a young age and had faced all the difficulties anyone would dread to endure so young. They were fostered by Colin until he eventually went a step further and adopted them. They weren't brothers by blood, but if you passed them on the street, you'd think otherwise. And now they were adults in their thirties and a long way from those formative years, they were free to do as they pleased. To make their own decisions in life. Colin had taught them everything he knew. The magic, the rituals. Through Colin, they had discovered their true will.

And now it was time to take him out.

They were in the living room. Darren had masterfully constructed a raging fire that crackled loudly and threw out extreme heat.

'Should've done it years ago,' Sam said. 'Poisoned the old cunt or something.'

Darren nodded. Took a drag on a smoke as he crouched by the fire and threw another log on. 'I've felt like it for a while now. We'd be doing him a favour. You know how he is. His health's fucked. Can hardly bloody breathe.'

'Let's do it, then,' Sam said. 'Put him out of his misery. No one will know. It's not like anyone ever gave a shit about this place. He wouldn't be missed as he never shows his face out there.'

'Got us two doing everything for him,' Darren said.

'Yeah, and for what? So he can do his sacrificial shit and feel good about himself for killing. You know he loves that power.'

'It's a great feeling,' Darren said. 'And you know it. But you know what? I think he wants us to take him out. He's just waiting to die, anyway. You've seen him on that bloody oxygen. Like a fucking crack pipe for him.'

'How many has he done now? Three?'

Darren nodded. 'Three women. She'll be the fourth.'

Sam grinned. He knew that Colin wanted him to bring her down to the chamber of horrors and administer the drug while he did the rest. Cutting her heart out was the easy part. Burying her under the farm was where the work came in.

Sam didn't know why they'd waited for so long. Not that he was complaining as they'd had a little fun with her while she was here. But still. It was best to get it done sooner rather than later. Before she went of her own accord. She was weak now. Very weak, actually. And it wouldn't surprise him one bit if they went in there and found her dead of hypothermia. It was cold enough for it, anyway.

'You really believe he wants us to do it?' Sam said. 'You know, to take him out?'

'Think about it,' Darren said. 'He's had us training for it all this time, hasn't he? This place is now ours. It was always destined to be this way. We can do him in, and fucking bury him with the rest. And when he's fully rotten we'll take his skull and put it on the altar. You know that's what he wants.'

'And then we don't have to do this anymore,' Sam said. 'We can just do what *we* want instead. Not just his dirty work. No more of this bullshit. I might even get myself a normal job.'

Darren had to laugh. There was nothing normal about them and he knew it. And that was part of the thrill. Sam laughed, too. Even though they weren't brothers, it felt like they were.

'So,' Darren said. 'How are we gonna do it?'

Sam frowned. 'Well, I think we have to do the woman first. Let him have his final kill before he goes himself. And then when she's done, one of us can pull the trigger.'

'Not the head, though,' Darren said. 'We'll need his head in one piece. Won't we?'

'I'll do it,' Sam said. 'After her. I've been fantasising about it. Blow his fucking heart out. Might even see him leave this world. Wouldn't that be something?'

Darren nodded, grinning. 'There's a search party out tomorrow. Have you seen that?'

'If only they knew,' Sam said. 'We'd better get it done before there's any chance of finding her.'

'It won't come to that. And even if it did, so be it. Prison won't be so bad.'

'You sound like you're not even arsed.'

Darren shrugged. 'Well, are you? After all we've been through. All those years. I'd feel better in jail, if I'm honest.'

'Yeah, but you won't be able to get your kicks,' he said. 'It'll be the other prisoners getting a kick out of you, if you know what I mean.'

Darren shook his head and showed Sam his phone. The woman on the screen—the copper—was pretty fit.

'She's my hot date tomorrow night,' he said. 'I'm gonna get what I can out of her before we sort the woman in the barn. Just in case it goes tits-up and I do end up getting bent over in the showers in bloody Broadmoor or wherever.'

'It won't come to that if we're careful,' Sam said. 'That's another reason for taking him out. He's fucking nuts. All this *hiding in plain sight* bollocks. He's asking for trouble. He doesn't give a fuck now because he knows he'll be gone. But us? We'd have to take the punishment if it came to it. We'd be the ones suffering in the long run.'

Darren nodded. 'You're right. The sooner we do it, the sooner we can bury it all, for good. No one will ever know what's underneath this place. It can be our secret forever.'

'Unless we get caught and go to prison.'

'That's not gonna fucking happen, bro,' Darren said. 'And you'd better believe it.'

'Tomorrow the day, then?'

Darren nodded. 'Tomorrow or Saturday. I'd prefer Saturday. You never know, I might get lucky and end up back at hers. Wouldn't that be good?'

'You'll have to lay on the charm if you want to get into her knickers.'

Darren tapped his temple. 'Got it all sussed. It's gonna be the best night of her life.'

KEL MCCULLOCH KICKED off her boots and crashed onto the couch. God, what a day. The weekend couldn't come soon enough. Get away from all this nonsense for a bit. All the bloody animals and missing women. Some sanity for once.

She poured herself a large glass of Malbec and flicked the TV on, just for the background noise. There was nothing worth watching. Never was. Yet what she really needed right now was a bit of escapism. Try to shake the job from her head for a while. Thank fuck she'd booked the day off tomorrow. Though admittedly, she felt somewhat guilty about not turning in when the search party was out. So, she would make the effort and show her face, if only for an hour or two. Shows commitment to the job, doesn't it? Not like she was committed, though. Maybe she was getting just like Rob in that regard. Maybe she'd reached the end of the line in her police career, too.

Perhaps a transfer to another department would be the

sensible thing to do. Maybe move into something else so she wouldn't have to deal with all this bloody murder and violence. She'd questioned whether she was mentally strong enough for it over these past few days, and concluded she wasn't. Yet she knew she'd face these tests, these challenges, when she took the job on.

Detective Sergeant Kel McCulloch. It sounded good. And she was proud of herself for coming this far, but she'd never let the career get the better of her. She had a life, for fuck's sake. A life outside of work. She'd never be one of those people married to the job. Not a chance. It was important to separate it from real life. Which is why she was so looking forward to tomorrow night.

She might even get lucky.

It had been so long now.

She'd arranged with Jen to hang around nearby with her mate, Cassie. Just in case things went awry and he ended up being some kind of weirdo nut job. Not that she thought he was. Looking at his profile now, he seemed okay. Just your average, clean and sensible guy. Looked like he enjoyed the nice things in life. Attractive. Sexy, even. Looked like the kind of guy who worked outside for a living. A rugged type. She wouldn't know for certain until she met him, of course, but he looked like a good, decent man. And that's all she wanted, really.

A good and decent man.

She took herself upstairs and ran a bath. Brought the bottle with her and threw on some Nina Simone. Lit a few candles to make it extra special. She would have a long soak, dig out her outfit for tomorrow, and pick out something to watch on Netflix. It was important to her, these little rituals. Living alone was a lonely affair. Yeah, she had friends who'd pop round now and then, but in the main, she was a one-woman band. She had to keep herself entertained so she wouldn't go stir crazy rattling around the flat.

She ordered a takeaway from China Rose—a treat—and went to let her cares drift away in the bath. She would make the effort tomorrow on the search. Just to keep herself involved. But all she wanted was for it all to end.

KURT HAD PARKED the car just up the road from the Kirkland place. He'd picked a spot that was near enough to be able to see what was happening in and around the house, and far enough away to be inconspicuous enough for no one to care.

There was no car on the drive. He knew Paul Kirkland wasn't home because he'd watched him leave the house, get in the car—a BMW—and leave the road in a careful and measured manoeuvre through the snow.

He just wanted to watch, that was all. Just to see if he could pick anything up from them. Anything unusual. Watch their comings and goings, see if they were giving anything away. He knew what people would think about him if they could see him now. They'd think he was being paranoid. They'd think he'd perhaps lost his way a little bit. Maybe even lost his mind. But they'd be wrong. This was just a concerned boyfriend looking out for his girl, making sure everything was in the correct order. He wasn't paranoid at all. He was *focussed*. Focussed on what he had to do. Focussed on the job at hand. Focussed on putting things right.

Okay, he knew he shouldn't be drinking and driving. As a professional driver, it was even worse that he was casually taking the odd nip from his hip flask. But what the hell. It's not like he didn't have the skills to cope behind the wheel.

It's what he did for a living, and in a far bigger vehicle than a fucking Volkswagen. He was used to it. He could handle it. And he was careful enough to take it easy. Besides, there was hardly anyone else on the road right now. The weather had seen to that. He'd never seen a winter like it. The roads weren't fit to drive on, really. It was fine if there was only the odd car knocking about, but that was all. Most people wouldn't cope in these conditions. Most vehicles weren't in the right condition for these roads, even his. The pensioners would be having fucking kittens.

He unscrewed the cap and took a nip. He was a whisky man, through and through. Loved that feeling of the burn on his throat, the warmth sinking into his chest.

He looked out over the road. It was still with snow, the streetlights illuminating the cul-de-sac in an orange glow. Footprints ran along the pavements on either side and into the road. A few tyre tracks led in and out onto the main road behind him. There'd been plenty of activity, but it had seemed to settle right down now. It was almost seven o'clock. That time of the evening when the dullards would be settling in to watch their soap operas or one of those excruciating reality shows. The town was quiet, with barely a soul around. It was the perfect time to go for a wander.

He retrieved the blade from the inside pocket of his coat. It was nothing special. Just a kitchen knife. A chef's knife, no less. Perfect for dicing vegetables. It was a pretty expensive one, he knew that. He turned it over in his hands, ran a finger over the sharp edge, watched the light glint off it. Remembered the day he'd taken Cait up to the Lake District where there was an ultra-expensive kitchen shop. She'd bought a set of them and brought them home, happy as you could get. She was a bit of a cook. Loved being in the kitchen, loved making these amazing dinners. How ironic that now she was gone, he was going to avenge her death with the very thing she loved.

He knew she was dead. *Knew* it. And he knew the police were hiding the truth from him. If it wasn't for Lisa Kirkland, she'd still be here now, with him, where she belonged. Well soon she was going to wish she'd never thrown that fucking party in the first place.

He put the knife back in his inside pocket and stepped out of the car. The cold hit him immediately. It was bitter, like his mood. He shut the door, locked it and stomped off towards the house. This was just something he had to do.

As he approached the gate, he could see the kitchen light was on. There was someone in there: probably her. Had to be her, really. He knew she was alone.

He stepped onto the empty drive and up the front path. The snow had been clumsily cleared with a spade and salt spread around. Pointless, really.

He stepped around to the side of the house. There was no gate, which seemed careless. His boots crunched in the snow as he approached the window. He could see her in the kitchen, wearing a black top and jeans. There was music playing and she seemed happy, dancing by herself, throwing something into a pot and stirring it.

She was cooking up a storm.

LOGAN WENT THROUGH ALL the things he had to do in his head as he pottered about the kitchen. He was on his third cup of tea of the evening and hanging around at the table—his favourite place to avoid the rubbish on TV and the chaos of Izzy's toys littering the carpet—and trying to piece together recent events. He was finding it hard to think and wanted nothing more than to see this through to the end, which couldn't come soon enough. His phone was fully charged, and he was jittery for an update: a call to say Chris Kearney had found the source of the dark site or something from Murray or Dr Graham about the Rottweiler. So far, nothing.

But tomorrow was going to be an eventful day. He knew that much. The search party would kick off as soon as it was light. By now, of course, the whole town was talking about it. Parents would be joining in after the school drop-off. The marine unit had been put up in a nearby hotel and were preparing for the job at hand. Warburton and Sanderson had been busy coordinating the logistics of it all. The search would continue throughout the day until darkness fell. It was hoped, of course, that by then there'd be an outcome, good or bad.

He expected the worst. Perhaps he could be forgiven for wanting them to find a body. Of course he didn't want to see the poor woman gone, but he expected it. He hoped tomorrow would bring closure. For the police, for himself and Kel. But, more than anyone else, for Kurt Chadwick. He knew the poor guy must've been suffering badly and was no doubt very fragile. He only hoped he wasn't planning on doing anything silly, like take the law into his own hands. He knew how such a tragedy could bring more tragedy in its wake.

'You look deep in thought, love,' Vic said. 'Everything okay?'

Logan snapped himself back to reality as she stepped into the kitchen. Outside, it was snowing again. He could see the flakes billowing in the wind out the window.

'I'm alright,' he said. 'You know. It's the job.'

'Getting to you, isn't it?'

'It's this case, that's all. I just want it done with.'

She came over to him, massaged his shoulders and kissed his head. 'Spare a thought for that poor man. He must be in such a state.'

'I don't know what I'd do if you went missing,' Logan said. He knew he'd said this before, but it was true. 'Don't know how I'd cope.'

'No one really knows how they'd cope in such circumstances, love. It must be such an emotional struggle.'

'I dread to think how he'll react if a body turns up.'

'Oh, God. You think it will come to that?'

He sighed. He couldn't really say anything more about what he'd seen on the CCTV or what he'd seen on the dark site. 'I can't see any other outcome.'

LATER, after Izzy had gone to bed and Vic had retired to their room to read, Logan hung around downstairs, trying to switch off from the case but failing miserably. He flicked through the news channels, browsed various YouTube videos about guitars—was he really ready to plunge into learning an instrument?—and read a few articles on the latest football stories. He felt disembodied from it all, as if he wasn't really taking part in this reality. He didn't need to examine why. He couldn't get Caitlin Slater out of his head.

He fired off a quick text to Murray, asking about any progress on the dark site. While he waited for a reply, he thought about what usually happened in those detective novels Vic was so in love with. Just about now, the detective would be pacing around the living room, looking for a bottle of whisky. He might put some music on, some country or some jazz or even some opera, just to try and take his mind off the job. He might sit in an armchair and examine his past or call up his mother for a row. He'd pour the whisky and down the first glass. He might savour the next one while he chain-smoked and let the ghosts of long-dead murder victims come back to haunt him.

But this was real life. He grabbed a can of beer from the fridge and stared out of the kitchen window at the snowfall. Right then, he decided he wasn't the hero in a crime novel or ITV drama. He was just a copper like any other, and not a very good one if he was completely honest with himself.

His phone buzzed. A reply from Murray:

CHRIS THINKS the source is definitely here.

HE DIALLED HIM UP. There was no answer. He left the window and went pacing around the house. Thought about those gunshots again.

Could it be?

Could they get a search warrant or was he clutching at straws? And even if they could, time was against them. Caitlin Slater could turn up dead tomorrow, but what if she wasn't? What if she was being held somewhere against her will? What if she was at that farm?

The phone rang. Logan took down half a can of beer and answered. 'Go on.'

'Just to run tomorrow by you,' Murray said. 'First light should see everything in place. There'll be a group of about forty people, mostly volunteers, going through Redisher Woods from top to bottom. The marine unit will be out scouring the River Irwell. They'll start in the centre of Bury and move up towards Ramsbottom and beyond. We'll have a search party of ready and willing coppers on foot across the moors. We'll also have a small team out across Two

Brooks Valley and up to Affetside. It's no small operation, Rob.'

'Just a bit.'

'You'll be out with DS Hussein. Probably going from place to place in a pool car, though we're not fixed on that yet. And a word of warning, Rob. This could be a long day.'

'Could be a short one, too, if she turns up.'

'There is that, but we're covering a huge area, as you know. So far, we're not finding signs of her anywhere. No one seems to know anything.'

'That's because she was taken, sir,' he said. 'You saw the CCTV of that van.'

'But we didn't see her get in it.'

'And we didn't see her continue her walk either. Any news on the van? Have we at least identified the vehicle type?'

'We can't find the current owner as there's no number plate. But we think it's a Ford. A fourth generation Transit, probably around 2014. That's just going off the images, though, so hardly conclusive. Without the vehicle in our possession, it's hard to nail down.'

'Could be thousands of them across the city.'

'Exactly.'

Logan thought about whether he'd seen that van parked up at the farm. He knew he hadn't, though he had seen a Toyota pick-up. And he'd also seen it on Google Earth. He wondered if he could find it again and dig the number plate out. They could check the PNC for any data on the vehicle.

'Look, sir. Seems like a good time to mention: I've been on Google Earth, looking at the farm for anything that might jump out. Came across a Toyota pick up. I'm sure I've seen it before.'

'Is there anything on that?' Murray said.

'I'm gonna try and dig a number plate out. I might need to enhance the image somehow. Blow it up, you know.'

'If you manage that, let us know.'

'I'll get onto it right now. Maybe we could justify a section seventeen search warrant?'

'Okay, see what you can come up with, but listen. It's an early start tomorrow. I'll be up at the crack of dawn. I expect you in at six. Don't forget, half the bloody town's shut off. It's snowing again now, so the gritters are out all night. But expect it to be bad.'

'I know.'

'I'd get prepared, Rob. Mentally, I mean. We could be retrieving a body tomorrow.'

'Any news on Kurt Chadwick? How's he bearing up?'

'I've not heard anything, but I expect he's hiding away in the house. Poor bastard's not expected to be out tomorrow. As you can imagine, his head's not in it.'

'Could do with getting him looked after a bit better, sir. We've not exactly been on top form with that.'

'I know. I believe DI Sanderson is taking care of that. Right, listen. I'm getting my head down now. And you should, too. This could all be over by end of play tomorrow and we'll be back to the usual shit.'

'How is Clarky, by the way?'

'Strangely, we've not heard a peep from him since he threatened to throw himself off The Rock car park. Right, I'm off. Remember. 6am. See you then.'

Logan locked up the house and turned all the lights off before retreating to the office. He fired up the Mac and went to Google Earth. Repeated the process of finding the farm and retraced his steps to find the Toyota pick-up.

He found it pretty quickly and zoomed in on the registration plate. Tried to enhance it, to find a way to make the image clearer and less blurry. It was proving a tough task. He took screenshots of both the pick-up and the quad bike and emailed them over to Murray with a short note that they consider a search of the property, if it was even remotely possible. He kicked himself for not pursuing this further days ago. Now it seemed that time was running out fast.

There was nothing left to do but catch up on sleep now. In an ideal world, he'd be stretched out on the couch watching some comedy or catching up on current affairs or a food programme with Vic, perhaps sharing a bottle of wine. But all that seemed a distant memory. All he saw was Caitlin Slater's face in his mind, screaming out for someone to save her.

COLIN WAS IMMERSED *in oxygen therapy. Breathing in, breathing out, the mask over his face like he was sucking at life itself. He liked to sit in darkness while he was taking it into his body, that desperate air, and he found it easier and more relaxing to do it that way. If he'd have known he was going to end up at death's door like this, he would've been much more careful in life. Though where would be the fun in that?*

He'd given instructions to Darren and Sam to bring the girl down on Saturday, as planned. He'd been getting impatient and felt he had to do it before his own time ran out, which he knew was soon.

It was a sacred thing to him, taking a life. To the average person, this was murder, pure and simple. He knew he would be judged that way. But it went deeper for him. Much deeper. To have control over somebody's destiny was true power and exercising that power was a sacred thing. It had been his destiny from the beginning. It had been his true purpose, his true will. He couldn't have changed it if he wanted to. This was him. He was ready to step into the other side in the knowledge that he'd taken lives so very easily. He'd been calm about it. He'd accepted his mission. And now, soon, he was going to meet his own maker. It was exciting. Thrilling. His heart beat hard at the thought of it all coming to an end soon.

Leaving the farm to Darren and Sam had been his plan all along. He knew they would respect and continue his legacy. He'd raised them well, even though at times they were a handful. Still, it was the right thing. The only thing.

Everything was in its right place.

He took one last deep breath and removed the mask from his face. He rested it on the stand and pushed the machine to the side, leaving his chair in a less than graceful way, but he was beyond caring about that.

He'd spent a few years in isolation. It had been perfect, away from the noise and chaos of society. A glorious time when he could focus on his mission in peace. But now his mission was almost over. Just one last kill and that would be that.

He shuffled forward and stepped through the black curtain into the adjacent room with the altar. Spent a few moments breathing in that darkness. The place where the magic happened. He knew she would be coming soon. Relished it.

He couldn't wait to get to work on her.

FIFTEEN

Kurt stood back from the window, hiding in the shadows. The last thing he wanted was for Lisa Kirkland to catch a glimpse of him. That would be the end of the operation. Instead, he hovered just out of sight, far enough away to be invisible. Car headlights danced into the street from somewhere behind him and he froze. Could it be her husband already? The headlights briefly illuminated the cul-de-sac then died away. The vehicle must've turned into a nearby driveway, but he instinctively ducked into the wall in a vain effort to make sure he was unnoticed.

When the danger had gone, he positioned himself carefully again and crawled under the window. He knew he was out of sight now, even if she leaned and looked out. If she did, she wouldn't see him. Just the falling snow against the streetlights. She would have to step outside to catch sight of him, but that would blow everything. His whole plan ruined.

He crouched beneath the window, flush against the wall. He could hear her now, tossing kitchen utensils into the sink, singing along to the song coming from the speakers on the side. 'Everybody Wants to Rule the World'. Tears for Fears. He almost laughed at the serendipity of it. A song he'd always liked himself, especially when it came on as he drove his truck on the motorway. Now, under these different circumstances, the song brought a strange new feeling.

HE SAW Caitlin in his mind then. Saw her screaming out in a sea of black. Had he come too far? He could stop it anytime. He could stop it right now, but he felt compelled.

All of this was Lisa Kirkland's fault. If Cait had to die, she would, too. And then he would sort himself out if he had to.

As the song played, he made his decision. It was now or never. He was finally at the point he'd seen in his mind: the moment he'd planned for. He took the knife from his pocket and gripped it tight. The blade was cold as hell.

Kurt crept past the drainpipes. He stood and leaned against the back door, calming himself, taking a deep breath as the snow fell. Was this really him? Maybe it always had been.

He knocked on the door before he could stop himself, feeling his knuckles cold and hard against the wood. There was a brief moment that seemed to last forever, and when the door opened, he caught his breath. It was her, standing right there.

'Lisa Kirkland?'

'Yeah?'

Her eyes fell to his hand with the knife. She tried to slam the door on him, but he was bigger and stronger. He leaned into it and forced it back open. She was too small to hold him back and in that split second, he lunged, the blade bright and silver and ready to kill. Caught her on the shoulder blade and she staggered back, screaming. He knew he had to shut her up quickly, so the only way was to lunge again.

This time, the blade caught something hard, probably a rib, then went into something soft. Blood spurted out in a fountain, spraying his face, which shocked him. He knew he was only half done so he pulled out the knife and went for her again.

The barks were loud and violent as the dog crashed through a door from behind her as she fell back. The animal jumped at him. He tried to plunge the knife into it, too, but its jaws snapped into his face and he fell back and landed hard, crashing through the door he'd just forced himself through. He dropped the knife.

He'd fucked up.

The dog's teeth snapped at his face: biting, pulling, tearing into the flesh. The animal ripped at his throat with its sharp and heavy claws, then wrapped its jaws tight around his neck, and he felt something pop.

The dog was overpowering him, easily as strong as he was. Maybe stronger. He could feel the dog's power as it ripped into him, could feel it tearing into his face like it was a piece of meat. His eyes swam with blood. The liquid in his mouth choked him and he wondered if he was going to drown in it, thinking that wouldn't be so bad after all.

Then the world went black.

LISA KIRKLAND CRAWLED across the kitchen floor. She tried to call out, but the words wouldn't come. She clumsily pressed a hand to her chest, but she knew it was pointless. The blood beneath her was slick and shiny and had pooled.

This would take a lot of fucking cleaning, that was for sure. When she tried to call out again, she coughed, and more blood splattered from her mouth.

She pulled herself up using the kitchen cupboards. It took all the effort she had, especially now that everything had gone blurry and her head spun. The curry she'd been making still bubbled on the hob, and now that was ruined. Blood had splattered onto the pan and oven door. It seemed to be everywhere.

She gripped the worktop, knowing her phone was there somewhere. Bear came in, whimpering, licking at her, trying to get the blood off her. He barked and barked, going in and out of the back door, panicking. She willed him to carry on, to go to the neighbours, anything. Go out into the street and bark his fucking head off until someone comes.

She spotted her phone. Tried to grab it but couldn't feel anything in her fingers. Her hands had gone numb but she gripped it, anyway, trying to make her hands work, then fell back to the floor. The phone dropped into the pool of her blood as the music played, the sound feeling like she could hear it from under water.

The pain in her chest was excruciating.

That fucker had *stabbed* her.

She didn't know where he'd gone, whoever he was, but thank fuck Bear had come to protect her. The only trouble was, she felt it may have been too late.

Oh, Paul. Why did you have to drive to the bloody supermarket now?

Just before she passed out, she thought she could hear people somewhere outside. She lay face down in her own blood, willing the whole world to come until everything went white and she could feel snow falling on her face.

. . .

PCs Claire Walton and Stefan Hartmann had been talking to a group of teenage boys about hanging around on the streets in such cold conditions when a call came through on the airwave radios. For Claire Walton, who had been counting down the hours for her duty to finish, which would be at 22:00 hours whether the gaffers liked it or not, a hot bath was calling.

It was bloody freezing out here. Throughout the shift, they'd clocked up three hot coffees and a pizza, spending most of the time in the pool car with the heaters on and the radio tuned to Radio X. With barely a few hours left to go, they were just killing time, winding up the local youth about how schooldays were the best of your life and they would one day look back upon their bravado right now and cringe.

'Shouldn't you guys be on your Xbox or PlayStation or whatever?' Hartmann had said, his German accent making the boys smirk. 'Somewhere in the warm?'

'Stefan, this one's for us,' she said, dragging him away from the boys and back to the car. 'We've gotta move right now.'

'What's up?'

'Stabbing. There's an ambulance on the way.'

'Oh, fuck.'

Walton fired the car up and put it into gear, pulling away from the side street by the park and straight onto Brandlesholme Road, heading north. Hartmann flicked on the blue lights and the siren kicked in. The gritting lorry pulled over and she manoeuvred past it, careful to keep the wheels straight in the snow. The surface was slippy, the black ice treacherous. There were a few vehicles on the road, but most people had shown the good sense to stay at home.

'Three zero, one zero,' Hartmann said into his radio. 'We're on the way to the scene. Over.'

There was a moment before the radio crackled, and the operator spoke again. 'Suspect is believed to be deceased.'

'Suspect?' Walton said. 'What about the bloody victim?'

Hartmann thought about the last time he'd attended a stabbing. A fifteen-year-old whose life had been taken over a bag of weed. The kids they'd just spent the last ten minutes chatting to seemed a far cry from the night he'd tried to stem the flow of blood from young Diallo Abimbola's neck under the strip light of Salford Precinct two summers ago. The image remained there fixed in his memory: probably the worst night of his career. And now here was another one, at a nearby house. Perhaps it was a domestic gone terribly wrong or an intruder caught in the act who had panicked and struck out. Or maybe it was more than that.

'You ready for this?'

'Can't say I am,' Walton said, wrestling with the wheel. 'Never seen anything like this before.'

'At least there's an ambulance on the way as well,' Hartmann said. He called in for more units, thinking that it was probably best they weren't alone for this one.

A moment later, as they approached the road in question, a response came from Unit 4978. They were on the way from the opposite direction.

Walton pulled a right into the road, both sides thick with snow. A small crowd of people stood in the front garden of a house on the turning circle of the cul-de-sac. Walton and Hartmann were the first on the scene, though they could hear the distinctive ambulance siren somewhere on the wind, which whipped the snow around them like sharp little arrows. She left the car in the middle of the road and they both got out, Hartmann taking the lead and heading into the group. They made room as he moved towards them, parting like the seas. An Alsatian moved keenly between the bystanders, looking agitated. The blue light flash flickered on all the distressed faces.

Hartmann headed into the kitchen of the house through the back door. There were several other people in there, too, looking frantic. The ambulance made its way down the narrow path, filling the road.

'Okay, what's going on here?' Walton said.

'See for yourself,' a man in a layered lumberjack shirt said. He grabbed her by the arm, leading her over to what she now saw was a male body lying flat on its back in the side garden by the back door. 'Whoever's stabbed her is dead. We heard the dog and—'

'Okay, calm down,' Walton said. 'What's happened?'

Another man, flanked by a woman Walton assumed was his wife, spoke up. 'A woman's been stabbed. In the house. She's called Lisa. Lisa Kirkland. We don't think she's gonna make it.'

Two paramedics rushed past. One knelt beside the male on the ground and then quickly left to follow the other into the kitchen.

The commotion was frantic. It seemed like everyone was trying to speak at the same time, calling out names, the dog barking, the lights flashing. More neighbours hung around in their front gardens looking worried.

'We came out to the dog barking,' a young woman said. 'We think he's attacked the man and bit him or something and the woman in the house has been stabbed.'

Stabbed came out in a sob, an incomprehensible gasp. Walton went over to the male body and the group stood back and gave her room, most of the faces turned away. She spoke into her Airwave radio, asking for more units. There was no answer. She looked down at the man's face. It was a red maw, the blood congealing. His hands were ripped to shreds, fat and red like crushed raspberries. The dog hadn't held back.

'Fucking hell,' she said. 'Jesus...'

Behind her, the voices in the kitchen were loud and urgent. Another siren was getting nearer. Walton suddenly felt immobilised and useless. This was a scene she wouldn't wish on her worst enemy. The trail of blood ran into the kitchen through the snow, which had turned pink around the back door. She shivered against the cold, tried to focus on the job at hand. But she couldn't for the life of her think of anything.

'Claire, let's make room,' Hartmann said, appearing beside her. 'The woman is still with us. Claire, come back to me.'

She snapped out of it and called for the small crowd that had gathered to make way. The paramedics came out, bringing Lisa Kirkland on a stretcher, with an oxygen mask over her face and a huge, bandaged tourniquet around her chest. A paramedic conducted CPR as they moved. Kirkland didn't look conscious, but her eyes flickered beneath the lids. The crowd parted and there were sobs and tears, a few words of shock and panic. The dog ran between the forest of people, barking out loud and whining.

Walton looked behind her again to see Hartmann knelt beside the dead man. Then two more familiar faces—PC Cooke and PC Nuttall—came around her, Nuttall dominating over everyone with his massive shoulders. The paramedics got Kirkland into the ambulance as Cooke joined Hartmann and the dead man. The ambulance sirens kicked in loud and lively, and the vehicle backed out of the cul-de-sac.

An incident unit van pulled up and four coppers in hi-vis coats jumped out. A police Land Rover spun around from somewhere on the main road to act as a support vehicle.

There was a tap on Walton's shoulder and she turned.

'I've managed to get the dog,' a man said. 'I'm one of the neighbours. Mike. I don't know where Paul's gone. His car's not on the drive.'

'Paul?'

'Her husband. He must've gone out. I didn't want the dog to go wandering off, you see, and I think he might've done, as she doted on it all the time and... Fuck. Is she gonna be okay?'

'I don't know,' Walton said. 'I'm sure the medics have it under control.'

'He's dead, isn't he?'

'Did you see anything, Mr...?'

'Baker. Mike Baker. I live at fifty-seven if you need me to make a statement or anything. I can take the dog into mine until this is all sorted. I'll look after him.'

She was about to thank him, but Nuttall ran past her armed with a yellow blanket and some police tape. Four incident unit guys came tearing past, too, and she followed, doing her best to look like she knew what she was doing. Now it seemed like the Airwave radios were filling the whole neighbourhood. The onlookers and bystanders were beginning to retreat inside, as much to get out of the cold as anything else.

The unit guys sealed off the house and the van moved into the spot vacated by the ambulance.

WALTON RETURNED to the car and started her up, just to let the engine warm through. Christ, it was bloody cold. Hartmann returned to join her as she moved the car to make some space. He opened the passenger side.

'God, that was fucking awful,' he said. 'It *is* awful.'

He let out an exasperated sigh and held his head in his hands, sinking back into the seat as the heating kicked in, blowing warm air into the car. 'Looks like the dog killed him.'

'Those stab wounds. Fuck me. He must've gone into her with some force. She still alive?'

He nodded. 'For now. I don't know for how long. Control are sending up a serious crime unit. We can expect a detective soon enough.'

'Any point in hanging around?' Walton said. 'I was hoping to finish on time tonight.'

Hartmann shook his head and was about to say they'd need to stay behind to file a report, but he was cut short by the sound of a man screaming.

Not in agony or pain, but in heartbreak.

SIXTEEN

Logan was woken at 3am by his bladder, which had taken him right out of sleep and wouldn't let him back in again. He went for a piss and got back into bed in an effort to return to the depths of slumber, but it was pointless. Vic slept deeply beside him, her breathing soft and steady. Careful not to wake her, he left the bed again and tiptoed downstairs, where he made an ultra-strong coffee and sat at the kitchen table, not fully in the room. A part of him still remained in whatever dream he'd abruptly left. He couldn't remember it now but was certain it had something to do with blood.

His phone buzzed. Strange time to be receiving a text message but then he saw it was from Murray.

KURT CHADWICK FOUND DEAD.

'AH, FUCK.'

Then another.

. . .

He tried to stab Lisa Kirkland to death. She's in the Manchester Royal Infirmary. Phone me when you can.

He sat and drank the coffee as the snow continued to steadily fall outside. Dead? Chadwick's welfare had obviously been overlooked. Surely heads would roll if this turned out to be preventable. Which it obviously was. Caitlin Slater's disappearance had clearly had a very negative effect on him, which begged a question: if he was capable of murder, which seemed his intention, what else had he been capable of?

The fact he'd gone for Lisa Kirkland told Logan it was a revenge attack, and a misguided one. It didn't take a genius to work out where he'd laid the blame for Caitlin's disappearance.

And poor Lisa Kirkland. If she'd been stabbed, it could go either way depending on where the blade had struck and what kind of blade it was.

He picked up the phone and fired a text back.

You awake?

A moment later, a reply from Murray confirmed he was.

Logan dialled him up. 'What the hell's going on?'

Murray sighed. 'Exactly what I said. The timing could've been better, that's for sure.'

'What happened?'

'Call came through about nine. PC Walton and PC Hartmann attended first, followed by half the bloody station. Turns out Kurt Chadwick had rocked up at the Kirklands' place and tried to kill the poor woman. Apparently he'd gone to the back door, gave it a knock and when she answered it, there he was with a bloody kitchen knife.'

'Jesus.'

'And then he went for her. We only know it's him because her dog mauled him. Identified by the driving licence in his wallet. His car's still parked up on the Kirkland's cul-de-sac, but I expect it to be taken away shortly. A thorough forensic examination will be made of his premises. I hope we've not missed anything glaringly obvious. And he wasn't just mauled, either. The dog ripped half his fucking face off.'

'Christ.'

'Also chewed up his throat, I believe. Which was enough to take him out.'

'What, the dog killed him?'

'The dog killed him,' Murray said. 'It's been taken to a police kennel in St Helens. I'm still getting updates but as far as I'm aware, Lisa Kirkland is still in the MRI.'

'How's she doing?'

'It's touch and go. Husband's in a state, as you can imagine.'

Logan let his head fall, then brought it back to reality. 'I'm coming in now. No point hanging around scratching my arse.'

'It's not even four o'clock, Rob. You'll be hanging around until six at least.'

'I'll be all the more prepared then. I can't sleep, anyway. I'll see you there.'

'Don't think I'm dragging myself in right now,' Murray said. 'I'll see you later.'

Logan hung up and spent the next ten minutes in the shower. Vic stirred as he was getting dressed. He resisted the temptation to get in beside her, and kissed her forehead before she turned over again. He checked on Izzy, who was fast asleep surrounded by her bear gang. Sometimes, when he looked at his daughter, he longed for that life again. Childhood. A time when there were no real cares or worries or fears. No responsibilities. And certainly no burglaries to deal with or murders to investigate. He closed her door and tiptoed downstairs, leaving the house quietly.

Looking at the state of the street and the main road beyond it, he wondered if taking the car was a silly idea, but he had no other option. He shifted the snow from the windows and the roof and scraped away the ice before getting in. It was like sitting in a freezer. Although he was wrapped up in industrial winter-issue police gear, it was still like the bloody Arctic.

He started her up, put her into gear and carefully drove out of Cemetery Road. In the cemetery itself, about two hundred yards behind him, he knew the local ghosts would be stirring, watching his every move. And as he pulled a left onto Bolton Road West, the freshly fallen snow pristine and untouched, he half expected to see a few hanging around.

THE STATION WAS QUIET, though not completely dead. He pulled into his usual spot and killed the engine. The car park had been gritted as a priority. Up above, an ice-cold moon shone down through a break in the clouds. Over beyond the back wall, a fleet of vehicles had been mobilised for the day's search. Logan was surprised they were pulling out all the resources, though not so sure the top brass would be happy about it, especially now Caitlin Slater's grieving partner had tried to commit murder and was now dead himself.

The world was one fucked-up place.

He climbed the steps and made his way upstairs, making sure he signed on for overtime first. The custody desk was empty and quiet, but there was a light on in the adjacent CCTV room . Logan walked over, groggy and tired and thinking about risking a machine coffee, when DS Becky Mortimer popped her head out of the door and waved.

'I almost shit myself,' she said. Her local Bury accent was fully loaded. 'What're you doing here at this time?'

'Got a call so I came in,' Logan said. 'Please tell me you've got a kettle in there.'

'I only do Taylor's Java,' she said. 'Best coffee you can get. You want one?'

His look said it all, so she ushered him inside and flicked the kettle on.

'I don't think Martin would be too happy to see you brewing up in his room,' Logan said.

'Oh, he's a pussycat,' she said, busy at the makeshift brew station. 'He brought the whole thing in for me.'

There was a comfortable-looking couch that had been brought in as well, not to mention the two computers Chris Kearney must've rigged up especially for her. If it was a heart-warming family film she was watching, or a gripping historical drama, Logan could see the set-up would be worth it.

But it wasn't.

'What's happening with the footage?' Logan said.

She handed him a fresh coffee, black. 'Not much, I'm afraid. Certainly no movement on any of these bloody live cams. You can see for yourself. There's nothing happening.'

'Nothing at all?'

'Nothing. And as for the website itself? Jesus. God help those people. I dread to think what happened in their lives for them to get into such shit, you know.'

Logan thought the same. 'You must be out of your mind with boredom.'

'I'm keeping myself busy with a few books. Got PC Carver and PC Drysdale helping out as well. We all take it in turns to monitor the bloody thing whenever one of us wants a little kip. We're coping, so far.'

Logan sat himself down at the terminal and moved the cursor around the screen. Aside from the bizarre and disturbing photographs, including those of animal heads on spikes and piles of bones, and a bonfire with a figure standing beside it in a Gandalf wizard mask, there wasn't much else he hadn't seen already.

'I reckon there's a few hidden things,' Mortimer said. 'Has to be. I know Chris Kearney has been around this thing twenty-four seven, but there's got to be something more.'

'Probably,' he said. 'Makes you wonder what makes these people tick. What motivates this kind of depravity.'

'I've seen some things on here, Rob,' she said, 'that would question your sanity. The amount of times I've thought, fuck it, let's go get a beer, you know? It's beyond my pay grade, if I'm honest.'

Logan nodded and drank his coffee. 'I can see that. The sanity bit, not your pay grade.'

She smiled and yawned at the same time. 'Gonna be a long day, eh?'

'You can say that again. You joining us for the search?'

'Gotta stay here. Could do with the fresh air, though. Getting a bit claustrophobic.'

'You hear about Kurt Chadwick?'

'Kurt who?'

'I guess not then. Doesn't matter.'

There was more movement outside the room: a few night coppers logging on and an army of cleaners moving down the corridor. Logan drained his coffee and wished Becky well, reminding her to let him know immediately if anything happened on the live cams.

He made his way upstairs as the night duties headed out. It would be a few hours at least until the sunrise. Right now, he felt like a night copper himself. And it would be way past his bedtime when he finally got home late tonight. In the future, Friday would forever be known as Rob Logan's Day Off. He would make sure of that. Because after this one was over, he swore he'd never work another in his life.

ALMOST TWO HOURS LATER, Dave Murray turned in with a face like thunder. Seems someone had nicked his parking spot. Logan was in the middle of coffee number three and by now the darkness was fading and the sunrise was a distant speck on the horizon. He looked out across the hills and the town below, feeling like the day needed to be over sharpish but knowing it would be a long, long time before he could switch off.

Either Caitlin Slater was out there, alive, or she was dead.

Long dead.

'Come and join me in my office, Rob,' Murray said. 'I'll get the kettle on. Asif Hussein's on his way, stuck in traffic. And I tell you what, I've seen a lot of snow in my lifetime, but this takes the fucking biscuit.'

Logan followed and weaved his way through the incident room, which was filling up fast. As he neared the door, he spotted McCulloch entering through the back, covered from head to toe in a wraparound quilted coat. She spotted him and shuffled through the crowd.

'Thought it was your day off?' Logan said.

'I'm only staying for the morning bit, eh? Thought I'd show my face.'

'Fair enough. You didn't have to.'

'I know I didn't have to, Rob, but I wanted to. I won't be here all day. And in all seriousness, I'm sorry you had to take the short straw for tonight.'

'You still meeting this date later?'

'Yeah.'

'Don't expect me to keep an eye on you.'

'As if I'll need it, eh?'

They went into Murray's office as the room filled up behind them. He looked genuinely surprised to see Kel McCulloch, and vice versa.

'I just wanted to show my support, sir,' she said. 'I'm not gonna be here that long, eh?' McCulloch said.

Murray nodded. 'Shows commitment to the cause. Though perhaps not that much, eh, Kel?' He smiled.

'Well, I'll fuck off home then if you want me to.'

'I didn't say it wasn't appreciated. Now, listen up, both of you. Ah, here he is...'

'Sir.'

Logan and McCulloch turned to see Asif Hussein standing in the doorway. Murray ushered him in.

'Fuck me, I'm half expecting the wicked ice queen to drag me out of my bloody car,' Hussein said. 'Some right whoppers out there. Have you seen some of them coats?'

'Right, Asif and Rob. Your Land Rover is in the undercroft. Kel, if you want to join them, that's up to you. But this is supposed to be your day off, so—'

'You're saying I won't be paid for my time?'

'Well, no one asked you to come in, Kel,' he said. 'But thanks for your efforts all the same.'

McCulloch paused. Thought for a split second about what she was about to say, then said it anyway. 'Well in that case, sir, I'll fuck off home, eh?'

'If you like.'

'Fucking gladly.'

'Shit, Kel...' Logan said, going after her. But she'd vanished in the crowd of coppers and disappeared down the stairs. He saw her run off through the double doors at the bottom and out into the cold. He watched her go.

When he got back, Murray was putting on his outdoor gear.

'No need for that, sir,' Logan said. 'She was only here to help. On her day off. She didn't need to be.'

'It's just a pay thing, Rob,' Murray said. 'That's all. If it was up to me, I'd have had her on the payroll, no problem.'

'There's a better way of putting it, sir.'

'All right,' Murray said, pulling on a massive overcoat. 'You've made your point. Now you know where the keys are, both of you. Let's go.'

'IT'S ALL A BIT POINTLESS, if you ask me,' Hussein said. 'We'll never find her, even if half the town's out.'

'You seem convinced.'

'Aren't you?'

Logan had to admit that he was. 'I'm surprised she's still not turned up, to be honest. But now her boyfriend's gone. You hear about that?'

Hussein nodded. 'A bit much, taking it out on the birthday girl. You think she'll pull through?'

'Hard to say. A stabbing like that...'

'Crazy.'

Logan took the Land Rover up Turton Road with Two Brooks Valley on the right a winter wonderland. Maybe Hussein was right. Maybe it was all a bit pointless. And even if they did find Caitlin now, alive, they'd have to break the news that her man was gone, killed at the culmination of a chain of wild events. Mauled to death by the family dog that Paul Kirkland had locked in the kitchen during his and McCulloch's visit.

'Is McCulloch okay?' said Hussein.

Logan pulled the Land Rover through the snow at the crest of the hill by the handful of massive barn conversions and farmhouses. 'I think so. Murray pissed her off, that's all. Murray being Murray.'

'Time of the month, maybe.'

'Who knows? She's got a date tonight. She tell you that?'

'No. Who's the lucky guy?'

Logan shrugged. 'Don't know, but I worry about her sometimes. She's that desperate for a man she'll go out with anyone, you know.'

'Surprising, really, innit?'

'What?'

'That she's single. She's a good-looking woman.'

Logan grinned. 'You fancy her, don't you?'

'Nah, just—'

'Asif and Kelly sitting in a tree...' Logan sang.

'Fuck off.'

They laughed and it broke the tension, just for a moment. When they reached the top end of Turton Road, just before Watling Street and the big curry house on the corner, Logan pulled in behind several more Land Rovers, each manned by a detective and a crew of willing PCs. DI

Sanderson was giving out instructions to a group of officers in heavy terrain gear.

'Sir,' Logan said as they approached. The winter chill was biting hard.

'DS Logan,' Sanderson said. 'DS Hussein. All I want you guys to do is a winter walk across the valley. Spread out. You'll be joining up with a group from the local TA in Bury, who've kindly volunteered to help out with the search. You'll see them down in the valley as you go into it, down that track over there.' He pointed to a gate beside the farmland behind them, on the opposite side. 'I see you've come well prepared.'

Hussein was busy zipping himself into an overcoat and testing the two Airwave radios they'd been given.

'Luckily, it's early enough for us to get through a lot of the terrain,' Sanderson continued. 'DCI Warburton's down at Ramsbottom, where a lot of the locals are out in force.'

'Wonder if they'd be out if they knew Kurt Chadwick was now dead after trying to murder another local woman,' Logan said. 'Fucked up, eh?'

Sanderson nodded. 'You could say that.'

'Is she gonna make it, you think?'

'I'm waiting on an update. She's not out of the woods yet, but she might pull through. The bastard punctured her lung and broke a rib. But you know what stabbings are like. An inch either way could be fatal. I'm told she lost a lot of blood. Husband's on the rampage. We've got PC Donovan down there with a liaison officer. She's probably in surgery as we speak, so should have some news soon.'

'Look, sir,' Logan said. 'Tell me it's none of my business if you want, but this dark site...'

'Murray's filled me in,' he said. 'And it looks a worry, for sure, but I don't think we're at the stage yet where we can take any action, even if we find where it's being run from. There's no evidence of a connection to Caitlin Slater. If there was, well, that's a different ball game entirely. But for now, there's nothing.'

'The white van with the Rottweiler dump is the same one she got into.'

'Might've gotten into. And that's the difference, Rob. We don't know for certain.'

'But it's looking that way, isn't it? We've got half the town out looking for her and she might just be holed up somewhere. Being held against her will, something like that.'

Sanderson nodded. 'I can see your concern. And I share it. I really do. But we have to—'

'This seems like a waste of resources, if you ask me,' Logan said. He waved his arm at the vast expanse around them. 'It's like a needle in a haystack, sir. I mean, look at it out there.'

Sanderson sighed, let his head drop a little. 'It's a challenge, I know. But it might bring us something, anything to get us closer to where we want to be. We have until darkness falls, about four o'clock this afternoon, to get a result, even if that's just a piece of clothing or something. We've got to be seen to be doing something, Rob. No one said this was gonna be easy.'

'Seen to be doing something?' Hussein said. 'So this is all a public relations exercise?'

'I never said that, Asif.'

'Something to keep the community happy? Make us look good?'

'It's not like that,' Sanderson said. 'Though I appreciate how it might look. It's not a futile exercise. I'm sure you understand. Now, a quick briefing. The marine unit are down at the Irwell in Bury and they'll make their way up the river, throughout the day. They've got sonar out and all sorts. The fire service are helping at the river, too, especially with the conditions. Some of it's iced over.'

'Not surprising,' Logan said.

'So, it's dangerous. I'm sure you agree.'

There was a rumble overhead and Logan looked up to see a helicopter search unit flying low, its rotor blades whizzing.

'Helicopter, as well,' Hussein said. 'I'm surprised all of this was signed off. '

'Your cynicism knows no bounds, Asif,' Sanderson said. 'But, as I was saying, the local TA will be taking on Holcombe Moor and the woodland around it. The local community, all the volunteers, will be in Redisher Woods and anywhere else they want to look. Back gardens, sheds, that kind of thing.'

Logan nodded. 'Murray said there'd be a forensic search of Chadwick's house. That true?'

'Happening as we speak,' Sanderson said. 'If it brings anything up, I'll let you know. In the meantime, now that we have light, it's time to get to work. There'll be hot drinks, and pie and peas provided this afternoon. We got a local caterer to sort that for us. Don't say we don't do anything for you. I'll see you both later.'

SEVENTEEN

They trudged through the snow a hundred metres apart. Logan reckoned they would find a big fat nothing and end up with frostbite if they weren't careful. The scene before them was beautiful, without a doubt. But the landscape was wild and rugged and not without its risks. It wouldn't take much for someone to drop off a small ledge or twist their ankle in a rabbit hole.

He looked out to his left, where twenty-odd territorial army guys were scanning the ground, stretched out in a line across several hundred feet. Hussein was to his right, looking like he was out for a Sunday afternoon stroll.

Already, Logan's feet were frozen, like blocks of ice. He thought about McCulloch, who was probably feeling a bit embarrassed by this morning's little exchange with Murray. He took his phone out and dialled her up.

'Hey,' she said.

'You okay? Murray can be a bit of a dick, can't he?'

'God, he's such a wanker at times, eh?'

'He said if it was up to him he'd have had you on the payroll without question.'

'I know. He's just a bloody jobsworth. Daft wee arse too scared to bend a rule. No wonder he's a bloody DI, eh?'

'You okay, though?'

'Of course I am. How's it going out there?'

Logan detected a croak in her voice but didn't say anything. 'You know what we expected. Not much happening, to be honest with you. But it's early yet. You still going out tonight?'

'You're damn right I am.'

'It'll be bloody freezing. You must be mad.'

'It'll be warm in the pub, Rob.'

'There'll be no one out. Have you seen the forecast?'

She paused. 'Aye, but the town centre's in good shape. Besides, I can't cancel now. Mark's all up for it. I like that about him.'

'Mark?'

'The guy I'm meeting. He's pretty fit, if I'm honest with you.'

'Spare me, please.'

'Right up my street, you know.'

'Jesus...'

She laughed. 'Anyway, don't forget. You're on duty tonight, aren't you? If you let me know where you are, I'll bring you a nice hot coffee.'

'There'll be no need. I think I'm just gonna hang around at the bus station. I can nick a brew or two from the bloody TfGM office.'

'But you know what those drunkards are like, Rob. You'll probably have your work cut out.'

'Yeah, but it's the post-Christmas lull, isn't it? I'm betting I'll have nowt to do all night. Anyway, you heard about Kurt Chadwick?'

'No. He been in the station again?'

He told her all about the events of last night, at least everything he knew. About how Lisa Kirkland was clinging on, about how her dog had mauled Chadwick so violently.

'You know, I kind of feel sorry for him,' she said. 'Despite what he's done. He's obviously been through the mill mentally.'

'Alcohol's probably been a big part of it, too. His car's been seized and his property's undergoing analysis. I guess we'll find out more as the days go on.'

'How could we miss this, Rob?'

'I don't know. It's like Kayleigh Matheson all over again. Failings all round. I guess heads may roll.'

'It's not as if he had to be looked after twenty-four-seven, though, eh? Not as if he was on suicide watch.'

'No, but still. He'd been in the station causing grief, pissed up. That should've been a warning sign. Now an innocent woman is fighting for her life.'

'It's a bit of an extreme reaction, eh?'

Logan pondered for a moment. 'Maybe we were wrong about him. Maybe he really was capable of murder. Well, we *were* wrong. That's a given. Anyway, listen. Enjoy your day off. And do me a favour. Send me a text later tonight. Or give me a quick call, just to let me know you're okay.'

'God, you sound like my Dad.'

Logan didn't let on that he sometimes felt like it. 'Have a good night.'

'I will. And any updates, you know where I am.'

He hung up and dug around for his police-issue mittens and fumbled to get them on. He looked out across the valley, clouds off vapour blowing into the freezing air, the sky clear but probably not for long.

His Airwave radio buzzed and crackled. He could hear DCI Warburton on the other end, giving out instructions to anyone who would listen. It was early days, but it seemed like the search party had kicked off without much fuss. It seemed organised enough. And maybe it would achieve something other than a few hundred freezing pairs of feet.

He got his head down and marched on, scanning the ground for anything that caught his eye.

But it was a red pick-up truck he saw instead, driving along Turton Road and down into Tottington. He watched it fade away and disappear behind the hedges.

AT ALMOST TWO hours into the search, Hussein gravitated closer. Logan couldn't blame him.

'What did I say about this being pointless?'

'I know,' Logan said. 'You're not wrong. Look, we'll walk down to that bloody golf course in Greenmount and come out at Holcombe Road. Sanderson said there's pie and peas, and a hot drink for us this afternoon. I think we can take a short break near lunchtime and get something. Come to think of it, I've had nothing all day.'

'Good. I'm bloody starved. Bet it's not *halal*, though.'

'Like you give a fuck. Come on.'

They walked on through the valley, taking it slow. Out to the west, the army volunteers seemed right up for it, shouting instructions to each other. Logan couldn't make out what they were saying, and he didn't care. As far as he was concerned, Caitlin Slater wasn't here and wouldn't be found. He couldn't explain it or put his finger on why he felt it, but he felt it all the same. He was convinced this was a pointless exercise.

His Airwave buzzed again.

'Logan, you receiving?'

It was Murray. Logan pressed the talk button and Hussein listened in. 'Receiving, sir.'

'How are you getting on?'

'Bloody freezing is the main gist of it, sir. If I'm honest, I can't see where this is taking us.'

'Well, I just wanted to let you know a few things. I've just heard from the liaison officer down at the MRI. Lisa Kirkland's out of surgery and is stable. All the signs are good, and we think she'll pull through. Looks like the dog's a hero. Might even make the *Bury Times*.'

'That's good. I'm glad to hear it.'

'The other thing is that CCTV from inside the Hare & Hounds has been looked at from the night in question and it checks out. I'm told there's a still image of a male in the same shot as Caitlin Slater. Here's the important bit. He was also seen getting into a white van that was parked up on Lumb Carr Road.'

'You're kidding me? What, the same white van?'

'Hard to say right now. Though when I get back to HQ, guess what I'm doing? Don't forget, though, that you're on the graveyard shift tonight. I won't say anything if you need to sneak off for a little kip this afternoon.'

'Hardly,' he said. 'Is that it, then?'

'Actually, no. There's something else. You'll probably like this. It looks like it's all over, bar the shouting. The marine unit have found a body. It's a woman.'

'Fuck off... Really?'

'River Irwell. Up in Rammy, near the train station. So, all of this wasn't a waste of bloody time after all. Now, I'll meet you down at the old school in Greenmount in half an hour. There's a load of pie and peas that will not be going to waste.'

Logan took a moment to think. A body. A woman.

Caitlin?

So, that was, it then. Whatever had happened to her between the party and the walk home was now somewhat irrelevant. She was gone, after all. A part of him hoped it wasn't true, that he'd end up finding her alive somewhere. In a state but alive. But maybe she'd been dead all week. Maybe it had all been quite straightforward in the end. Maybe there could now be closure, of a sort. There was still a crime to solve, a murder to investigate. But they had a body, finally.

It was over.

He felt relieved, yet sad. For her, for Kurt Chadwick. Sometimes tragedies came in twos and threes. Sometimes people were dealt a hand that would lead to the ultimate ending before their time.

Sometimes life wasn't fair.

And neither was death.

HUSSEIN LED the way to the school building, looking hungry. Logan followed into the warmth and spotted Murray in the far corner, devouring a plate of food. There was a crowd gathering, the atmosphere subdued. Word had gotten round about the discovery of the body in the river, and there was a lot of talk about the media, both press and TV, turning up at the scene.

'Logan,' Murray said, between mouthfuls. 'Hussein. The body's already been retrieved. Makes no sense to prolong it. We don't want the community getting unnecessarily alarmed. We're working on identification but it's nailed on it's her. The SOCO boys are on site with a tent. Shouldn't be long now. Anyway, go and get yourself something to eat. It's bloody outstanding.'

Logan went over to the counter by the kitchen and

found a pretty-looking woman serving up something that looked quite divine. 'I'll have some pie, if that's all right.'

'You want peas and gravy with that?'

'Please. And a cup of tea would be good.'

She got busy portioning it up and Logan got a bit distracted by her heavenly rack. He quickly snapped himself back to reality when she offered him a plate with a mountain of pie on it. He left her to the queue and took the food and tea away, knowing it would probably be the last thing he ate until late tonight.

The old school had been sanctioned as a hub for the search operation. There was another one at a pub in Hawkshaw, though Logan was thankful he hadn't been drawn to that one. The temptation of a pint, especially after the news of a body and the promise of a conclusion, would no doubt prove too much.

'So there she was, apparently,' Murray said, mid-swallow. Logan saw his plate was almost clean. 'Face down in the water, fully clothed.'

'Not a suicide?' Logan said. 'After all this?'

Murray shook his head. 'Too early to say right now. We'll need to look further into her mental state. Talk to people who knew her, that kind of thing. As far as I'm aware, we don't know much else.'

Logan nodded, then ate, feeling a little bit empty. Perhaps this wasn't just the end of a life, or the investigation, but also the end of his police career. He'd been thinking about it. About calling it a day once and for all, and now seemed the perfect time. He'd considered mentioning it to Murray and, looking at him now, he'd figured it wasn't quite the right time. But that conversation was coming, for sure.

'Listen, sir,' he said, 'I'm gonna head back. I think I'll take you up on that offer and duck away somewhere for a little sleep.'

'You can take yourself home for a bit if you want?'

'Nah,' he said. 'I'll never come back out again, especially in this weather. Where's Asif gone now?'

'He's gone back outside to wait for the Land Rover. I got a lowly PC to bring it down for you. I expect he'll give you a shout when it's here.'

A moment later, Hussein called Logan from over near the door and dangled the keys. It looked like he was about to take the wheel, which made Logan nervous. From this point, the only operation Logan would be conducting was Operation Career Change.

IT WAS PUSHING two o'clock by the time they got back to HQ. Hussein parked the Land Rover up in the undercroft and they made their way inside.

'So,' Hussein said. 'She probably had enough and did herself in. That's my feeling.'

'We don't know that for certain,' Logan said.

'Nah, but it looks like it. Makes you wonder what was going on at home.'

'Yeah, well it's easy to speculate after the fact, isn't it? Whatever happened, the poor girl's life ended in tragic circumstances. I think that's enough for us.'

'Doesn't explain all that stuff with the dark site, though,' he said. 'Or the fact she got in that van.'

'Murray would say there's no certainty it was the same van. He probably doesn't care either way now. For him it'll be case closed, move onto the next one.'

'He say when we can expect an ID?'

Logan shook his head as they climbed the steps up into

the station. 'I think they'll want something pretty quickly. Wouldn't surprise me if they had Dr Graham making her way in as we speak. Seems like it's just a formality now.'

Inside, the incident room was busy. There were plenty of coppers who had started to come back from the search. Logan was torn between making himself a standard coffee or disappearing to the canteen for a long nap. Maybe he should save it for later, when he'd need it to perk him up for the night duty with the StreetSafe team. He watched Hussein disappear to his terminal to work on another case he'd been handling, then went back downstairs to find Becky Mortimer to see if she had any news on the dark site.

Mortimer was busy with her head stuck in a book when he walked in. She looked up over her glasses like a librarian when she realised he hadn't knocked.

'Just checking in,' Logan said. 'See if you've managed to spot anything.'

'It's like watching paint dry,' she said, putting the book down. 'So boring. But then I suppose that's a good thing, eh? All seems a little bit pointless now Caitlin has been found.'

'She still needs a definite ID,' Logan said. 'I expect it'll happen quickly. As soon as they bring her in, I reckon.'

'So, it must be case closed for you lot then?'

'Yeah, but we still have the mutilated animals. And this site was found through another site, which I only discovered because of a mutilated white rabbit. A pretty sad way of getting your kicks.'

'Takes all sorts.'

Logan nodded. 'Listen, I could do with speaking to Chris Kearney. Don't suppose you've seen him, have you?'

She shook her head. 'Might be his day off?'

'No, I think he's supposed to be hanging around so he can trace where the dark site's being run from.'

'I believe it's based in Bury somewhere.'

'I know, but that's the million-dollar question. Where exactly?'

'Well, don't ask me, I wouldn't know where to start.'

Logan eyed several balls of wool sitting on the couch beside her. 'What's all this?'

She followed his eye and laughed. 'Thought I might as well take up knitting. I've got to do something to occupy my time. I've gotten into making woolly hats. I'll have to do you one. I reckon a rainbow one will look good on you.'

Logan smiled politely. 'I'd rather have a scarf.'

'Oh, yes! Like Harry Potter. I'll do you one of those...'

'I was only joking, really.'

'No, I'll do you one. Call it a late Christmas present.'

Logan left and asked her to update him immediately if anything happened on the live cam.

Then he went to the canteen for a much-needed sleep.

HE WOKE around half-six to Dave Murray shaking him.

'Time to get your stab vest on,' Murray said. 'It's Street-Safe time.'

'Fuck...'

'Now, don't be like that, Rob. And like I said, it won't go unnoticed that you've stepped in at such short notice. Really good of you.'

He sat up and shook himself from a dream about an empty town square. 'Thanks to you. Has the woman's body been identified yet?'

'I'm told Dr Graham is conducting an autopsy within the hour. So we should know by close of play tonight.'

'Keep me updated.'

Logan got to his feet, which felt numb, and psyched

himself up to move downstairs and out to the StreetSafe unit: a van that had been painted up in a punter-friendly fashion. Top brass felt it was important to strip away barriers between policing and the community. As a small part of this effort, a more community-focussed and friendly vehicle was stationed in the same spot every weekend on Silver Street in the town centre. The StreetSafe team was really just a bunch of night-shift PCs who took turns on a rota basis. They were always joined by a duty DS and usually shared the evening with a couple of local paramedics who were stationed nearby.

Tonight, Logan was that duty DS. What fun.

'The good news,' Murray said, 'is DS Carmichael's wife gave birth about an hour ago. A girl. Mother and baby are doing just fine.'

'And the bad news?'

'It's snowing again. Come on now. They're waiting for you.'

EIGHTEEN

McCulloch couldn't decide between the little black dress or the jeans and top. In the end she'd decided it was way too cold for the little black dress, even though it was a thick woollen thing, and went for the jeans and a top. She slung a fancy overcoat on and felt a thousand times better for it. She'd also gone for the smart leather boots over the casual shoes, which added a bit more height. She'd pushed her boobs up with a magic bra and made her lips look perfect.

There'd been a little doubt about whether she was doing the right thing. She deserved a night out, but she questioned if it would've been wiser to go for a coffee or something first. Maybe a walk around the lake, that kind of thing, instead of a full-on drink in a bar.

'You're a daft wee girl, Kel,' she said to herself in the mirror. 'But he's worth it. And you're worth it.'

She'd asked her friends, Jen and Cassie, if they could hang around in a nearby pub, just in case things went tits-up and she needed a quick escape, but Jen had already made plans and Cassie was working lates. It was no biggie.

She didn't anticipate things being that bad. She'd been on plenty of shit dates before and she'd probably have a few more in the future, that was what the dating game was all about.

The phone rang. She left her dressing table, thinking it was the Uber she'd ordered ten minutes ago, but then clocked it was Logan.

'God, what the fuck do you want now?'

'And a good evening to you, too,' he said. 'Just checking in to let you know the news.'

'Let me guess. Murray swallowed a doughnut and it's choked him to death?'

'They found a body. Well, the marine unit did. We're waiting on ID, but it looks like it's her.'

'What, Caitlin Slater?'

'Yeah. So. That's it. Back to the boring stuff from now on.'

'Our comfort zone.'

'Well, not necessarily. I'm still looking at knocking it on the head. This shit's taken it out of me.'

She peeked through the curtains and saw her Uber had pulled up. Got a ping on her phone to confirm it. 'I know the feeling. Look, I'll fire a text over to you later, like we agreed. But don't go bothering me all night like an overprotective father. I'm just going on a date, that's all.' She left the flat and headed down the stairs to the car.

'Okay, well I'll leave you to it. And spare a thought for me out with this lot. I think I'll need a stiff drink when I get home.'

She hung up. So, that was it. Caitlin Slater dead. Kurt Chadwick dead. Some people just weren't meant for this world. She checked the time on her phone: almost quarter past seven. She was set to meet Mark at half past. She had to admit, she was a tad nervous, and she took that as a good sign.

DARREN LIT UP and paced the kitchen, peering out into the night. The snow had eased a bit but was expected to come down heavy again by ten o'clock. He'd planned that by that time, she'd be well on her way to being drunk. If he could persuade her to take him back to hers, all the better. Nevertheless, there were one or two back alleys he knew around town that would be easy enough to coax her down. He also had a few pills tucked away should he need them. Even half of one would be enough to knock her for six.

He'd made a considerable effort to dress well for the occasion. Understated, but cool. Not over-dressed. He didn't want to look like he was going out for a night at the fucking opera or something, but he did want to look decent enough for a bar and a good restaurant, if it came to it.

He was looking forward to it. Looking forward to spicing things up a bit. Looking forward to putting on the charm. Looking forward to playing a few games. And looking forward to being with a woman for a change.

'You ready for this, then?'

He turned to Sam. 'Yeah. You?'

'I'm gonna go get her sorted soon,' he said. 'I could really do with a hand, but I guess you've got better things to do.'

'Too right I have,' he said. 'I've gotta make a good impression if I'm gonna get what I want out of tonight.'

'Which is?'

'Well what do you think?'

Sam shrugged. 'I can guess.'

'You're just jealous,' he said, laughing. 'Admit it. Here's me out on the town with a copper and she hasn't got a fucking clue. I suppose you'll just have to make do with old Colin down there. Won't that be fun?'

'I've loaded the shotgun,' he said. 'Everything's ready for tomorrow. I'll bring her up tonight and take her down to the dungeon. The old cunt will be wanking himself silly over it all.'

'Please...'

Sam cracked open a cold beer. 'I might as well, if you are.'

'Don't wait up.'

'You will let us know what's happening, won't you? If you manage to get your end away with her, make sure you're back in the morning.'

Darren gripped Sam by the chin and kissed him on his lips. Ran a finger down his shirt. 'Don't be jealous. You'll get your turn soon enough.'

Sam watched him leave the house by the kitchen door. Darren got in the pick-up and started the engine, the headlights illuminating the fields beyond, and slowly drove away from the farm.

There was something about tonight. Sam hadn't been this excited in a long time.

He drank and smoked in the kitchen, occasionally hearing Colin moving around downstairs. The house was empty now, and creepy as fuck. He would give it half an hour before he went to fetch her. Pretty soon, she'd be going down to join the rest of the bodies.

It was going to be magic.

PC BLACKFORD HANDED Logan a hot coffee and a cheeseburger. He nudged over and sat in the passenger seat.

Logan ate hungrily and rested the coffee, black and bitter, in the holder on the dashboard.

'I don't understand how anyone can be out in this,' Blackford said. 'I mean, it looks nice and all that, but fucking hell, talk about cold. Is this really the worst winter we've ever had?'

'Feels like it, doesn't it?'

Logan kept an eye on WPC Starling, who was busy nailing her third smoke of the evening in front of the van, shivering. 'Give me a glass of whisky and a roaring fire. That's me these days. Seems like all the pubs have shut now, anyway. It's not like when I was younger.'

'When I was a lad,' Blackford said, mocking.

'Yeah, yeah. But it's not. Most people can't afford a night out these days, anyway. Especially with kids.'

'God, I'm never having kids.'

Logan looked at him. 'How old are you, Joey?'

'Twenty-five.'

'Plenty of time yet.'

They sat and ate while they watched the punters out on the streets, some moving from bar to bar in groups of five or six. Couples out on dates, gangs of drunken teenage girls pretending to be older than they really were. Logan had once done the same thing, long before he became a copper, and long before he met Vic. It seemed a different world away now.

'You always wanted to be a detective?' Blackford said.

Logan almost laughed. 'Me? God, no.'

'So why, then?'

'It seemed a good idea at the time. Now it doesn't really do it for me. It's much worse than I thought it was and not at all like I thought it'd be. Why? You fancy it?'

'One day, maybe. If I'm good enough.'

'You don't have to be good,' Logan said. 'You just have to be a bit mad.'

But Joey Blackford wasn't listening. He was far too busy devouring his fried chicken.

Logan finished his cheeseburger and was about to dive into the coffee when his phone rang. It was Murray, probably phoning to take the piss about having his feet up with a beer in front of the telly.

'Yeah?'

There was a massive sigh on the other end. 'An update. I've just had DCI Warburton on the phone. Dr Graham's carried out an autopsy and we have an ID. It's not Caitlin Slater.'

Logan felt a chill fall into his chest. 'What you mean?'

'I mean it's not Caitlin Slater, Rob. This poor woman's only been dead twenty-four hours, if that.'

'Well, if it's not her, who is it?'

'It's Louise McDonagh. It's her friend she went to the party with, Rob. Can this get any more fucked up?'

'What? McDonagh? But we only spoke to her yesterday. Really? Are you sure?'

'Of course I'm bloody sure. She'd cut her wrists. Probably taken some drugs or something to help her along the way. Dr Graham says she'll have to send off for a toxicology report. As far as I'm aware, there are no relatives living nearby. We'll have to carry out a full forensic search of her property as well.'

'Jesus.'

'Ain't it just wonderful?'

Louise McDonagh, dead. Did she seem suicidal when they called round to her house? Not really. A little bit on edge, but not suicidal. Maybe it had been an impulse thing, but it would have to be a pretty strong impulse to do that.

'So, what now?'

'We're back where we were,' Murray said. 'Caitlin's still missing, presumed dead, and we have to bloody find her. Though now her boyfriend's gone, it's hardly a priority to get her back.'

'You heard from Chris Kearney? Any location for the dark site?'

'I've not heard from him but that doesn't mean he isn't on it. You know what these bloody computer geeks are like. He's probably deep into some video game as we speak. Anyway, that's that. How is StreetSafe?'

'Shit and cold.'

'Well, keep up the good work. If I hear anything else, I'll be in touch.'

SHE'D BEEN DREAMING about Kurt. He was in a field, lost in the snow, a blizzard swirling around him and the wind howling hard. She called out to him, trying desperately to reach him, but every time she thought she was getting close, he was pushed further away from her. When she looked down to see why her legs weren't working, she saw they were naked and pale white, covered in goosebumps.

She was woken by a thick finger that reeked of nicotine. It was tracing a line across her cheek. She wanted to speak, to say a big fuck-you to her captor, but she simply didn't have the energy for any of that.

He'd brought something into the barn with him. It was too dark to tell for sure, even with his bloody torch that he'd put down on the cold hard floor, but she instinctively knew it was something for her.

'I'm gonna unlock all this now,' he said. A dirty, foul voice. 'Take you down to him. It won't be long now, I promise. I know

you've had to put up with a lot but that's just the way it is. And when it's over, you'll go someplace much better than here. Won't that be worth it?'

Fuck you...

He jangled those bloody keys as the freezing air ran into the barn. She could see that blizzard blowing outside and wondered if she was still trapped in the dream. Maybe Kurt was out there? Maybe he'd really come for her?

She felt the clasp around her ankle loosen and fall away. Then the chain around her waist slid off her, too. Lying there, unable to move, all she wanted was to be somewhere far away. And if that meant them taking her life, so be it.

He pulled her up and she slumped. So weak.

He slung a blanket over her and grabbed her by the waist, moving her into a wheelchair, then grabbed her feet and put them on the supports.

'I'm taking you away from here now. It has to be this way. I promise I'll make it easy for you. Nothing will hurt you. Shhh.'

Fuck you...

'I'll get you warmed right up. Won't take long. And don't even think of running. You'd never find your way out there in this snow. It's way too dark, as well. You really wouldn't stand a chance.'

He wheeled her out towards the barn doors. As she got closer to the air outside, her jaws chattered hard. When the air finally hit her, she sucked in, gasping. She hoped and prayed that breathing in that fresh, cold air would be her very last action. And she went on breathing it in as he pushed her along towards the house, imagining an angel flying out of the sky to come and carry her away.

. . .

INSIDE, it smelt of burning wood and alcohol, mixed with a musty odour that reminded her of old men and dried mud. It was a strange feeling to be in a different place. Her perspective had changed so dramatically, she felt detached from her body.

He had wheeled her into a large living room, the furniture covered in unwashed clothes, with dirty plates scattered around. A half-empty bottle of brandy sat on the mantelpiece and she remembered how she loved brandy in front of the fire. She was in front of the fire now, thawing out and feeling half-dead. She remembered how that was her plan when she got home from the party: to sit in front of the fire with a warm brandy and wait for Kurt to get home.

Oh, how she wished she'd just gotten a taxi instead of walking. How she wished she hadn't gone to that bloody party at all. She sat there in that wheelchair while he moved around. Sat and watched the flames flicker and felt the heat tear into her.

Her phone. Her bag.

What the hell had happened to those?

She darted her eyes about the room, looking for any sign of her things hanging around. Looked out of the big window to her right for any sign of her knight in shining armour.

And then she heard music.

NINETEEN

McCulloch ordered a large Malbec. Part of her thought fuck it, let's just get a bottle, but she knew that would be reckless at this early stage. The plan: a few drinks followed by an impromptu meal. There was a decent Italian just around the corner.

She had to admit it. She was so nervous. She stood at the bar, looking like a total lemon, drinking the wine much quicker than she'd have liked, and was trying and failing to look relaxed and chilled, like she did this stuff all the time.

But then she thought that maybe he was as nervous as she was and that calmed her down for a minute.

She realised why she was so nervous. It was because she placed so much importance on it. Was she really that desperate for a man? Love and sex, sure. Companionship, yes. Friendship, of course. All of these things. She wanted children and time was running right out the door.

And she wanted more. Someone to look after her, someone to protect her. Old fashioned things, but things she valued. Yeah, she could look after herself. Yeah, she could probably survive on her own, no problem. But she didn't want to and that was the difference. In short, she just didn't want to stay alone and single for the rest of her sodding life.

She wanted a man.

She turned and scanned the bar. It was a small place. She'd chosen it well. It was close enough to Silver Street, the centre of the action, for her not to feel too wary. It was close enough to see lots of other people, so she wouldn't feel isolated if she didn't like him.

Just as she was about to drain the glass, in he walked. He was tall but not too tall. Dark and handsome with rugged features and quite well dressed, though she cringed at the silk shirt. She suddenly felt a flush of anxiety.

Bloody hell. This was it.

First impressions? He wasn't exactly what she'd hoped for, but then that was okay. She watched him walk towards her and break out in a grin and that just took away all the anxiety in one go.

'Is it Kel?'

'That's me. You must be Mark, eh?'

He kissed her on the cheek. He felt warm.

'Great to meet you. You look amazing.'

She blushed. 'Thanks. Shall we...?'

'Please tell me you're drinking Malbec.'

'How did you know?'

'How about a bottle? My shout.'

He led her to the bar by the elbow.

'AND THAT'S when I decided to become a gardener. I always really enjoyed doing Betty's front garden. When she died, I realised I missed her. And I missed her garden.'

'Aw, that's so sweet.'

Darren smiled. 'Fancy another?'

'Another bottle?'

'Or something else. Whatever you think.'

She thought about this for a moment. Was this worth pursuing? Maybe. He was okay. Not amazing, but she quite liked him. She didn't *fancy* him, though, and that was the deal-breaker for her. Funny how someone can look so different from their profile photos. She wondered if he was even the same guy.

Another bottle would get her tipsy—a bit too tipsy—and she never liked not being in control on first dates. Maybe now was a good time for a quick call with Rob. And she needed to pee.

'I'm just gonna nip to the ladies. I'll have a think while I'm in there.'

'Hey, maybe a cocktail?'

Not a great idea, she thought. She pulled a face to let him know she wasn't up for that. 'Nah. But I am hungry, if you fancy something to eat?'

'Yeah, sounds good. I think they do food in here.'

'I'll be back in a minute.'

The ladies were quiet, which was just as well. She locked the cubicle and did her business while she dialled up Logan.

'Go on, then,' he said. 'How's it going?'

'Not too bad,' she said. 'Though I'm not so sure about him now I've seen him close up. And he smokes. I can smell it on his clothes.'

'That's not you, Kel.'

'No. And he's full of all these stories, you know. I'm not sure I believe him.'

'So, he's bit of a bullshitter.'

'I never said that, eh?'

'What's he after? A quick shag and a curry?'

She tutted. 'Rob... There's absolutely no chance of that, I can assure you.'

'Not with him at least.'

'Not with anyone. Especially on a first date. God, what do you take me for? Anyway, how's StreetSafe? You keeping busy?'

'Nothing happening other than Joey and Rachel arguing about whose turn it is to go get us a brew.'

'Oh, shit. I said I'd bring you a coffee, didn't I?'

'Nah, don't worry. I've got my little underlings to fetch and carry instead.'

Logan thought about telling her of Louise McDonagh, then realised it might ruin her night, so steered clear.

'Right, well,' she said. 'I'd better get back to him. Listen, I might call it a night by ten if he starts boring me.'

'Sounds like you're not feeling it.'

'Is it that obvious?'

'Just be safe. Trust your instincts. We'll be out here until midnight if you want to escape. You know where we are.'

'Aye-aye, Captain. I'll give it an hour or so. Will let you know.'

When she finished peeing, she checked her face, then the time. Almost nine. They'd drank that bottle pretty quickly. She really fancied a few more but wasn't entirely sure about spending the evening with him.

But she'd give him a chance. It was only fair.

THEY'D DECIDED to stay in the bar, moving to a booth over by the back wall. The place offered tapas, Greek dishes, steaks and burgers, a bit of a mixed bag. She went for a grilled halloumi salad with couscous while he ordered a messy burger that was as big as her head.

It put her off him immediately.

God, the dirty bastard was shovelling it in like his fucking life depended on it and talking with his mouth full.

'And so I left,' he said, chewing as he spoke. 'She's probably still in Newcastle.'

Another bullshit story about how his ex had poisoned his daughter's mind and turned her against him.

'So, have you seen your daughter recently?'

He shook his head. 'Donna won't let me. She's a real bitch.' He took a long drink on his beer and wiped his mouth with the back of his hand instead of the napkin in front of him. A pet hate.

'Shame.'

'So, what about you, then? You been single for long?'

Too long, she thought.

She shrugged. 'A few years. I'm used to it now.'

'But you're looking for someone, right? Otherwise you wouldn't be here, yeah? You know what those dating sites are like. I bet you've been on a few dates recently.'

'Not really. Trying to find the right bloke, eh?'

He seemed to be looking right through her, which gave her the creeps.

'You're a very good-looking woman, Kel,' he said. 'I'm not normally this forward but... well, I really fancy you, I've got to say, and I just wanted to tell you that.'

'Right.' God, no. How cringey.

He leaned in to kiss her and she backed off quickly.

'What's up?'

'Nothing, I just. I'm just not feeling that.'

He grabbed her wrist tight, gripping with his thumb and forefinger.

'Get off me.'

'You know you want it,' he said, spittle flying out between his gritted teeth. 'Don't be a tease.'

She wrestled her arm away and stood up from the table. 'Get the fuck off me!'

'Sit down. You're making a scene.'

'Fuck off.'

She dragged on her coat and went straight for the door, her eyes scanning the small crowd of people to see if anyone had seen what he'd tried to do. But there were so many people in deep conversations.

'Wait!' he called.

She ran through the door and out into the cold, a little disoriented and blinded by the falling snow.

'I said, fucking wait!'

Her mind had gone blank, and she tried to remember where Logan and the StreetSafe team were.

He grabbed her from behind, pulled her into a side street. Covered her mouth and nose with his thick, pudgy hand. She tried to shin him with the heel of her boot, but he shoved a knee into the small of her back and she yelped in pain. She tried to call out, but all she could manage was a muffle.

He pulled her into an alley behind the art gallery, of all places, and pushed her up against the wall.

Punched her.

Put his hand where he shouldn't and fumbled with her fucking zip.

Bit her neck and grabbed hard at her breasts.

She brought a knee right up into his bollocks, hard, and stamped on his toe with her heel.

It was enough to let her break away and run.

God, how could she have been so bloody stupid?

It seemed like the world was now empty of anyone who

could help her. She called out. Screamed for someone, anyone, thought about ducking into the nearest pub.

'Help!'

She just kept running, blinded by the snow, skidding through the pavements, slipping on the ice. She went over and smashed onto her back, which took the wind out of her and almost knocked her out. She quickly rolled over and came to, her clothes soaking wet, her head pounding.

She got to her feet and ran into the road. She stood out the front of the library on Silver Street, trying to spot the StreetSafe van but only hearing the noise from the nearby bars, the laughter and the shouts, the music and the...

The...

Her legs had turned to jelly.

Her head spun and she went dizzy.

The fucker had spiked her drink. She turned to see a Toyota pick-up tearing towards her, its headlights on full beam and blinding. She jumped to her left with everything she had but it wasn't enough. The world had gone upside down and took her leg with it.

'SIR, WHAT THE FUCK WAS THAT?'

'What was what?'

'Oh, shit,' Blackford said. The streets suddenly went from relative quiet to hysterical screaming. 'Someone's been run over.'

Blackford was at the wheel and started her up, spinning it out of the side road and down Silver Street in a matter of seconds. Logan was on his Airwave, calling for more units and the paramedics. When Blackford skidded the van to a halt, Logan dived out and saw the Toyota pick-up screeching off and away. McCulloch was lying in a heap, her right leg bent and broken.

'Aw, shit. Kel. Kel, come on. No!'

He knelt beside her. She was shaking violently but breathing. There was a nasty gash on her forehead, but it was the leg he was concerned about.

'I need more units here and a fucking ambulance, fast. It's DS McCulloch, involved in a knockdown. Suspect has left the scene at speed in a red Toyota pick-up. I need all units in pursuit. It's travelled east onto Jubilee Way. I repeat, I need all available units in pursuit of a red Toyota pick-up truck heading east on Jubilee Way. DS Kel McCulloch is down in a hit and run!'

'Fuck!' Blackford paced up and down with his head in his hands while Starling tried to administer first aid. It was pointless. Her leg was a mess.

You bastard. You bastard. You bastard.

An ambulance screamed into the road and came to a stop. Two paramedics jumped out and the coppers asked the crowd of drunks to step the fuck back. Logan was out of breath, trying to piece shit together in his mind. Starling handed him McCulloch's phone and he pocketed it without thinking.

'Jesus, Kel. You know how to pick 'em.' He got down beside her. 'Kel, can you hear me? Kel, it's Rob. Can you hear me, love? Don't fade out on me now, love. Kel!'

She blinked, then her lights went out.

TWENTY

It was almost midnight when they parked the StreetSafe van up in the undercroft. Logan had called Vic, desperate to talk to her, and had spoken at length about what he'd just witnessed. She said she'd wait up for him and there was nothing else he could do but leave the medics to it.

He'd informed Murray, who got in a taxi straight to Fairfield Hospital, and assured Logan he would update as soon as he knew more.

A search unit helicopter—probably the same one from this morning—had spent the remaining hours of the night searching for the Toyota. It was found abandoned and set alight on a dark country lane in Affetside. Several units went up there, including a fire engine, and the Toyota's number plate identified the owner as one Darren Harris of Northolt Farm, Ainsworth.

It was the same farm Logan suspected had been involved in Caitlin Slater's disappearance. The same farm he'd found on Google Earth. The same farm he'd looked at with McCulloch the day before. The same farm where they'd heard the gunshots. The same farm where the bird skulls sat in the windowsill.

'You okay?'

Back at HQ, DS Becky Mortimer had retrieved a blanket from her comfort couch in the CCTV room and wrapped it around Logan's shoulders.

'Not really,' he said. 'If anything, I'm tired. Shattered.'

'She's gonna be okay, Rob. You know that, don't you?'

'Her leg was a mess. She's lost a lot of blood. I tell you, Bex, if I ever get my hands on the bastard, I swear I'm gonna fucking murder him.'

'Sir?'

Logan looked up. It was PC Joey Blackford. 'Yeah?'

'I can give you a lift home. I'm heading that way anyway. It's no trouble.'

Logan's car was parked outside but he was in no fit state to drive himself. For one thing, he'd be too sleepy to keep his hands on the wheel. 'If you don't mind, yeah.'

They left the canteen and DS Becky Mortimer to her observations. There was nothing more anyone could do about McCulloch now. None of it was anybody's fault.

As Blackford drove them home in his beat-up Fiesta, the windows open to keep the windscreen from steaming up, Logan let his head lean out, where the air was fresh and freezing.

The snow on his face felt good.

HE GOT BACK HOME AROUND 1am. Vic was waiting for him by the wood burner with a large whisky. He took it and drank, his hands shaking and chapped from the cold. It burned his throat but in a good way. He crashed into the couch and closed his eyes, figuring they'd open when they were ready.

'Come to bed now, babe. You've had a really long day.'

He forced his eyes open and drained the rest of the whisky, then followed her up to fall into oblivion.

SATURDAY MORNING BROUGHT GREY CLOUDS, heavy with another forecast downpour. Logan groggily sat in the living room and nursed a tea with toast. Izzy hopped between cushions she'd slung onto the floor and his head pounded, with the stresses of last night still fresh.

He checked his phone. There had been several missed calls. Two from Murray and one from Becky Mortimer. He called Murray first.

'Logan,' he said. 'How are you feeling?'

'Tired. How is she?'

'She's stable and she'll live,' he said. 'That's the main thing. She had surgery in the early hours. Doctors reckon they've saved her leg, but she might have mobility problems for a good while. She's out of it right now and it's the best thing for her. She's gonna be in a good few weeks at least. Probably longer.'

'Thank God.'

'Indeed. Listen, I've been fully updated on last night's events. We'll be sending several units to make the arrest of Darren Harris a priority. He'll no doubt be charged with attempted murder, certainly manslaughter. I've got a couple of officers reviewing CCTV from the library and the bars down there to build evidence. And we'll of course be getting a statement from Kel as soon as she's able.'

'That's good,' he said. It felt like progress. But there was a nagging feeling that something was missing.

'And one other thing, Rob. I want you to take a few weeks off. You need a break, and you deserve one.'

He wasn't about to decline the offer. 'Thanks, sir.'

'Don't mention it. Right, I've been here all night. Time to head home. Phone me if you need anything else.'

But Logan could hardly think straight. He finished his tea, feeling sick to the back teeth of coffee, and waited for Becky to call again.

He fell into a daze, almost back to sleep, then snapped out of it when the phone rang again.

'Yeah?'

'You had some sleep?' Becky said.

'I have. You?'

'Yes, but not much. Okay. There's movement.'

'Come again.'

'On the live cam. The dark site. Something's happening.'

'You're kidding me.'

'I wouldn't joke about this, Rob. And it's pretty bloody disturbing. I don't know what to do.'

'Tell me what's happening, Becky.'

'There's a girl in a wheelchair. Just sat facing a wall with her face away from the camera. I can just see the back of her head, that's all.'

'Shit! Can you describe her?'

'She looks painfully thin. Like she has an eating disorder or something.'

'Listen, Becky, I need you to get hold of Chris Kearney. Tell him to call me as soon as possible. We need to know where this place is.'

'It's here, Rob. In Bury. Chris has already said he thinks it's here.'

'Yes, but *where*?'

'I don't know, I just think—'

'I'm hanging up. I need Kearney fast.'

He didn't bother showering. Just threw on some scruffs

to make do. As he was pulling his trainers on, a text message came through.

DON'T FORGET Izzy's birthday party. Invitation's in the rack on the windowsill.

FOR FUCK'S SAKE! There was absolutely no chance of that now. He watched his daughter forward-roll across the floor, oblivious to everything, and dug out the invitation so he could rip the fucking thing up.

He stared at the picture on the front: Alice in Wonderland dancing with the Cheshire Cat.

On the other side, an image of a white rabbit had been superimposed over the handwritten invitation. Logan held his breath and read it.

YOU'RE INVITED to Caitlin's party!
11th January, 1pm
Balloons! Prizes! Party Games!
Northolt Farm, Ainsworth.
Follow the white rabbit!
(Fancy dress only).

'HOLY *FUCK*.'

He picked up his phone again and called Vic.

'BABE,' he said, when she answered. 'Is there a Caitlin in Izzy's class?'

'What? Why? I'm not sure.'

'What do you mean, you're not sure? It's pretty bloody simple, love.'

'She's your daughter too, Rob.'

'Yeah, but you deal with all the school stuff, don't you? It's the name on the invitation. Can you not ask one of the other parents?'

'Give me five minutes. I'll check.'

She called back in less than two as Logan was pacing up and down the living room. 'No, love. There's no Caitlin in her class. And no one knows anything about a party.'

'Jesus...'

'What is this? What's going on?'

'Nothing. Listen, I need to go out. To work. I'll leave Izzy with Fiona over the road.'

'What? Rob!'

'There is no bloody party, Vic. The only Caitlin is Caitlin Slater.'

'DS Logan?'

'Yeah.'

Logan had dropped Izzy at Fiona's and was now running over ice back to the house, cursing himself for not driving his own bloody car back home.

'It's Chris. Chris Kearney. Look, I know you've been trying to get hold of me, but that's just it. I've been busy with this tracing thing. Thought there wasn't much point in updating you if I didn't have the right information. But now I think I do.'

'I already know,' Logan said.

'Come again?'

'I said I already know where it is.'

'How? That's impossible.'

'Good old-fashioned detective work, Chris, that's how. Do me a favour and tell everyone down there to get to Northolt Farm, fucking sharpish. And send Asif Hussein to come and get me, fast. They're gonna kill her at one o'clock on the dot.'

TWENTY ONE

Logan kind of knew it would come to this. He stood out on the street in the freezing cold, watching out for any sign of Hussein in a pool car. He paced up and down, each long second drawn out and lasting a lifetime, until the Land Rover came careering around the corner and skidded to a halt. Hussein looked hyped. Logan pulled the passenger door and jumped in.

'Stab vest,' Hussein said, indicating the back seat. 'Get it on now. We've got two tactical aid units and about six cars. Murray and Sanderson are on the way as we speak.'

They bolted away at speed, and to hell with the road. Logan fired on the sirens. The farm was ten minutes away.

'We've had reports of gunshots,' Hussein said. 'That same bloody shotgun, I reckon. Could get ugly, this.'

Logan looked out the window and up at the sky as they approached the farm. A helicopter was circling the house, low and loud.

'Ever handled a firearm?'

'No,' Logan said.

'Me neither. Let's leave that to the bloody professionals, eh?'

Logan was delighted to see the first tactical aid unit on the scene as they arrived. Hussein pulled into a lay-by and they both got out, stab vests on, each carrying a cosh. There were four armed officers ahead of them, taking up position by the back door.

Logan ducked by the wall. Checked his watch. It was 12:57. He dialled up DS Becky Mortimer. She answered almost immediately.

'I need your eyes and ears, Becky. What's happening?'

'Fuck, Rob, he's injecting her with something.'

Logan guessed it was either xylazine or ketamine, or both. 'Where is he injecting?'

'Looks like her neck.'

'Fuck. They need to get in there fast.'

There was a sound like thunder as a battering ram slammed into the back door once, twice, then a third time. The door flew off its hinges and the four armed officers ran inside. Another TAU van skidded to a halt behind them and six more operatives with machine guns belted into the property. Loud shouts and commotion followed, accompanied by a piercing scream and the unmistakable sound of the shotgun he'd heard days ago. It was followed by a hollow explosion, like an underground bomb had gone off, and a fireball ripped through the top windows.

Logan and Hussein dived for cover in the snow.

Logan passed out. When he came to, his ears were ringing. He was on his back. And when he opened his eyes to look up, all he could see was a billion flakes of snow.

Or ash.

TWENTY TWO

Caitlin Slater had been rescued and taken to hospital with a police escort. Her condition was critical, but she was alive. She could so easily have not made it at all.

She never said a word in the days following her ordeal and it was expected she wouldn't for some time. A decision had been made to not break the news of Kurt Chadwick's death until she was deemed fit and ready to hear it. But the professionals around her were all convinced she knew, anyway. In time, she would find out the truth, if she lived that long.

Logan had a feeling she would. In time, a healing would come. It may take years but Logan felt she was mentally strong enough to rebuild, even after her ordeal.

Colin and Sam Harris were killed when the firearms officers entered the property. Sam had already shot Colin in the chest and the oxygen tank he'd been dragging around exploded in the assault. He'd left the valve open in the hour prior to Caitlin's injection. No one would ever really know the reason why.

Darren had abandoned the Toyota pick-up and was currently missing and presumed on the run. A public warning announcement had been made, with the police cautioning against approaching him.

A manhunt was underway.

Northolt Farm was searched and examined in close forensic detail over several months. Sixty-two skulls, seven of which were human, were found, along with the bones of several men and women stashed in the walls of a tunnel beneath the farm. Computers and photography equipment were seized, as were over twenty personal diaries and journals of Colin's. The house and attached land was full of the ghosts of the unwilling dead, and locals rightly wanted the whole place burned and destroyed.

LOGAN KNOCKED and opened the door, popping his head through the gap.

'Can I come in?'

McCulloch smiled and ushered him through. 'You don't know how good it is to see you, Rob.'

He gave her a hug, but she was still too weak to move much. She'd been bed-bound for two weeks now, her broken leg raised slightly and heavy in plaster.

'Brought you something.'

'I can see what it is already, eh?'

He pulled it from behind his back and handed it over. 'Thought it might keep you busy.'

It was the jigsaw puzzle of a ram in all its glory: a large five-thousand-piece beauty. It would take some doing.

'That'll keep me busy all right. Now, more importantly, what about you? Have you come to a decision yet?'

Logan sighed. 'I've had a long chat with Vic and a few

others. In the end, it was an easy decision. I don't know why I ever doubted, really. This is me. This is my job. And if you're still hanging around, then I am, too.'

'I'm glad to hear it, eh?'

He nodded. Now that he'd made the call, he felt he could move forward again. 'There's one more thing.'

'Oh? What's that?'

'You seen the weather forecast?'

She shook her head, so he went to the curtains and opened them. Bright sunlight filled the room.

'Spring is coming at last,' he said, arms open wide. 'It's finally melting, Kel. The snow is finally melting.'

THE END

ACKNOWLEDGMENTS

Special thanks must go to my editor, Andrew Lowe, for his expertise, his keen eye for detail and his patience. Also, much kudos and appreciation to Staurt Bache for the great cover, as ever. Also, how could I forget my other half, Kelly-Ann, for keeping me well fed and motivated? Thanks, love.

ABOUT THE AUTHOR

P.F. Hughes was born in Manchester in 1976. He's worked in many jobs over the years and continues to work on the DS Rob Logan and PI Jim Locke series, among other forthcoming projects.

He currently lives somewhere between the city and the Lancashire countryside with his partner, Kelly- Ann, their two children and their dog.

Join the author's mailing list for regular updates on forthcoming releases and more.

ALSO BY P.F. HUGHES

The P.I. Jim Locke Series

A HARD RAIN

PLAYING WITH FIRE

BLOODLINES

THE P.I. Jim Locke SERIES BOXSET 1-3

Printed in Great Britain
by Amazon

45017159R00178